LIQUID

LIQUID

A Love Story

by

Mariam Rahmani

ALGONQUIN BOOKS OF CHAPEL HILL   2025

Published by
ALGONQUIN BOOKS OF CHAPEL HILL

an imprint of Workman Publishing
a division of Hachette Book Group, Inc.
1290 Avenue of the Americas,
New York, NY 10104

The Algonquin Books of Chapel Hill name and logo are registered trademarks of
Hachette Book Group, Inc.

The Hafez quatrain (Rubaiyat No. 10) is translated from the Farsi by the author.
Quranic verses 78:8–14 are translated by the author, adapted from The Quran:
Saheeh International English Translation, with reference to Tahereh Safarzadeh's
Farsi translation.

Excerpt from *Love in the Time of Cholera* by Gabriel García Márquez, translated
by Edith Grossman, translation copyright © 1988 by Gabriel García Márquez.
Used by permission of Alfred A. Knopf, an imprint of the Knopf Doubleday
Publishing Group, a division of Penguin Random House LLC. All rights reserved.

Printed in the United States of America.
Design by Steve Godwin.

This is a work of fiction. While, as in all fiction, the literary perceptions and insights are
based on experience, all names, characters, places, and incidents either are products of
the author's imagination or are used fictitiously.

The publisher is not responsible for websites (or their content) that are not owned by
the publisher.

Library of Congress Cataloging-in-Publication Data
Names: Rahmani, Mariam, author.
Title: Liquid : a love story / a novel by Mariam Rahmani.
Description: First edition. | New York, NY : Algonquin Books of Chapel
Hill, 2025. | Identifiers: LCCN 2024055109 (print) | LCCN 2024055110 (ebook) |
ISBN 9781643756509 (hardcover) | ISBN 9781643756523 (ebook)
Subjects: LCGFT: Romance fiction. | Novels.
Classification: LCC PS3618.A3837 L57 2025 (print) | LCC PS3618.A3837
(ebook) | DDC 813/.6—dc23/eng/20241120
LC record available at https://lccn.loc.gov/2024055109
LC ebook record available at https://lccn.loc.gov/2024055110

Printing 1, 2025
First Edition
LSC-C

عزيز

And We created you in pairs
And made your sleep rest
And made the night a cloak
And made the day for work
And built over you seven strong skies
And there made a burning lamp
And sent down from rainclouds rushing water.

—THE QURAN 78:8–14

He had taught her that nothing one does in bed is immoral if it helps to perpetuate love. And something else that from that time on would be her reason for living: he convinced her that one comes into the world with a predetermined allotment of lays, and whoever does not use them for whatever reason, one's own or someone else's, willingly or unwillingly, loses them forever.

—*Love in the Time of Cholera*, by Gabriel García Márquez, translated by Edith Grossman

LIQUID

PROLOGUE

Friday, June 16, 2017

THE NIGHT I WAS awarded my doctorate, I had sex with a stranger on the beach. It was easy to get there, to that point of false intimacy. I'd seen the script.

Pick the most attractive person at the bar. See that they're unattached.

In this case, a twenty-something cisman crooked over his phone, bench-press-produced chest curling like paper.

Order a drink without consulting the menu.

At a civilized bar like this, a whiskey sour—an egg-white sour requires a kind of quotidian violence, and violence is the sign of civilization.

Wait.

I sat, sipping my drink and studying the other women in the room. Women who'd gotten all dolled up on a Friday night for men or for each other but most of all, I chose to believe, for themselves. To feel the weight of your lashes cloaked in black, the pinch of no-stretch denim against your depilated thigh.

And just like that, he set his phone down and turned to me.

"Come here often?" he asked.

So we were sharing a script. Indeed, as time would soon tell, in the hours wedged between that predetermined line and our so-to-speak roll in the hay (i.e., sand), little about this man surprised me. But I surprised myself. My hunger for risk. (According to the rules of straight respectability, a first encounter should not end where I took it.) My interest in power. (Was it his or my own limits I wanted to test?) My modest shame. (It clung to me like the sand that stuck to my pubes for days, materializing on clean sheets and the wet shower floor.)

Now I reminded myself to smile.

"Every now and again," I said.

In fact it was my first time. The place was way too pricey.

"What about you?" I asked.

"Almost every night. I work just around the corner, on Rose."

At the word "work" his chest broadened. He sat up straighter. Wrinkle-free athleisure and suspiciously white shoes: today's version of the gray flannel suit.

My phone pinged. A text from Adam, offering to "brave" the Westside to take me out for a celebratory drink. He'd grown up in Venice, but now, like everything that breathed except me, lived much further east.

"What kind of work do you do?" I asked the guy.

"Standard Silicon Beach," he said. "But I'm a poet at heart."

Was he being ironic? Though I supposed it was no concern of mine if a bunch of softhearted white techies ran out the softhearted white hippies who'd run out whoever was here before that. And as for Adam, he only stood to profit—his mother still lived in the neighborhood, and she owned.

I turned my phone face down.

"So what're you trying to 'disrupt'? Duvets?"

"Not exactly," he laughed.

He talked, I listened. At some point he mentioned a motorcycle. What was the make of his bike? And oh wow, he'd fixed it up himself?—from there, my work was done. I said "yes" to another round, my drink joining his tab. Night was falling outside, clarifying our shared objective. I wrapped my fingers around the stem of my coupe.

I smiled on cue. If it weren't for my boycut I would've flipped my hair. Fresh off a six-year PhD and just five months into a presidency that had decided to define itself by a Muslim ban, I wanted, for just one night of my life, to coast.

He asked about the oysters that lay at the barman's back in a glass case, on a bed of ice. He ordered a dozen of the kind that was described as "easy to shoot" plus two glasses of white. I didn't care for oysters. All those wet and briny folds—the allusion was too obvious. But now I ate my fair share. Like the light fare my department had served after the hooding ceremony, it only left me hungrier.

My solace lay in the mediocrity of the wine, an oaked California chardonnay that was so buttery it could've used its own pairing to cut the fat. Any adult would have gone for "brightness" and "minerality"— I found myself reassessing our age gap. I'd half expected the barman to correct his order, before remembering that a man is seldom corrected, even less so in public and never when paying.

After a plate of kanpachi crudo, plus fries and a bread basket; after another up-and-down to check he hadn't misjudged my waist size; after the immense relief of a trip to the bathroom; and after the closing of the tabs—mine as light as the foam on that first sour, which through the sparkly tulle of my intoxication now seemed so far away—we left.

To the beach, for a stroll, like lovers do.

Across Main, across Pacific, and into the maze of multimillion-dollar bungalows. Through a latch-gate into the courtyard of a weed shop. Onto the empty boardwalk and, kicking off my heels, into the sand. It was cold, and the air was colder. There wasn't anyone around, outside of the tents pitched before the tide.

A few paces from the water we paused. He kissed me. There was nothing to be done, of course, but that.

I kissed him back. He kissed me again, harder, and I kissed him again, harder. He used tongue, I used tongue, he kissed my neck, I touched his fly, he touched my breasts, I lay down, he lay on top—the syntax of straight sex is straightforward; every book, every movie, every song and sleepover and bridal shower, every set of his&hers sinks and soaps and towels, conspired to teach you its grammar, and now I let this language do the work, dictating my body and his body, ridding us of the burden of meaning-making: Penetration.

Just then a camera flashed. Some sicko on the sidelines, watching from the darkness—but I guess if you had sex in public, you didn't have the right to complain.

I stood and brushed the sand off my back. Shimmied down the hem of my skirt suit. Reclaimed my things. Bag, shoes, phone.

At the edge of the road, I called a car. The guy left without a word. I'd proved myself no lady, and he'd tired of playing the gentleman. A pair of piercing brights announced my ride, and I checked the license plate before climbing in.

I scrolled through my phone on the way home to Mar Vista. My mother had emailed her congratulations in lieu of flying to LA for commencement. Never mind that I was her only child, or that she'd pressured me to do the PhD in the first place; it was her policy never to apologize. My father had left a missed call from a +98 number, the Iranian country code the better excuse for being absent, but not by much. This was the right time, he suggested in a follow-up voice memo, to start thinking about marriage.

Ignoring my parents, I texted my friend Adam back, taking a rain check on the French 75. I didn't tell him about my hookup.

I lay back against the headrest, spent. The Greek that Adam had tattooed on his bicep—a pale but admittedly sizeable canvas—genied before me:

γνῶθι σεαυτόν

"Know thyself," the great Delphic command.

There had been a single hiccup in the sentence between me and the handsome stranger, an em dash in a comma's place: he'd paused when

I reached to unbutton his jeans. Clearly I wasn't the woman he thought I was, and this was not a woman's place. To want sex with a stranger in public. To go cruising.

Only then did it occur to me, tucked safely in the back seat, that this man had what, six or seven inches, on me? And a solid seventy or eighty pounds; mostly muscle, by the look of his pecks. The slightest shift in power, and desire could've turned to mere consent, and consent was a hair's breadth away from violence.

Know thyself. It seemed to me now that this, if anything, had been whispered in Eve's ear at Eden, this had caused humanity's fall. Each day on earth this edict drove us, self-knowledge an asymptote that only death would collapse.

Or maybe chlamydia. I set a reminder to stop by the health center for an STD screening in the morning. Now wasn't exactly the best time to start teasing out the galaxy of selfhood, at least not its sexual frontiers. I only had health insurance for another week.

LOS ANGELES

ONE

1

Saturday, June 15, 2019

TWO YEARS LATER I was still broke, still single, and still clean. Defying the teleology of progress that is the promise of American life, finishing my degree had only made my life worse. Cruelly evicted from graduate student housing the second I wasn't a graduate student, unable to afford Westside rents without the university's sfumato touch on the LA rental market, I'd moved across town. Morning after morning, kicked out of the Wi-Fied cocoon of the free university shuttle and more appalled than ever by university parking rates, I took the No. 2 bus ten miles down Sunset, riding westward alongside wage workers and the homeless between whose under- and uninsured ranks I oscillated depending on the quarter, to teach whatever courses the department chair begrudgingly passed off. A lowly adjunct, I haunted the library. Trying and failing to turn my dissertation into a book. Trying and failing to land a real job. I read and reread, wrote and revised, abstracted and excerpted and applied and reapplied in a cycle of creation and destruction whose semblance to Nietzsche's eternal recurrence I would have found more amusing had I not been made to live it.

My career had gone nowhere. My love life was nonexistent. And as for sex, here I was, home alone on a Saturday night with a chick flick playing on my laptop because I didn't own a TV. You can draw your own conclusions.

At 7:33 I saw Adam's name flash on my lock screen: *accept* or *decline*. On my laptop Sanaa Lathan was watching her childhood best friend and neighbor, now boyfriend, dance with another woman at a party at USC.

I hit pause.

"Are you dying?" I answered.

It wasn't that no one ever called—though truly, no one ever called—but more so that Adam was a control freak about language. Texts could be edited and agonized over, as was his poet's way. Oral communication was more unruly—sometimes even impossible, evidently. Adam's low moan came over the line. Then, finally:

"Julia's killing me."

Julia was Adam's on-again, off-again girlfriend of too many years. "Eight" years—given all the breakups, I contested the count.

But that was the allegation, according to an anniversary reel he'd posted that very morning. Julia, smoking in her backyard in Silver Lake; Julia, grabbing birria at that spot by Skid Row; Julia, cresting the Wisdom Tree hike, looking twiggy and messy and perfect.

As Adam now explained, he'd made a reservation for the two of them tonight at an exclusive farm-to-table in Ktown whose produce traced its provenance to the chef-owner's personal Long Beach backyard. The rez was for eight o'clock. It was now 7:34. At precisely 7:31 he'd canceled on her. Julia had cheated, again.

I put on closed captions, muted the movie, and unpaused. This was going to be a while.

JULIA WAS HOT IN that white-girl way without having to suffer—or so she claimed—the whiteness: no hips, no boobs; she was a body without matter, pure form.

In a climate in which whiteness was passé and yet somehow still the rule by which all was judged, folks found in Julia cause to "celebrate" difference without having to reckon with it. Hers was a body that upheld, rather than challenged, the impoverished aesthetic of whiteness. White people saw their reflection in her, while simultaneously flattering themselves with their own antiracism: they liked liking her. Boys and girls both. Though such queer admiration typically remained unconsummated—until about a month ago, apparently.

Today, sometime between photographing the roses he'd preordered to take to dinner—posted on the reel as its culminating shot—and lunch, Adam had discovered that Julia was having an affair. Yet another affair. A friend had tipped him off, and when he confronted her some minutes ago, she hadn't denied it.

THE FIRST I HEARD of Julia's heritage claim was well over a year into knowing her. We were at her first big opening, for a group show that soon got reviewed in a roundup in *Artforum*. In print. Julia was mentioned by name.

The work was savvy. Understood as a durational performance, it consisted of dead skin that had been dry-shaved and pumiced from Julia's hands and feet during routine mani-pedis, the labor of darker-haired women who chatted in one or another tonal language as they worked. Displayed at the gallery in the sorts of tiny jars and vials used at makeup counters for packaging samples, this dead skin was, naturally, for sale, thus producing capital from the usually unmonetizable medium of human biowaste, and catering to critics and gallerists alike, in that order.

As numbers dwindled at the opening, the gallery's wan pinot grigios long drained, I went to congratulate her. Julia stood in a one-hipped lean by her curator, scanning the room, clearly impatient for us plebes to go home so she and Adam—then taking a piss—could move onto the more exclusive gallery dinner.

"I like how you implicate yourself," I said. "In critiquing white femininity and whatnot."

As far as I saw it, the real problem with Julia was that she was smart. It made it much harder to hate her.

"Implicate how?" Julia said, with a manicured wave of her lychee-flavored vape pen.

"This piece is about labor," the curator said. "And the ambivalence of identification across class."

She was quoting herself. I had the print-out in my hand.

"Sure," I said. "But race and class rely on each other, you can't have one without the other." I turned to Julia. "It's a performance of white womanhood, right? I mean, you're literally charging money for your skin."

But instead of Julia, the curator took me up again.

"I think talking about white adjacency is frankly pretty—" she paused. "Let's just say, *reductive*, of the Asian-American experience."

Julia smiled sweetly, as though harnessing a truculent child. By then Adam had sidled up to us, and he leaned in to whisper:

"Julia's part Asian."

"What part?" I said none too quietly, eyes on the fingers pearling against her vape pen's matte black skin.

Julia had either enough tact or scorn to ignore me. I wondered what otherness meant without surface, without signs. Whatever it was, I hardly had reason to trust it.

UNABLE TO AFFORD THE luxury of professional attention, I was attending to my own pedicure under the glare of my laptop when Adam finally got to his ask.

"You free for dinner?"

It was 7:41 and counting down. His sob story had run over seven minutes, long enough for Lathan to confirm her man's infidelity in the daylight and dump him.

"What were you doing all afternoon?" I said. "You've known about this for hours."

For years, I wanted to say.

"I was at work."

"And? It takes about two seconds to tell someone to go fuck themselves. But you waited till the ninetieth minute to text her."

I'd by now accustomed Adam to this fobby idiom, a soccer reference lifted from my father's Farsi. Rewatching *Love & Basketball* every couple years was about as close as I got to American sports.

"To make her suffer," Adam said. "Obviously."

Julia wasn't the only one who played dirty. Adam had waited until 7:31, so that he could be sure that she'd already spent an hour soaking in the tub and shaving her legs and drying her hair, and another hour agonizing before the mirror in her walk-in closet, half its normcore contents piled on the floor, sweatshirts and khakis galore. He had waited until exactly twenty-nine minutes to the reservation, when Julia was throned on the leather seat of an Uber XL, floating from the hills of Silver Lake down to Ktown in the calm ripple of Friday night traffic. Only then, only when she'd texted him to say that she was on her way, or rather, "omw!"—when it came to men, Julia was not one to be cowed by an exclamation mark's alleged uncool—did he tell her not to bother. Keeping the reservation for himself was, in the corporate lingo of Adam's day job, a power move.

Or would have been, had he not followed up with missives long as novels that were oh so obviously drafted beforehand with painstaking care.

I could see for myself, as forwarded messages flooded my screen. Therein was detailed: 1) the contours of Julia's recent infidelity as related to him by the aforementioned friend (where the term "contours" operated strictly metaphorically); 2) the sincerity of his attempts to love her these past eight years, which no one had any reason to doubt, not

Julia, and certainly not me; and 3) the corresponding depths of his despair—though all of this more earnestly put, or so I trusted; focusing on the cuticles of my toes, I only skimmed the texts. Julia, I was sure, had done the same; she was never much of a reader.

Unlike Adam, who had for as long as I'd known him—thirteen years, since freshman year of college—trapped himself in an intellectualized passivity rivaled only by Rodin's thinker, Julia was all about action. (I'd once asked Adam to please explain the attraction, and he'd shut me up with Goethe: "Elective affinities.") Upon being ditched and dumped at 7:31 tonight, Julia had promptly rerouted her car and sent Adam a screenshot, her new destination a dive bar on the border of Boyle Heights made to double as an artist powwow, meaning, a tequila-soaked promise of getting picked up and laid. The old German Orientalist, that lover of Hafez, that self-taught Sanskritist, had a point: Opposites attract. What could be more natural than the thinker and the thot?

"The carbon footprint's just too big," Adam said. "Don't let me do it alone."

The farm-to-table chef specialized in red meat. Eight courses of it.

I had a slab of farmed salmon thawing in the fridge and a grad-student party bound to be more flavorless than that lined up for dessert. But there was also the promise of watching Omar Epps/Quincy get his act together, babysitting courtside at the WNBA. That was the beauty of this film: the woman never compromised. A Black woman, no less. Lathan/Monica isn't punished for following her dreams; she's rewarded with love. *Love & Basketball* wasn't just the ultimate LA love story. For the woman of color in America, it was career inspiration.

"Thanks but no thanks," I said to Adam. "I have a house party to go to."

"Where?"

"Mar Vista."

"Weren't you just out there?"

"I was not."

We'd been texting that morning on my way to campus to drop off some books. As an adjunct I didn't retain borrowing privileges at the library over the summer. Another summer of unemployment loomed.

"The Los Angeles campus of the University of California is located in Westwood."

"Same difference. You're seriously saying you're gonna go to the Westside twice in one day—that's the contention?"

It's simply not done, it was true.

"Well I was going to drive."

I sounded more defensive than I would have liked. I capped the polish, admiring my work. Neat harlot-red toes.

It was Adam's security that crippled him. If only his mother had been more withholding, he wouldn't have spent his twenties—indeed, wouldn't now be spending our thirties—running after a serial cheater. He took it for granted that, deep down, Julia wanted him.

"Dinner's prepaid and I'm buying drinks. Please?"

Via a jump-cut, Monica now found herself abroad, playing for Barcelona. Later, her success would taste sweeter for how circuitous the route. I figured my factory fish could survive another day.

ADAM STOOD BEFORE THE glass door of the restaurant, nose in a thin book. He cut quite the figure. Gray linen suit over a white shirt, collar points buttoned to spare the need for a tie—he was the last man in Los Angeles to follow such antiquated rules. Except he wasn't wearing socks, and an ease hung about him. ("I shall wear the bottom of my trousers rolled.")

He was so absorbed by the book that he didn't register my

stiletto-clicking approach, and I saw him flip one page, then another—
what was he reading, Marcus Aurelius? His other arm lay limp at
his side, Julia's bouquet upside-down, ready to dive head-first to the
ground.

I reached for the bouquet, and Adam looked up with a start. Taking
her roses as I'd taken the rez, it struck me as fair that Julia had never
liked me.

"One, two, three, four—" I made a show of counting each flower's
pretty face. "Eight roses, eight years, eight o'clock, eight courses—"

It was a lazy rhyme scheme, internal and identical. Exactly the type
of thing Julia would have found "just adorable." Between the saccharine tone she adopted around men and her cheating, she had quite the
conventional idea of romance.

"—a little on the nose, don't you think?" I said to Adam, nipping a
closed rose bud and letting it drop.

I was of the opinion that a man worth his salt should never be complimented. The world did enough for his ego.

Adam shut his book.

"Good evening to you too."

Sarcasm was a positive sign—maybe in the last half hour he'd
recovered his personality.

For a moment, neither of us moved. The bise that we usually shared
as a kind of joke seemed all too real, dressed like this at a place like this,
and our bodies didn't know what to do.

Breaking away, Adam held the door.

"After you."

The restaurant was composed of a single countertop in dark wood.
A neat line of Edison bulbs hung from the ceiling—cheap anachro-
nism, and yet you couldn't help but take pleasure in the effect. Like a
full moon, they cast a light at once rich and withholding. A pudgy man
with a topknot I took to be the chef-owner—too proprietary an air for

an employee—nodded us to our stools. Two other duos I took to be couples were already seated at the counter. Far at the other end, a lone stool stood unclaimed.

We shimmied into our seats.

Between our two plates, a single sheet of cardstock detailed the menu in language as angsty and enigmatic as a teen's attempt at poetry. (Of this, a choice example was tacked to the fridge at Adam's childhood home in Venice, relic of the early aughts.) I flipped the menu over: only wine. Liquor licenses were, in this city, famously few. Scanning the list, I mentally landed on a Burgundy white to start, for myself, and straight to a gamay for Adam, who didn't like a progression unless it went from wine to booze.

"Two glasses of champagne, please," Adam called down the counter.

The chef-owner was busy organizing linens and silverware—and yet he swept over, coupes in hand. Man to man, it seemed, one might speak out of turn. But it wasn't like Adam to do so.

With a pop the chef-owner decanted the creamy sap of a true capital-C Champagne into our coupes' gaping mouths. Touching their lips together then to ours, we drank—Adam, for inappropriately long. I didn't dare interrupt. Maybe the mood around here would improve.

"I see we're still feeling a tad dramatic," I said when he came up for air.

Our first course arrived: the slightest bit of caviar on a dollop of cream, no carbs. Adam's glass was refilled, and in unison we spooned the products of other creatures' reproductive cycles into our mouths and swallowed, chasing them with drags of bubbly.

I raised my glass. "To Julia."

Champagne and caviar is hard to argue with, and I was beginning to enjoy myself.

"To you," Adam said, as we clicked coupes.

An image of him, doe-eyed and red-faced as he drained a bottle at Julia's twentysomethingth birthday party, came back to me. A few years ago, Julia's parents had shipped a case of Veuve that sent us and her supremely unlikeable, fuckable crew of friends reeling through her Reservoir-side bungalow. It wasn't a round-numbered birthday. Julia's life was like that: Champagne just appeared on the doorstep. And she wasn't even paying for the doorstep.

"How's your heart?" I asked.

Adam shook his head. "No, no. Too early in the night for that."

"Fine."

I nodded ever so slightly at the straight couple on Adam's other side: a bottle blonde encased in a bandage dress, aging stomach beaten flat by Pilates, and a sunspotted puddle stuffed into cargo shorts and a Polo. Safari-goers from a much richer neighborhood.

"Beverly Hills or the Palisades?" I asked.

"Laguna."

Two wedding rings shone in their midst.

"But which one's got the money?"

"Easy." Adam didn't lower his voice. "He does."

"Do enunciate," I whispered. "In the off chance they don't know we're talking about them."

He bent toward me.

"The one with the money gets to look like shit."

"Right," I said. "Why is everything so lame."

Adam only shrugged.

"Sex work without the stigma—isn't that what your dissertation was on?"

"Thanks for the Second Wave read. And no, not exactly."

"But like, kind of." Adam held up scare quotes. "'An exploration of companionate marriage as a fundamentally anti-queering force'—I edit your cover letters, 'member."

I crossed my arms.

"You copyedit my cover letters. And apparently, it doesn't correlate with reading comprehension."

In my dissertation—in what, against increasingly bad odds, a part of me still hoped would be my first book—I had waged a critique of what scholars called "companionate marriage," aka the modern concept of liking the person you marry. Of being both friends and lovers. Before that, marriage was a contract. In both the West and the Islamic world, you traded goods, not feelings. Women offered sex and offspring; men, food and shelter. (At least in theory. When the woman was wealthy, the guy was just—around.)

With our third course—carpaccio, shaved melon—I ordered us both white wine. My long-intended Burgundy manifested before Adam could do more than pout. Left to his own devices, he'd have spent the entire night at the regionally regulated tit of true Champagne. Then tomorrow his head would explode.

"I mean what kills me"—Adam straightened, revived by the sugars—"is she isn't even attracted to women."

"Evidence would suggest otherwise."

Adam fished for a sliver of melon that kept sliding from his fork.

"She made out with this girl at a party one time and told me it felt like kissing Stuart."

"The dog?"

The dog was an albino greyhound bitch so lithe and prepossessing that confining her to a ten-by-ten concrete patio in her prime surely constituted abuse.

Adam put his head in his hands. I could see his breath rising and falling in his crooked chest. He looked so sad—there just wasn't any other way to put it.

"Maybe you can have her tried under Islamic law," I said, bumping elbows. "Nothing like a good old-fashioned stoning to cheer a person up."

Adam was my closest, oldest friend. Both scholarship kids, we'd met at a reception the first week of college, paraded before alumni who were trying to swallow a few canapes, and spit out as many allusions to

Milton, before death. Given that our particular grants came courtesy of the class of 1944, the alumni we'd been assigned to chat up were all white men, and few. Our college held the distinction of being the last Ivy to admit women, just one year shy of 1984, a date so dystopically futuristic that it had met Orwell's needs. Between alternately refusing to engage with me or laughing loudly at my nonjokes, their uneasiness around me provided a strong argument for coeducation. And that's not even getting into the race stuff: they either stared at my hijab or clung to eye contact, awkward and unblinking.

But Adam was a hit. When he approached, the men's shoulders sighed, and the accordion folds of their frowns fell open. It wasn't just that he was another white guy—after all, he wasn't one of them. They were rich, and he, at least poor enough to be on scholarship. What Adam had was charm. A charm so practiced, it came naturally: jokes seasoned with sincerity; a slight leaning-in when he spoke. But over the men's hunched backs, he locked eyes with me conspiratorially. Rolled his eyes at the next inanity, or slipped me a wink when they pretended we had something in common. Moneyed Americans want nothing more than to feel middle class—not to be, but to *feel* like they're just like anyone else. If I learned one thing in college, it was that.

Adam already knew. He had spent his preteen years making himself scarce as his mother conducted studio visits in the living room of their Venice Beach bungalow, and his teenage years doing the Thursday-night gallery circuit with her, studiously attending other people's openings. He'd fancied himself an artist at age ten. As fate would have it, his confidence was less misplaced. Where his mother, Sharon, had all the pretensions that console the failed artist, Adam enjoyed the slack elegance afforded by skill. We were still in college when his first chapbook was accepted for publication, winning a prize. Powered by senioritis and cafeteria coffee, we burrowed through Manhattan and into Brooklyn for the better part of an afternoon, surfacing deep in Bushwick, where he collected his ten author's copies and thousand dollars, in the form of fifty rumpled twenties packed in a recycled manilla envelope.

Still a working poet—meaning, he wrote poetry while working in marketing—he'd published two books since. He had a third manuscript ready—I'd sent him notes last week. With each book his art had matured. The poems were frank, embodied. And generally improved, I was sorry to admit, by his dysfunctional relationship with Julia. Heartbreak is rich soil for the artist, and he'd gotten at least three— heartbreaks and books—out of a single relationship.

But book to book to book, the best poems turned on an unrequited love. This "Y" haunted his oeuvre. She predated Julia, and I assumed, would outlast her. A fiction, as far as I could tell.

"So how's your life shaping up?"

Adam speared a piece of meat—what number course, I'd lost track—and kept it on the fork.

"I'm a thirty-one-year-old without a summer job."

"Sex life?"

He took the bite.

"None to speak of."

"Love life?"

Another bite.

"Even less."

"What about fall teaching?" His hands lingered over the dish, which was seemingly replenishing itself with each bite. "Can you make up for the loss?"

My plate was already empty, and I had a passing urge to throw it at the wall.

"The chair's ignoring my emails. And my parents think I'm an old maid."

I'd received a disconcerting email to this effect just last week, sent from my father, with my mother cc'ed. The threat of a setup was closing in.

"Between your mind and whatever you've got going on here"— Adam waved a hand up and down, catching my knee. It rested there—"you're the definition of marriageable."

The Champagne had taken root. Gently shaking off his touch, I gestured to the lines on my forehead that were daily becoming more defined.

"Not for long," I said. "This city is poison."

"I'll buy you sunscreen for Christmas."

"I need to leave LA."

"Hey." Adam kicked my stool. "Don't say that."

The couple next to him was laughing about something. Authentic, joyous laughter. That they shouldn't be suffering in their cliché of a life was a gross injustice.

"So what's the backup plan," Adam said, less a question than a demand.

I didn't have a backup plan. I'd never needed one.

"Sell the family jewels," I said.

"Are there any?"

I took a scoop of the elevated baby food that had arrived with our next course—the only vegetables, I was beginning to gather, we were likely to catch hint of all night.

"Maybe the matchmaking's not the worst idea. Just marry rich."

Adam pointed a thumb at the couple, which I quickly covered in my fist.

"Right. Find a nice doctor in Oklahoma who's cousins with my parents' friend's nephew from the mosque."

"Like a real doctor or your kind of doctor?"

I arched my eyebrows, and he smiled sheepishly.

"Okay, this stuff doesn't exactly help"—he sipped his wine—"but hear me out here. It's 2019 and you're an academic, which means you're not much better off than the heroine of a nineteenth-century novel. Finishing your PhD is like your dad dying—the house is going to some idiot third cousin who fancies himself a philosopher, and you, meanwhile, the legit brains, are about to get shucked out on the street."

"It is a truth universally acknowledged—that's your big advice?"

"Either you get hitched to someone with an inheritance, or you can give up on ever reading another book, let alone writing one. You won't have time, working at the factory."

"Okay, yeah, I'm on it."

I took his glass and drained the white.

"When I die," Adam said solemnly. "You can take the house."

"You mean the one that's not yours?"

He smiled. "That very one."

Scholarship kid or not, Adam had the security of a pending inheritance. When she got pregnant with Adam during her senior year of college in '87, Sharon was bought out by her boyfriend's old-money Pasadena parents. They offered her a rundown bungalow in a then-undesirable part of town, on condition that she leave their WASP son alone to do his WASPing in Pasadena in peace. Three decades later and Sharon was now sitting on a goldmine that mined itself. Assuming the LA housing market continued to climb as steeply as it had since the nineties, by the time Adam's investment vested—that is, when Sharon dropped dead and the house became his—you could depend on astronomic returns. This windfall, due sometime in our sixties, would neatly ready Adam for retirement, regardless of what came of his day job.

"And what about the Mrs.?" I now asked Adam. "Whatever waif's willing to take the title."

"I'd still call you 'Dr.'"

He looked me straight in the eyes. Popping the head off one of the roses, I tried to make light of things.

"And how much do you make these days?" I plucked a petal. Then a second petal. "Let's talk figures."

I refused to look at him but could feel the weight of his gaze on my body.

"Where's that dress from again?"

I'd thrown on a plain silk slip from Goodwill—the big one, in Atwater, which sold by the pound. The airy silk had come in under a dollar, leaving ample room to pay the tailor.

"I can't remember," I said.

Adam gently took the decimated rose and brushed the petals from my lap. I had thick tights on—forget the pedicure, I hadn't waxed my legs since last quarter—and again, even through layers of fabric, my stomach shrank from the thrill of his touch. It was like discovering a seashell I'd once hid in a shoebox.

"You really do look—" He gestured around. "It's like all this was made for you."

Another course came and went. In our wine glasses, the sun set from white to orange; soon, to red. Our knees were knocking, and my head was swirling—this wasn't supposed to feel like this. Suddenly we were all clapping. One of the gay guys in the couple next to me had proposed. I withdrew my leg.

"Fifty bucks says you're back with Julia by Monday morning."

"I'll raise you a hundred." Adam raised his glass.

"Come on. Why else send you that screenshot of her Uber ride?"

Giving Adam the address was a taunt, but also an invitation.

"It's like, 'fuck *you*' and '*fuck* me' all at the same time."

Adam put down his silverware. I attacked my plate, speaking between bites.

"You both do it. Punish each other. You're here with me, she's at the bar, and you know how to find her. Tonight, makeup sex. Tomorrow, tears, apologies, promises. Monday, you're back together. Except there's even less trust, plus the high of the whole mess, to say nothing of the fact that Julia's constitutionally unfit for monogamy."

He crossed his arms.

"Whether it's in a month or a year," I continued, "the cycle's doomed to recur. The only way out is to change the terms. Just admit you're in an open relationship."

Clearly I wasn't the only one who needed to revisit my Nietzsche.

Adam stared at me, tapping a finger against his knee. Eventually it slowed.

"I know it's hard for you to have feelings," he said. "Or to have other people have feelings."

This was the problem with friendship: sometimes you got read.

"But—" Adam sighed. "This is for real."

What is? I wanted to ask. Julia, or something else, or both?

I rose, mustering as much drama as my stilettos could support. Not much—my ankle rolled, and Adam reached out a hand. I didn't take it. Putting my shoe back on, I grabbed my clutch, and announced with utmost dignity: "I need to pee."

On the can I thought about money. Kicking off my peep toes (Vintage YSL, sixty dollars at a yard sale), I climbed up onto the seat and squatted with my tights bunched down. It took all my core strength not to fall in. Apostate or not, I still had some Muslim in me: I'd sooner eat my own flesh than sit on a Western toilet in a public bathroom.

I ran through a few calculations. The prix fixe was priced upwards of two-fifty a pop, dessert not included; I'd looked it up on the ride over. Add another couple hundred for the wine, an extra thirty bucks for Adam's hangover-inducing second glass of Champagne, tax, tip, and, of course, dessert—Adam was nearly a grand out. Wiping my ass

I contemplated whether he hadn't been planning to propose to Julia tonight. He'd fully intended to blow one thousand post-tax US dollars on her. On someone who could've picked up the tab without having to do the math. (Infinity minus something equals infinity.)

Dry if not clean—the toilet lacked a bidet—I realized I still had a little more to go.

By now quite literally in a sweat, abs burning, I flirted with the idea of splitting the bill. Sure, Adam occasionally picked up the check. He made more money than I did, he said, and it was only fair. Plus, there was the unspoken: though now a mere working man, a poet, Adam effectively possessed—in the form of a 90291 bungalow—a couple million in the bank. Which didn't mean that his poetry wasn't good. It was. (Sometimes, the math got quite complicated.)

Impatient for my departure the automatic flush went off, again. I started to login to the bank app on my phone. All said, the bottom line was this: I wasn't his girlfriend, and you didn't spend a grand to take a friend out to dinner.

My foot slipped—straight down into the toilet bowl. The other leg folded like origami, my hands shot out, and my phone clattered to the floor. Cursing myself, I peeled the tights off, stood on one leg, and extracted my foot to let it drip over the toilet bowl. Thankful at least for the overactive flush.

An angry knock came at the door, and I suggested not in so many words that they kindly fuck off.

I hopped over to the sink and stuck my entire foot in like I was doing wudhu, Sunni-style. First one, then the other. Feet airdrying on a wash towel, I pushed down the pretty gold stopper, filled the sink, and plunged the tights into the soapy tub. If only I'd waxed I could dump them in the trash, but I was too invested in normative femininity to go back out baring my hairy legs.

I dug elbows deep into my handwashing. Even in our dysfunctional department, fall adjunct appointments were made by the prior spring.

By now the jacarandas by my old place in Mar Vista had committed suicide. Spring was over. Time had all but proven what I'd suspected weeks ago, everyday reiterating, by way of my bare inbox, that same claim: I was out of a job.

I rubbed and scrubbed. As for love, what was I doing out with Adam in this dress, these shoes? Black silk and Shiraz-red stilettos with a man who was unavailable, to say nothing of being my best friend. I stuck my tights under the hand dryer.

And I hadn't had sex since—what? I wracked my mind, turning a Rolodex of drinks and parties that, I now realized, only thinned nearing the present. It was like a bad CV. The last time I went out, as in out-out, past closing time, I'd tucked myself into bed. There was the Silicon Beach guy, Venice. But that was two full years ago. Graduation night. My life had ended with my PhD.

Several long minutes later, my tights at least approximated dry. I reassembled myself. Applied a fresh coat of lipstick for good measure. Used a spritz of the full-size perfume—between the sofa and supplies, you could spend a week there and want for nothing—and slipped my stockinged feet back into my stilettos.

I stepped back to look in the mirror. YSL and a tailored LBD. I dressed best when most depressed. Suddenly the signs were everywhere.

Finally, I gathered the courage to face my phone. It had landed at the foot of the toilet, and gingerly, I flipped it over. The case was cracked but not the screen. And the balance on my account was so inconsequential it wasn't worth citing.

I supposed it was the thought that counts.

I EMERGED TO A nearly empty restaurant, music lowered to a murmur. The other couples had paid their bills and left.

"What happened, you fall in?"

"Precisely."

Adam laughed, taking my monotone for sarcasm. My foot squished in my shoe as I slid back onto the stool. I sank my fork through the refreshingly conventional slice of chocolate cake that sat between us. He'd waited for me to start.

"You're gonna be okay."

"Don't be offensive."

He found my gaze and held it.

"Seriously. You're too talented and—"

"Remind me of your pub date."

I was his most faithful critic, a role that had once kept us from speaking for weeks. This round I'd found disappointingly little to critique.

Adam smiled.

"You can't take a compliment."

His manuscript, this next book, ended with a sonnet that pulsed on the page. One of the "Y" poems. My pulse had skipped. Now he offered me the last bite of cake.

The chef-owner bid us a happy anniversary as he slid Adam the bill. Adam didn't correct him, and in my embarrassment over the check, I protested, rather too loudly, that we were just friends.

"Just?" Adam said.

"Look," I said. "I know it's hard. The breakup."

"I know you know."

When the chef-owner finally circled back with Adam's bill, he set two tulip glasses before us, slips of digestif aglow. "Compliments of the gentleman." He nodded toward the far end of the counter.

The lone seat. Someone so monied he needed neither company nor cause to justify a dinner like this. Someone for whom a bottle of cognac is kept behind the bar at a spot without a liquor license. He raised his matching glass.

Smartly cut trousers, a shock of black hair. There was a shimmer about him. Maybe Adam was right. The lighting had been tuned to the likes of me, the chef and this man and me—calibrated to show off our skin. From ten to twenty-two karats, we sparkled under the naked bulbs like settings that outshone their diamonds.

The man rose and zipped his jacket. Left ring finger bare.

I walked over. Stopped where I could smell his cologne. Orange rind and sandalwood and underneath it all, dense and animal, musk. Terre D'Hermès. My father kept a backup bottle on hand.

"That was kind of you."

"Kindness has nothing to do with it."

The practiced line slid over me and down, carving out my want. I could almost feel Adam at my back, rolling his eyes.

With a flicker of his fingers, the man extracted a card from the inner pocket of his suit jacket.

"May I leave you with this?"

The paper was thick and soft. EUGENE KIM and a 310 area code— I'd no more than read it than he was gone.

"Expensive stuff." A hand reached over to rub the corner of the cardstock—Adam had come to collect me. My jacket was slung over his, my purse cradled in his arm. "Kind of tacky, isn't it."

With Julia gone—or more likely, on hold, for about as long as it took to get from Ktown to Boyle Heights at this traffic-free hour—his jealousy needed a canvas. I took my bag from Adam and tossed the card inside.

"Just taking your advice."

He frowned.

"Yeah. Right."

We stepped into the night. The chill on my skin felt just fine.

2

Sunday, June 16

I AWOKE THE NEXT day to a barrage of texts from Adam that colonized my lock screen and sent pings into the air. I rolled onto my back to read. The only significant line was that he'd slept with Julia, a climax so quick I felt cheated. This confession was followed by a treatise of such delicate interpretative acrobatics that it would have made an ayatollah proud.

Justifications (loneliness, habit, maybe even still some kind of love) led to escalating truisms (can't live with her, can't live without her) that in turn led to self-flagellating existential doubt: "Do I have a soul after this Faustian pact?"

Given the elegance of a rhetorical question, I silenced my phone.

But there was no use trying to sleep in at this latitude, just past sunrise, and the room was already flush with light. The world outside my single-paned windows shone like the Reckoning had come.

I GOT UP. MY tights lay crumpled on the shower ledge, a jellyfish stranded ashore. My thrift-store stilettos had washed up onto the bathmat, scampering crabs. They belonged on the shoe rack, neatly coupled like their peers—and no matter how debauched the night, that's usually where they ended up. At least I'd had the sense to wash my face.

Eugene Kim's card lay on the toilet tank. The toilet was running, and undoubtedly had been running up the water bill all night. Delivering the card to safety, I lifted the lid and futzed with the float.

"Just marry rich"—something people only ever said to a woman, and it wasn't only men who did the saying. How many times had I heard a woman colleague laugh off a slight with that line? She discovers the new guy in her department enjoyed a starting offer $10k above hers. She gets an email soliciting her doctoral expertise addressed to "Ms." A sip from a stiff drink and it comes like a bad chaser: "I'm gonna quit and marry rich." Freshman year of college a few girls told me they were there for the "M.R.S." degree. It took me minutes to decode.

Now it took all of one second to see I was screwed. The rent for this leaky apartment ate up half my monthly salary, and I wasn't even salaried. I'd counted on teaching summer session.

Further horizons only proved smoggier. I was an adjunct. Unlike tenure-track faculty, I was compensated only for my teaching, and not well, at that. But without furthering my research I'd never move on, a Sisyphean struggle that kept me from the peak of true professorship.

You needed cultured people to produce culture. To make the movies we winded down to, Friday evening. To write the novels we snuggled up with, Saturday morning. To paint the paintings we breezed by after Sunday brunch. But no one was willing to pay for the educators who squeezed Tolstoy-reading, Kiarostami-watching, Hartman-quoting artists out of the ignorant pipsqueaks who walked through our classroom doors. American culture—such as it was—was dying.

Finally, inexplicably, the toilet stopped groaning. I put the lid back on the tank.

AT MY DESK AFTER coffee and a shower, I got to work. My first order of business was to text Eugene Kim.

Hey

I left it at that. Happiness, my immigrant parents had taught me, lay in leaving something to be wanted. (They also taught me that it was both unattainable and a poor measurement by which to judge one's life.)

In truth my dating experience was limited.

As a child I didn't go running around the playground referring to my "boyfriends"—my mother would've slapped me, and she didn't believe in corporal punishment.

I then spent my teens and early twenties in hijab, as a fuck-you-too to post-9/11 America. Between the Patriot Act and the War on Terror, between tapping Muslim family phones and spying on local mosques, the message was clear: American Muslims were Enemy Number One. My response was to mark myself with a bullseye. Never one to half-ass a project, I prayed at least once, if not actually five, times a day and fasted for enough of Ramadan that I figured God could round up. If I could've been one of those brown girls who sands her whiskered baba down to a prom-date-on-the-lawn-photographing American dad, I'll never know.

A decade after 9/11, my reactionary—but, I still hold, reasonable—anti-Americanism had faded, and with it, my faith. Even today, the only "boy" I'd ever brought home was Adam, as a friend, and that was only permissible because:

a) my mother didn't want to help me move across the country in my rickety Ford Focus when I got into grad school in California;

b) she was at least invested enough in my survival to recognize that a driving partner was preferable, if not strictly necessary;

c) my father was out of the country.

My first year in LA, I went on a couple dates, I lost my virginity. (To whom was incidental.) At a conference later that same quarter, I had sex with a woman. Most situations in life, you can "intuit" what to do from the movies.

My twenties progressed. What my department liked to call my Degree Progress progressed. I took classes, I taught classes, I sat exams, I saw friends, I had sex, sometimes. With men, it didn't take much work, and east of La Brea, queer women were out and about. I dissertated. The feminists and queers whose scholarship moved me wrote from experience, "theorizing from the self," as my advisor liked to say. But for me, books came before life. My own body did not interest me nearly as much as what I was reading. After all, it was not a work of art.

Fall 2016 something in me shifted. Squeaky, inchmeal change. I finished my last dissertation chapter. An Islamophobe was elected president, again. Ushered into Progress by my advisor, I went "on the market." All this really meant was that I spent weeks researching other universities to apply to jobs I'd never get, but now I could run into my cohort-mates and say, cuing a fog machine of self-importance, "I'm on the market." The experience was kind of camp.

At the same time, my mother recommended that I assess the going age for old-maid status these days, now that my research slate was opening up. My father had started his campaign a year prior, when I'd gone to Iran for research Summer 2015. With the benefit of a captive audience, he'd tried to set me up with a cousin. ("*Second* cousin!")

Winter quarter came and went with a flurry of interviews that resulted in no offers, personal or professional, like the snow in the San Gabriel Mountains that didn't stick. I was the only one in my cohort set to finish my degree on time, which would have felt like an accomplishment, had I anywhere to go. Dissertation done and dusted, I found myself studying how people flirted. In grotesquely upholstered hotel lobbies at Annual Meetings, on dance floors and kitchen floors sticky with booze, over the post-talk grocery store cheese plate in the department seminar room, on the arms of secondhand IKEA couches in my friends' shared apartments, and in the synthetic-stucco slivers behind their buildings billed on rental listings as "private patios"—the gestures were the same. Touching someone's arm to emphasize a point. (An excuse to break the seal of individual space.) Holding a light to the cigarette between another's lips. (The lips were hardly a metaphor; instead, the significance lay in the fire, the threat.) But I discovered that what was most crucial of all was this: knowing when to linger and when to leave.

From empiricism to phenomenology, almost without intending to, I started to have more sex that spring. A first-year in my department after an insufferable all-day pedagogy workshop. An atonal-jazz bassist after an afterparty. A Hollywood PA after the afterparty to an afterparty. (That was a real coup, because the friend I went with also triumphed, saving us twenty bucks each when we shared a car the next morning.) In short, May Gray was kind to me that year. Meantime, graduation loomed like a public execution scheduled for the next sunny day.

With the punctuality of a Shinkansen to hell, June 16, 2017, arrived. I was awarded a PhD. The climax to a decade of postsecondary foreplay.

Two years to the date, today.

Who is this?

A text from Eugene Kim floated atop my screen. Right. He didn't have my number.

Last night, I typed as I went to fetch a glass of water.

Ah ya of course, was my quick reward. *How's the aftermath?*

I tipped the end of the glass into the aloe plant that lived at the corner of my desk. It looked even thirstier than I was.

Better than I had right to hope for, you?

Love is neither necessary nor sufficient for a successful marriage, any fool could discern that. My parent's marriage was model enough: it worked best when they were on separate continents. Still, I liked to think that in this rainbow-striped wide world, I could find someone whom I wanted to kiss goodnight, if not good morning (I preferred a good tooth-brushing first). Someone on whose soft stomach I might rest my head at the beach. Someone whose grating laugh might pumice my ears. To locate this someone, I had to increase my candidate pool by manyfold.

How many fold? I googled the minimum sample size for statistical significance: one hundred. Strictly speaking, that meant a candidate pool of a hundred *first* dates—but handwaving at science was a human-ist's prerogative. I needed to go on one hundred dates. As impressed as I was by Mr. Kim's early application, one had to honor the process.

On my phone gray dots unfurled only to disappear. Zero dates in and I'd already been reduced to a girl waiting by the phone. But some-times the antidote lays in the poison. I had to get on the apps.

As with any new project, I moved to text Adam—only to find, entering our thread, that I still needed to respond to the memoir he'd released at dawn, finally in his own bed. With an ambivalence I couldn't help but betray precisely by veiling it—Adam knew me—I performed my social duty, consoling him with a lot of repetitive bullshit to show I cared. (Among friends, I'd discovered, clarity and concision were not valued.) I did care—about Adam. But Adam+Julia did not make a couple. How many times could this axiom be falsified before it was thrown out?

Starring on the newest BachelorX, I typed.

wanna consult?

He marked the line with a "haha."

Like actually tho

What're the kids on these days? Apps-wise

There was a slight pause before Adam wrote back.

I was more winedrunk last night than a whirling dervish

Like every literate American, Adam had dabbled in a little Rumi.

I'm waiting

You can't be serious?

Have I ever been otherwise?

This got a thumbs-down.

What if I'm looking for love

More ellipses.

You don't believe in love

I laughed out loud.

Fair. But also can't remember the last time I got laid. After a beat I added, *Asking for a friend.*

When Adam finally responded it was to recommend one app for dating, and another for "fucking." The word was usually so innocuous, but I sensed a censorious tone. What did Adam know about dating apps, anyway?—he, a devotee at the shrine of Julia.

Sources? I wrote.

There was another lag, long enough for the message to break through my lock screen:

Julia's already got both. She showed me her phone. Catholic-style confessional. Then, *ISO skilled couples therapist.*

I gave this a thumbs-up. Hopefully he was joking?

I downloaded first one, then both dating apps—absent religion and a crippling sense of obligation, I figured, sex was crucial to keeping a marriage together—and began to set up my profiles.

The dating dating app's ultimate purpose, according to the ad copy, was to be deleted: *Love is forever—so this app doesn't have to be!* My favorite pastime went from "reading Butler" to "iterative gender performance" to "walks on the beach."

In contrast to the dating dating app's shameless appropriation of a gay rights catchphrase in service of an anti-queer teleology of monogamy, the fucking dating app was at least more honest. Photos only. I scrolled through my reel. Adam was everywhere. On the beaches of Malibu last month, enjoying the rare spring scorcher. Under the spray of Switzer Falls, the mountain stream rushing with a post-drought winter's worth of melted snow. Over cake at his mother's two years ago, for the kosher version of his thirtieth birthday. Us, us, us, more us—the only reason he wasn't in my graduation photos was because I'd banned him from coming, punishing myself for my parents' absence.

Imposing the productive limit of excising Adam from the stack—I was, after all, trying to get laid—there was little left to curate. I happened to have the requisite swimsuit shot in classic red (I liked red). Risking redundancy, I added a bikini shot (I liked the beach). I topped these off with a shot of me in big butterfly sunglasses, hand on the hood of some braggart's street-parked yellow Rolls Royce.

But I couldn't use two swimsuit shots to find a spouse. The feminist revolution wasn't that successful.

I had no choice but to squash my dislike of selfies and take to my closet. Channeling sexy-professor vibes, I settled on an oxford shirt and painfully high high-waisted jeans (e.g., the contemporary corset), plus my usual tortoise-shell glasses.

Lacking a ring light, I headed outside. Most of the garden was too scrubby to warrant attention. But my eyes fell on the pomegranate tree, whose dark leaves were now peppered with poppy trumpets. Eyeliner drawn thick as kohl, features offset by pomegranate flowers, I managed a decent composition. A little self-Orientalizing never killed anyone.

BACK AT MY DESK, I opened Excel. Every weekday morning from June 2014 to June 2017, from advancing to Candidacy to finishing my PhD, I'd wrapped up a day's worth of dissertating by entering the date and wordcount on a spreadsheet titled "God's Work." Watching the number go up obfuscated my want of real progress.

According to the calendar that loomed above my desk, there were now a little over fourteen weeks left to the first day of fall term, which I had not—or not yet?—been contracted to instruct: Thursday, September 26. I started a new tab.

9/26/2019 Engaged to be married.

It was certainly ambitious, given American dating norms.

To market oneself, my advisor had once advised me as she had once been advised by her advisor, one must flip the script: they need you more than you need them. At the time, her "help" struck me as naive as the primary-colored plastic stool on which I then sat. (This jejune aesthetic was the only substantial cultural shift the department had adopted after a recent Title IX scandal: sofas had been outlawed in offices, as if no one ever fucked a subordinate on a hard surface.) In fact, there were hundreds of me desperate to fill each *Chronicle of Higher Ed*–advertised "need." The typical academic job got four hundred to a thousand applications.

My phone dinged. Once, twice, thrice—it was the fucking app clamoring for attention. Eight or nine dudes had slid into my DMs, plus one lady. I toggled to the dating dating app. Twenty minutes in, and I had two matches. My advisor finally made sense. What was marriage but tenure? Thanks to our society's ableist superficial values, this field, this market, was in some real sense available to me. I was a thin, educated young woman from a respectable family who knew how to cook; surely I could muster a few suitors.

I counted 103 days between 6/16 and 9/26, inclusive. But a date a day wouldn't cut it. My own preferences aside, no sane person would go for a shotgun engagement.

I could stack first rounds like office hour appointments, and go from there. Whittle down to a few finalists by early August, hit a hundred by midmonth.

8/17/2019 Date 100

That left forty days of dedicated courtship with Mr., Ms., or Mx. Right.

The glow of the vacant Excel blocks illuminated the veins running between my fingers. They bulged big and blue in the encroaching heat. It was half past ten. I got up, downed two glasses of water, and stretched. Then I sat my ass back down and got to swiping.

Soon a few rules emerged organically:

No dogs.

No cats, actually, either.

No photos with mom. (Selfies with dad were evidently not a convention.)

No references to cartoons, serialized fantasy novels, or other media deemed strictly suitable for children everywhere outside the US.

HOURS PASSED. I READ and analyzed and judged and discerned and hearted and passed. I fried the long-thawed salmon. I prayed I wouldn't get food poisoning.

My phone squawked again. Eugene Kim, offering a perfunctory *Ha.* Then, an invitation.

When are you free? Let me take you out

A contract with refreshingly clear terms: my time, his money.

Swiveling over to the bookshelf in my rolling chair, I picked my advisor's first book off the shelf. It was a slim volume: these three-hundred-some pages had gotten her tenure. I extracted the printshop-bound copy of my dissertation that sagged on the shelf below. Four hundred pages in five meaty chapters, excluding the introduction. I flicked a match and let the flame lick the corner. The Xerox paper took surprisingly long to catch. But when it did, it went hard, and soon, my fake book was but a slash of fire. My grip released only as the heat singed my skin. The smoke alarm screamed, the fire fell to the floor. Pure beauty.

Except this was not an abstraction. I stomped out the flames with a slippered foot and threw a pot on top to suffocate the embers.

A few minutes later, alarm quieted, windows open, I nudged the pot with my foot to reveal the damage. Several floorboards sported a black bruise. Notes of burnt oak laced the air, sweet and uncompromising.

Tonight, I texted Mr. Kim.

No time like the present, as they say.

Date #1: Town & Country

EUGENE KIM WAS A man of leisure.

He would arrive, at his leisure, at a quarter past the hour, strutting the line between charming and rude, and soon speak, at his leisure, about the detritus of half-completed degrees that littered his past, while then drinking, at his leisure, an alarming volume of vodka so top-shelf I hadn't known it existed.

As for me, I was unspeakably early. By which I meant on time. (Despite my parents' Germanic sensibilities—if they weren't five minutes early, they considered themselves late—I was perpetually stuck on CPT; I considered the former a sorry story of assimilation, and the latter, a strong case for genetic predeterminism.)

Beamed up to the thirty-fifth floor of the downtown Westin at six o'clock, as instructed, elevator doors sealing shut behind me like those of a spaceship, I found myself alone. The podium past the elevator bank stood unmanned.

Contra the pale concrete of the hotel's Brutalist exterior, up here things were friendly and soft. Cold tiles gave way to carpeting, and the art was appropriately anodyne. Propped on a pedestal by the far wall, fleshy pink curves gestured at the female figure. My own was outlined in a plunge-neck dress. Rich red crepe offset by glittery thigh-highs and athletic slides. At no danger of being exposed on a first date, I'd again put off waxing my legs, and the socks had required a hundred visions and revisions to strike the right note. With all the melancholy and indecision of a marginally chestier T. S. Prufrock, I had destroyed my closet. I was beginning to see why hot housewives didn't have time for jobs.

Noticing a set of stairs past the podium, I descended to meet a second podium guarded by a skinny hostess. I took it you were supposed to know to come down. She made a show of making me wait, flipping languorously through a handwritten ledger. Behind her, crescent booths and bubble chairs hovered around round tables big and small, like moons to sundry suns. The curved walls were but a ribbon of glass. Outside the city stretched far and wide, South Central graying under a southward gaze.

"Ready?" The hostess said, starting down the low steps to the recessed dining room. "Watch your step," she added, after I'd already tripped.

The ground under my feet was moving. Literally, like some cheap pun—it was a revolving bar. So this was what got them off, the rich? She deposited me at a window table, and I sank into my orb.

Now the polished thread of the 10 stretching from downtown to the Pacific Ocean had come into focus. I was in the eye of a camera marking a measured pan over Los Angeles. Slow, steady.

For long minutes, I waited, not daring to order a drink. It was one thing to land a lay, another to find a fiancé. I tried to muster the same confidence I'd had on graduation night, at the bar in Venice. Every scholar is at heart a contrarian. "What're you writing against?" my advisor used to ask. That night I was writing against myself. Rewriting the self. Sex on the beach—it was such a cliché they'd named a cocktail after it. Could I manifest a metaphor? Realize a fiction? For one night, I could. There's no high like a fresh PhD.

But the higher the high, the harder the comedown.

EUGENE KIM TOOK THE step I'd missed with the sparrow's stride of someone in his own living room. At the table, he gave me an unabashed lookover, then bent to kiss me on the cheek so casually that I trusted that this intimacy was right.

A waiter transpired.

"Martinis are the thing here," Eugene said, glancing at the menu I had open on my lap.

I shut it.

He took his "martini" sans vermouth, no twist, no olive. It was a generous interpretation of the word, all form, no content; crude vodka gussied up in a stemmed glass. Peasants' poison. I felt my spine straighten.

The waitress recognized Eugene as a regular, and I gazed out the window-wall as they flirted inoffensively. She was back at school for her BA. "That makes one of us," Eugene joked. Now my digits tingled: superiority, that dependable fix.

Behind the glass, the Los Angeles sky was blue and limpid, the city still, as though ten million souls weren't down there right this minute, walking and breathing and struggling against the oppression that was their miserable birthright, plus some bad luck, to boot. Struggling against people, it dawned on me, such as I was then: those with a view.

I ordered a dry vodka martini with a twist and asked after Eugene's day.

"Just a rinse of vermouth," I added before the waitress disappeared.

Smiling, I turned my attention back to Eugene. He breezed past the interruption.

"Got up at eight, stayed in bed till ten, and had about three pots of coffee before I could remember our date."

The man was wearing cufflinks and cologne, and his excellent jawline shone with a fresh shave—everything about him said "trying." In which case, we were even.

"Late night last night? After you left the restaurant, I mean."

"The standard."

"Uppers or downers?"

He smirked.

"Where there's smoke, there's fire."

I imagined meeting here every week for martinis, each of us flitting from the office at a job that was actually a hobby to the thirty-fifth floor of a rotating turret to tally the quotidian before taking the same car back home—it was a satisfying thought, a life with a man like this. I'd be reborn in his image, a woman sprung from his rib.

By Eugene's second coneful of vodka, I'd succeeded at navigating the conversation to the subject of family, meaning finances. Though Eugene had grown up respectably on the Westside, his father was from Echo Park "way back when," before fourteen-dollar juices and wood fences laid on the horizontal. Mr. Kim, senior, had made it big in construction, riding the wave of legally mandated retrofitting to build an empire of earthquake-proofing yet to be put to the test. (Faced with the Big One, one had to assume that such efforts would likely prove shakier than their profit margins suggested.) Eugene had drawn on these funds to then return to the ancestral homeland, that is, Sunset east of Alvarado. He "kept a place" in Echo Park.

The firstborn to whom he owed his freedoms was his older sister. As this woman shouldered the family business, Eugene was left to pursue his passions, including, but not limited to: pickleball, silk-screen printing, and a dalliance with doctoring that fizzled after half a postbacc. A couple summers ago he'd even picked up croissant-making at a crash course at Le Cordon Bleu. I asked, he talked. I complimented, he explained. All this while munching on Marcona almonds that came to thirty-five or forty cents apiece, their blanched flesh barely brushed by his fingerprints, before they were ground to a pulp and consumed.

A reverse Scheherezade, I even managed to extract the punchline of his parents' love story: his father had stolen his childhood best friend's fiancée on a trip back to Korea.

"My parents met at the MSA," I said. Eugene looked confused. "The Muslim Students Association?" I explained, and in that moment, I wondered what my appetite really was for difference.

"Oh right—hey, hold that thought."

He got up to go to the bathroom.

Lifting an almond with the faintest grip I could manage, I tried to mirror his elegance, his ease. Mimicry of the oppressor was a tool of the oppressed. I wasn't exactly a member of the subaltern, in the grand scheme of things. But in comparison to this kind of rich, it was easy to feel poor.

MY PARENTS MET IN the late seventies at jumma. At the meet-and-greet after the sermon and prayer, to be precise, over samosas that teetered on Styrofoam plates threatening collapse. That Friday my father led the service. As snow fell on the Michigan plains, inside a college classroom emptied of desks and laid with bedsheets in lieu of prayer mats, my father sermonized about hypocrisy. A lazy subject befitting an amateur: flip to the back of the Quran, find "munāfiqīn" in the index, and the khutba writes itself.

You couldn't really blame him. In this Great Lakes MSA, as in so many campuses across America, the role of Imam was not the special-ized clergyship that it was back home. Instead, male students signed up to volunteer on a roster pinned to a cubicle in the physics depart-ment. (Here was another mark of immigrant suffering: Excel wasn't released until 1985.) Whether in the form of pimply youths sent—and sometimes, sponsored—by their home countries to cultivate a little Western knowledge and sow the seeds back home; or just plain broke

FOBs who'd landed a coveted spot in the electrical engineering PhD at Michigan—either way, Imamate had been democratized in diaspora. If a marker of status, the title conferred a status as impermanent as this terrestrial life.

My father was one of the FOBs, fresh off the boat in bell-bottoms and a knit polo. That Friday in winter 1977 or 1978, the precise date a lacuna in my family lore, so uncharacteristically vague that I smelled a lie (clearly, my parents had skipped the courting and cut straight to the wedding, only to later realize that rushing into bed wasn't an appropriate example to set for a nice Muslim daughter)—that Friday in 1978 then, my father fell in love. Twice over: once with America, and once with my mother. Both would later spurn him.

It was his first time leading jumma. The forty-minute lecture was the easy part. What worried him was what he'd do with his hands as he led the foreshortened midday prayer, for all of two minutes. (On Fridays, God cuts the believers a break.) To let them lay limp at his sides would give him away as Shia; to fold them like a Sunni—like everyone else—would make him a hypocrite.

Sweat beaded on his forehead as he delivered his conclusion. By the time that day's muezzin (mech-e undergrad) finished calling the adhan, his white polo was gray at the pits. The room was silent. He stood. Took his place in front of the congregation, his fellow brothers in Islam shoulder-to-shoulder in the rows behind him, the handful of sisters at the back. He raised his hands on the first "Allahu-akbar"— then let them fall.

No one cared. A Shia imam for a Sunni congregation? Just another strange Americanism. Apolitical, a-historic, willfully naïve. Wonderful.

After a final, extralong prostration in which my father gave thanks— and, while he had Him, prayed for a grant he'd recently applied to and hotter hot water in the shower—my father rose to help clean up.

The brothers gathered the now dusty sheets and passed the dirty laundry to the sisters. They unfolded the legs of the splintered folding table rented from campus facilities, which was too small because whoever'd put in the order still didn't have a handle on the imperial system. They drew a plastic tablecloth over the table, cutting the roll with a pocket knife. The brothers watched as the sisters weighted the table with aluminum trays of samosas and pakoras and homemade chutneys so large that you'd forget how small their husbands' stipends were. With great chivalry, the brothers manned the serving spoons and invited the sisters to start. At which point the sole sister who wasn't pregnant or breastfeeding could only insist that she be served last, except, then it had to be considered that the other women, the wives, had done the cooking, excusing her from such labor because she was single and, more importantly, herself a graduate student whose time deserved respect and protection, which in turn, given that there was no world in which a hostess could eat before her guests, meant that the original sister did have to go first, after all.

This woman was my mother. Rewarded for her indolence as in any civilized culture, she stepped from server to server, from brother to brother. Immediately after the prayer, my mother had allowed her dupatta to fall to her shoulders, and now she appeared before them as she did in class—or the grad student lounge, or the library—lustrous black hair falling in waves down her back. Not one man would meet her eyes. Eyes my mother had met over cubicle walls and over the stale coffeepot labeled DO NOT REMOVE in Sharpie; eyes whose gaze my mother had followed to the glossy pages of a textbook to tackle the same problem—those same eyes she'd witnessed smiling at white women, all now dutifully trained down. Pious, duplicitous.

Until, there at the end of the line, standing over the green chutney, ready to serve, was my father. Sporting a caterpillar mustache, which was about as close to clean-shaven (i.e., anti-Fundamentalist) as fashions allowed, the top button of his polo already back to unbut-toned, the collar unyoked—this man; that day's imam; Shia, Iranian, and certainly no one intended for the likes of her Sunni Indian self, met her eyes and smiled.

Love at first sight, that's what they claimed.

SEVERAL HOURS LATER, TWO of which were spent chewing up the 10 in a custom matte McLaren, trap staggering through the speak-ers, I passed through the front door of the Kim family property in Palm Springs. And back outside, to the private courtyard. What had looked like any other Mission Revivalist ranch when we pulled up—red-roofed, stucco-sided, and of modest width—was in fact a U-shaped winged estate that stretched back, back, back into grounds so vast that their far reaches lay murky under the waxing moon. Tucked into the darkness, a broad pool reflected the moonlight.

As a matter of course, I was offered a drink, and as a matter of course, I accepted. Eugene slid through one of the many latticed doors that opened onto the courtyard, and a restaurant-sized kitchen lit up behind the glass.

I stayed al fresco. There was a niche carved into the house on the opposite wing. A fountain of sorts, mosaicked, Spanish-esque or maybe Moroccan—thanks to Islamic imperialism, the two were not so different. I crossed to look it at. The fountain was painfully sim-ple. Little more, indeed, than a brass spigot sticking out the wall. The spigot was off, but dripping, and the well underneath, wet. I remem-bered then that I hadn't waxed my legs. The evening should've already ended.

It was of course, by any measure, unhinged to be there. Why he'd suggested a two-hour drive to his parents' place in Palm Springs, instead of ten minutes to his own house in Echo Park, I couldn't say. Probably for the same reason we'd stopped at In and Out for fast-food burgers after running the bar tab at the Westin higher than an anesthesiologist going off shift. The truly rich lived by their own mores, I was learning, practicing a modesty so exaggerated, it was coy, then peacocking with the ardor of repentance. As for me, I said yes for the same reason you break into a locked closet at a vacation rental.

While Eugene pumped a cocktail shaker, I slid out of my rubber slides to touch a clothed toe to the tiles below the fountain. The ceramic was slippery with cold. But the terracotta floor remained, despite the desert night, tepid—the day's sun had been that relentless. I supposed that was why sane people didn't go to Palm Springs in the middle of June.

Eugene finally appeared, passing me a brimming glass. The martini sloshed onto my skin.

"Forgive me."

Relieving us both of our glasses, setting them on the lip of the fountain well, he took my wrist with both hands and wiped away the wetness. Then he let it go. Expectation sparkled on my skin. For some minutes he drank. I left my drink where it was, and when he was finished, stepped closer.

We kissed. His grip on my back was firm but gentle. His lips worked on my neck, then lower, and lower still. He got on his knees. With the back of a hand, he parted the slit of my dress as though a veil and kissed my thigh, above the elastic, where the socks cinched my fat and skin. My breath tightened. He used his lips. Softly, ever so softly, the touch of his fingers hardly discernible from his lips'. Like an oriental vase lent luster by a museum's wan lighting, I glowed under his touch. Empty, all surface. The kisses crept up, the fingers crept down, ghostly and teasing. Until they were no longer teasing.

My nails dug into his scalp.

A sharp shattering crashed into the night—we'd knocked my glass over. Shards of glass glittered close to my feet. His eyes, unwilling to meet mine.

WHEN WE'D BOTH FINISHED, Eugene assured me that he slept awfully fitfully. With the promise that I'd be better off alone, I was shown to what he called "the guest room."

Alone again, my body loosened with a relief I hadn't realized I craved. I lay down on the narrow bed. The room was hot and cramped, and the air weighed on me. I was sweating. I peeled off my socks, my dress, my underwear, unhooked my bra. I kicked off the sheets. Now I was naked, and still sweating. I forced myself back up, enough to try and crack the window above the bed. But there was no way to open it. The window was purely ornamental, sewing me in with the day's heat.

From behind the pretty picture window, the cool night taunted me. If I weren't so spent, I'd go sleep on the grass. I could. I could get up and go back into the night. To lie there, on that bed, was a choice.

I rose. Disentangling my dress from the bedding, I looked for somewhere to hang it. Other than the twin bed there was no furniture, and the only closet was stuffed with linens. Guest room, my ass. Servant's quarters, was more like it.

He'd seen through me, I had to give him that. Class was a border, and tonight I'd come up against routine policing. It would take practice to pass. This was going to be harder than I thought.

I turned the dress inside-out and, taking care to smooth any wrinkles, lay it flat on the floor. Tomorrow I'd have to wear it, dusty side against my skin. But outwardly I'd confront Eugene in the same clean crepe. I climbed back into bed and closed my eyes to welcome sleep.

3

Monday, June 17

MONDAY MORNING, AT HOME in LA at long last, my first order of business was to depilate.

In hopes of manifesting a future in which I was served and serviced by someone other than myself, I called around for an immediate appointment at a waxing salon. Unless I wanted to go all the way to Beverly Hills, pickings were slim. The first place on the Eastside that would take me was in Highland Park. They were charging a clean hundred for full legs, and the list of bikini services was as precise as butcher cuts. Evidently it took less time to flip a neighborhood than you'd think.

I changed into a cotton maxi dress and headed back out.

Sitting behind the wheel of my Focus felt like taking the throne. Several hours prior, making my way back from Palm Springs at the crack of dawn via the indignity of an intercity bus, ass stuck to the gray felt seats, I'd wanted to confide in Adam. But we hadn't spoken since 6:34 a.m. yesterday, according to the time stamp, when I'd metaphorically clucked, via an acid thumbs-up, my disapproval at his running straight back to Julia. The bluelit glare had put me off, and I'd opted for staring at the scenery.

Now I swung into a spot right by the salon, in front of a Mexican bakery that had somehow survived the wave of whiteness washing over Figueroa, so far.

Ten in the morning and the clinical waiting room was full of the sort of residents that usually made me avoid this part of town, new moms who still wore skinny jeans and hung whiteboards by the fridge reminding themselves to pick up more organic oat milk. Because it was LA, they weren't all white, just rich. Around here, this was what was meant by "diversity." But hey, I didn't make the rules. I took a seat between two other Asians, completing the continental spectrum from Southwest to Southeast. With some luck, I'd soon join their ranks as another moneyed wife from a white-facing minority. (Sans baby, thank you.)

As I waited, I scoured the web for digestible, factual articles on chronic depression. Too lazy to grope through the scientists' technical jargon yet loath to trust "content" distilled from Wikipedia by unpaid interns, I got nowhere. What little I gleaned only depressed me more: exercise, exercise, exercise. Studies showed that, over the years, routine running improved both mood and outlook better than antidepressants, given the latter's diminishing returns: the body built tolerance to drugs; less so, to its own chemicals. But I both didn't like running and already regularly went running. This was me on endorphins.

My name was called. Waiting by the desk to receive me, the aesthetician introduced herself as Juniper. She was almost as pale as her lab coat.

"Just this way."

She gestured down a hall of gleaming doors, and I followed down the hall, studying her hair. Ombré, shading from blonde to lavender, like a cloudy LA sunrise. Bald wrists poked out her sleeves. Her fingers were smooth as porcelain. Naturally hair-free, needless to say, and perhaps as liable to break.

She opened the door for me, and the scent of eucalyptus floated out atop local public radio.

"I'll let you change."

She smiled. I smiled.

Then I turned right back around and walked out.

There were some things you simply couldn't trust a white person to do. Waxing your bushy brown bush was one of them.

TWO HOURS AND A groin spasm later—if waxing your own bikini line demands acrobatics, the butthole is pure hubris—I inspected myself in the mirror, legs smooth as petals, privates blooming blush and beardless as an English rose. I turned up the disco. Donna Summer crooned about her cake melting in the rain in MacArthur Park, my laptop speakers doing the diva a disservice.

Folded wax strips lay scattered on my dresser like discarded folios. My plucked black hairs spelled neat lines in a nonsense language, or perhaps an ejaculation in one I knew. "Aah!" they yelped, alif after alif. "Aaah," they sighed, the cry of femininity signed in a prophet's script.

Date #4: The Untrained Algorithm

POST–PALM SPRINGS, SPIRIT RENEWED by anger, I began to institute more rules. Scheduling was strictly on my terms: a hundred dates was simply too many to leave to the vagaries of LA flakiness. But I let my dates pick the spot, so as to assess their taste. Though an important caveat had clarified: don't leave LA County.

After a couple whiffs on the earnest app, this particular prospect (*What do you do when you're not having fun?* "In production." *Ideal Sunday?* "Foraging for loquats to update the family pan dulce recipe.") had proposed ice cream on Larchmont.

Parking down past the meters, I started back up the road, past cottage homes in the 1.2 to 1.4 mil range (I'd spent some time on Zillow getting to know his neighborhood). I could smell the vanilla pumped out the ice cream "shoppe" vents from two blocks away. On a climate-changed summer day such as this, the line crept just as far, curling out the door and along the sidewalk. Frantic waving flagged me down. He hadn't made it very far.

"Hola!" He went in for a hug. By reflex, I shriveled into my silk romper and extended my hand.

Khakhi shorts, tucked-in tee; in short, the kind of guy who suggests an innocent cone as a first date. Why not drinks? Coffee? It was infantilizing. Though to be fair, the onesie was not doing me any favors.

Plus, his smile threatened to thaw me. He looked like a nice guy, not in the way people usually said that as a euphemism for a serial killer, but an actually nice guy.

FOR THE NEXT HALF hour, the counter an infinite limit I feared we'd never reach, we covered the basics. He asked, I demurred, he answered. Favorite foods: tacos, churros, ice cream, and really, just anything enjoyed with family. Family background: fourth-generation Chicano, albeit somewhat "diluted"—his word, not mine. Family goals: three kids, two dogs. (Admittedly a slight misalignment, but the man seemed pliable as honey.) Values: family. Or rather, "la familia." Here was a fellow on the marriage market.

We ordered. Single scoop in a cup, for me, and for him, a proper sundae loaded denser than my dissertation.

Taking to the sidewalk at a snail's pace, we then forayed, without any lag in cheer, into his anxieties. Evidently he was on some sort of roots journey. Whence, I gathered, the peppered Spanish; terms like "la cultura" continued to figure prominently. Had my own shrinking and crossbred roots not been shoved down my throat all my life—by my father, by America, and for the past decade, by myself, pursuing an entire PhD about my fatherland—I might have found this more inspiring. As it was, I had to ask myself whether Larchmont was really worth fighting for.

"Isn't this just perfect?" he marveled at some point, gazing at the blue sky, seemingly undeterred by his existential crisis from enjoying himself. "Life is *good*."

This kid was walking the world like an open wound when all of humanity was due for acid rain.

"What're your career goals?" he went on.

"Well," I said, dodging my tenth Dutch stroller. "I'm kind of in a transition moment."

"But what're you passionate about? Gut feeling."

I spooned the last of my scoop of California Gold Rush, which tasted like big-tub vanilla, despite being thrice the price.

"I'm trying to write this book but—"

"That's so cool!"

"Yeah, is it?"

Whatever happened to jadedness, I wondered. Ours was a decadent age.

"Anyway, I've run into this—funding issue, basically. I'm trying to work out how the pieces fit, you know."

"Heck yes, I can totally relate. I'm hoping to have my own company someday, instead of being some peon. I mean don't get it twisted, I'm super grateful, but well, you know, that's just not my dream."

I stopped us in front of an empty bench.

"That sounds capital intensive?"

"It's for sure tough."

We sat.

"But so, what's the benefit? Can't you just rise through the ranks at Paramount?"

"I definitely see that point," he said, in the way I'd heard other people's parents talk at Parents' Weekend back in college, encouraging while correcting. "But if you stay in the studio dining system, you're not calling the shots on quality. Like if they want to cut back, there goes the crushed pistachio your all-time favorite DP likes on his tuna, and forget about organic grape nuts—"

As dollops of mealy hummus and shrink-wrapped pitas floated through our conversation alongside actors' trailers and directors' chairs, I started to see my mistake.

"So you're not even a production assistant?"

He let out a good-natured laugh.

"You know those catering companies that show up at the way end of the credits? Like after the theme song's done playing out again and all that? I got my start as a dishwasher—"

Clocking his worn Vans, I glimpsed the gulf that stretched between being a producer and working "in production." This man wasn't working working-class cosplay. He was working class.

When it came to marriage, either he was still operating in a naïve economy, ready to marry for love, or we were direct competitors in the same market, each desperate for some capitalist to invest.

4

Later that week

SADEGH HEDAYAT's *The Blind Owl* is widely credited as the first novel in Farsi. A first-person fever dream, the novel plays and replays versions of the same story on loop, commonly interpreted as one long, opium-induced hallucination. The narrator is, as far as the book's sensibilities go, a half-blood, born to an Iranian father and Indian mother.

Hedayat wrote *Būf-i Kūr* while living in Bombay in 1936 or '37. He had to pay for the first printing himself. Early copies only circulated locally, on the outskirts of a shrinking Persophone world, and weren't typeset but stencil-printed, so readers enjoyed the intimacy of the author's hand. Official publication in Tehran only came several years later, and global recognition, another decade after that. In the 1950s, French and English translations crowned *Būf-i Kūr* as a work of world literature.

Let's open the book. Early on, we confront this central image: a young woman sitting by a stream near a cypress tree, offering a bruised water lily to a hunched old man. The scene is a painting by the narrator, obsessively painted and repainted for months—until now, when the image comes to life. The old man knocks on the narrator's door, introducing himself as the narrator's paternal uncle, and so on and so forth (the men aren't really my concern). The Iranian girl soon appears on the doorstep. Inviting herself in, she lies down on the narrator's bed. The air sparks with sexual tension.

Here it's worth pausing to note that the narrator's mother was a temple dancer, which, in this context, pretty much translates to a whore. His father was a merchant, meeting this infidel dancer on the road. Both parents were absent from the narrator's life, and he only remembers his nanny. This tortures him. In his imaginings, his mother operates as a kind of fetish object, at once desired and despised. Indeed, the history of Persian letters is rife with such Orientalization: India is demonized, considered uncivilized and dirty. In *Būf-i Kūr*, the hyper-sexuality of "the" (generalized, abstracted) Indian woman fuels the narrative, birthing the narrator's story—and the book itself—as it once birthed him. Now this female sexuality bubbles up, oozing out from under his bed, the pretty Iranian girl reclining on top. The narrator sits next to her, studying his subject, redrawing her eyes.

She's dead, by the way. He realized last night, the open eyes of rigor mortis providing a nice opportunity for his still-life. Satisfied with his work, he decides to hack her body to pieces. He arranges the dripping body parts—the faint hairs on her arms and legs slicked red, the blue tongue that now lolls out her slackened mouth—in a suitcase. The old man reappears as a hearse driver and helps the narrator dig a grave. When they're done dumping the mutilated girl in the dirt, the narrator realizes he doesn't have any cash to pay the guy. That's what he's worried about.

IT WAS THIS STORY that was running through my mind a few days into my project as I refused to respond to my alarm. A bar of light so hot it felt solid was cast across my chest, shooting through a gap in the blinds.

My ringtone took over the snooze. It was my mother.

Since I'd left for college, our habit had been to talk once weekly for an average of ninety-two seconds (I'd timed it). It sufficed to know the other was alive. No need to get into the details.

"Good morning," I answered.

"Good day."

I willed myself up. My mother woke before sunrise, and when the sun did finally rise over her Midwestern hamlet, it then took hours to creep this far west. You got the sense that by the time it was appropriate to call, she resented the very curvature of the earth for keeping her waiting.

"Are you familiar with a minor discourse called Orientalism?" she asked at second forty-three. "The name 'Edward Said' mean anything to you at all?"

Apparently, a couple weeks ago my mother had come across my job market materials in the wild, as it were. I'd applied to a postdoc without realizing that she was still "serving"—per the Service section of her CV—this particular humanities council. It was my statement of diversity, equity, and inclusion that my mother took issue with, starting with the opener. "Coming of age as a Muslim in post-9/11 America," I'd written. Though why she'd waited weeks to bring it up was beyond me.

"Throw the document out entirely," my mother continued her constructive feedback. "And reframe with something—friendlier. Cultural translation, bridge metaphors, nice, benign images."

When I'd decided to start wearing hijab back in middle school, she had been vehemently opposed. A-plus for consistency.

"But that's the critique," I said, my voice an octave higher than intended. "Extending Said's genealogy into the contemporary. Inserting an 'I,' but, like—but rather, historicizing it, feminizing it."

My mother hated it when I used fillers. Around the same time as my hijab controversy, she'd tried to scrub my vocabulary of the word *like*. I'd taken it under serious consideration, before realizing that was the only part of my vocab that sounded normal.

"Don't be naïve," she said. "Just because they want to hear the postcolonial critique doesn't mean they want to listen to the postcolonial subject. You do realize that Said was Christian."

"And Palestinian. So not even *post*colonial, really."

"That's not what the 'post' in post-anything means."

"Well it is, in theory," I outright whined. "Fanon in Algeria, Spivak and India, etcetera, etcetera. They were all writing after independence."

My mother, I thought as I rose to make coffee, was just starting grad school in 1985, when Gayatri Chakravorty Spivak first published "Can the Subaltern Speak?" (The answer is no.) Which was to say, my mother was late to the party—or would've been, had she ridden the tailwinds of postcolonial theory. Instead, she'd had the sense to stick close to whiteness, building on gaze theory, that favorite spawn of Second Wave feminism.

"You're missing the point."

She paused for emphasis. How I'd yearned as a teen to hear her story, but she eschewed theorizing from the self. ("Why should I read books by people who refuse to read books?") After six long seconds, drama evinced, she went on.

"They wouldn't have taken the critique coming from a Muslim. It took an insider."

SAID PUBLISHED *Orientalism* IN 1978, the same year my parents married, the same year they met. Within five or six years of that ill-fated eye contact some Friday in '78, my father graduated with a PhD in electrical engineering and started working at Ford. Within a year of that, my mother quit her engineering PhD to start all over in English. The sciences got her out of India, she liked to say; the humanities got her into America.

Contractually obliged to act as sole breadwinner according to their Quranically certified marriage—as she was quick to remind him—my father worked and my mother studied. He deposited her monthly wifely allowance, while her stipend lay at her own discretion. This freedom—soon to be a shackle, as so many freedoms are—allowed her to gain her footing. She leased a new car. She bought a Birkin. She had a baby. She actually read the books on her comprehensive exams list. Making quick work of it at a time when a PhD program in the humanities could easily underwrite ten or twelve years' worth of meditative walks and burnt espressos, she graduated in '91 with a dissertation on the gaze in Jane Austen.

The minute she finished, almost as if to spite her, my father's career took a nosedive. I supposed the American dream didn't need a reason to screw you. She held down adjunct appointments to support us, no time left to apply to real jobs or finally get that article through peer review. PMLA's revise-and-resubmit request yellowed in her mailbox cubby in the department mailroom. She returned the car. She sold the Birkin. Its cheerful red face still shines in old photographs.

BY NOW I'D GIVEN in to my mother's ad hoc advising session, taking my laptop and my coffee with me back to bed. As my mother proceeded to dictate corrections to my job market materials, complete with line edits—which I pretended to duly take down by clicking nonsensically on my keyboard—I toggled to the apps. A doctor, a lawyer, some girl with a PhD in chemistry who'd sold out to big pharma—my prospects were looking up.

"Why not 'and' rather than 'but' toward the top of graf three?"

Dutifully ignoring her suggestions, I made a few appointments. The jackpot, I was well aware, wasn't this kind of white-collar worker but someone who dealt in the business of money itself. That said, LA lay a long way from Wall Street. I powered through some new profiles, sniffing for green. Didn't this city have any banks?

"Graf break after 'as evidenced by the institutionalization of Sharia law in service of modern heteropatriarchy.' Oh, and do try 'substantiates' in place of 'as evidenced by,' it opens you up to an active construction."

I tried to square the ease of my mother's current patter with the grit of her immigrant story. It had taken almost a decade for her to plow through the shit fate my father had thrown at her, to land her first tenure track job. Her big break arrived only two years ago, right around when I finished my PhD. After decades of working twice as hard for half the pay, as it goes, she was promoted to provost. It was this coup that had justified missing my graduation. Then recently appointed as second-in-command at a no-name college that wouldn't be in business were it not for the insidious degree inflation that required every secretary and barista in America to hold a BA, my mother had considered it "simply nonnegotiable" to miss her institution's commencement, which had the misfortune of being scheduled for the same day as my own. Come June 16, 2017, she'd performed her provostian duties to the tee, lobbing each of her 296 "kids" into their uninsured, debtloaded, minimum-wage-paying futures with a smile and a handshake, while I, her only actual kid, walked Royce Hall without a soul waving at me from the audience.

Now, judging by the rare and unwanted attention she was paying to my research statement—"lines nine and fourteen, add the Oxford comma"—and no doubt thanks to her dedicated secretary, who in fact managed to singlehandedly run the college, and rather diplomatically, my mother, while the latter enjoyed annual raises that bloated the budget and, like any good, honest twenty-first-century college admin-istrator, made cuts to the humanities that would someday climax in the deletion of literature departments altogether, I could only conclude that she was finally so successful that she had nothing to do.

"As much as I hesitate to swell an already tumefied document—"

In a last twist of the knife, my mother had taken to my CV.

What do you do when you're not having fun? "Fintech." *What do you do when you're having fun?* "Fintech." On my phone screen I finally met a stone meriting the stumble. There were entire frontiers of exploitation I'd never imagined.

Still on speaker, my mother counseled that I add a brief "hobbies" section on page six to "humanize" me.

"I am a humanist. How much more humanized can I get?"

Ignoring me, she swerved off script.

"Are you talking to anyone these days?"

"What?"

In Muslim code, that meant dating. Hitherto my mother's approach to my love life had been that of patent, willful ignorance. She held the same policy on husbands as PhDs: one had to have one, but there was not to be any handholding in the process.

"Are you seeing anyone?" she said, painfully enunciating each word.

Thinking back to my evening with Eugene, to say nothing of graduation night, it occurred to me that the verbs were just right: good Muslims did only "talk" and "see" before marriage. Touching was for degenerates like me.

"A male person with a postsecondary degree and a retirement account?" Her exasperation was mounting. "Someone single, whom you might consider?"

I said nothing.

"Think about it. And seriously. Even in this country, there's a marriageable age, and then a point of no return."

"And that point is thirty-one?"

"Every society has its hypocrisies. They often concern women."

I heard the growl of the electric garage door. Soon after, the soft whir of her 2018 engine.

"What about that boy you brought here some years ago? With the Jewish nose?"

"Adam? My friend, Adam?"

"He was charming in his own way."

"What happened to marrying a Muslim—"

"Well, that's all I have." She turned suddenly cheery, as though wrapping a difficult meeting. "We have a luncheon for the game studies hire, and I need to get in at least ten minutes of this nonsense before I reach campus."

I heard the sage voice of an audiobook reader announce "Preface."

"Good night and good luck." My mother hung up.

I stopped the stopwatch: twenty-four minutes and seven seconds. A minute for every hour, a second for every day; in short, an eternity. This evisceration was my mother's idea of care. I imagined her waking to a green summer day washed by last night's storm, moved by the perfume of lake-effect rain to take pity on her fledgling offspring.

The last time we'd spent even half that long on the phone was years ago, to discuss a heart attack my father had suffered in Tehran. And that had included the ten minutes she'd put me on hold. We decided not to go see him in hospital.

THAT AFTERNOON I FORCED myself, for the first time in over a week, to go for a run. My mother's advice ringing in my ears, I'd spent the day cycling frantically through profiles and chats as the line of light between my blinds made its path across the room. I always left the blinds closed. Not because I was depressed—cyclic chronic depression didn't require darkness to survive—but because I didn't have AC.

Stuffing myself into biker shorts and a sports bra, I thought about Adam—I was surprised that my mother even remembered him, much less recommended him. Was my situation so desperate that she thought only a heathen would take me? Technically Jews were People of the Book, but she knew he was a poet.

The real problem, of course, was that Adam was already practically married; I could've just said that. To vindicate my worst suspicions of my friend, I detoured to my laptop. Adam had once tracked his phone from my computer, thinking it stolen after a house party that left him looking for excuses to hate our Adonis of a host, who, on top of being hot, was a white civil rights lawyer. "What a prick," Adam had fumed, fluffing my handwoven throw pillow rather too energetically for my tastes as he prepared to crash on my couch. "Fuck his shady friends."

His phone of course showed up, pinned in place in Ktown, safely at home.

But I'd never logged Adam out of the tracker. From time to time, I'd check on him, watching his dot move about the city, from his place to work to Julia's and back to his place in a monotonous loop. Which was exactly what I saw now: Adam's dot tucked into the high hills of Silver Lake.

So he was actually back together with her, and ghosting me because he was too chickenshit to admit it.

Motherfucker. I deleted the dot and clapped my laptop shut.

ON MY RUN, I compared my recent trajectory to my mother's.

Few abuses are more premediated than a PhD. The years spent writing the dissertation were only the final blow. Field, subfield, subject: each choice was agonized. Not only the material you studied but the people you studied with were researched, read. Hours, entire terms, perhaps years, were spent selecting and courting faculty to "serve" in these positions. You bought their books, scouring the internet for discounted copies. You took their seminars. You attended their office hours, where you unleashed subtle and precise references to their "contributions" to the field to flatter their egos. You contemplated whether sycophancy was a form of affective labor, hours of intellectual labor spent deciphering and disentangling and discussing capital-t Theory hidden in the very question. Since undergrad, since high school, since preschool, you'd been collecting As and recommendations and advice to land the right programs, the right people: you judged, and assessed, and yes, researched. Before the dissertation, there was the prospectus. Before the prospectus, comprehensive exams. Before comps, coursework. Before coursework, admittance. And before that, there was the agony of birth.

Huffing past my first mile marker, I eased into my exertion. What did I have to show for any of this? My mother had spent grad school versing herself in the vagaries of love spooned sweetly at teatime. I'd devoted my life to a literature—modern "Persian" literature—founded on violence against women. That, and an Orientalism aimed at its darker-skinned neighbors to the east. Every east has an east. Every Orient, its Orient.

People loved *The Blind Owl*. Not just Iranians, but also American elites. The butch professor who'd assigned it to the World Literature seminar Adam and I took in undergrad. The grad school reading group convened to celebrate a new translation out from a well-respected indie press. The editors at said indie press. I'd read the novel in Farsi, and English, and English again. Again and again I felt the caricatured Indian "slut"-mother as a slap against my own face—my own mother's face. I felt the blow of the narrator's dull knife as bruises on my body, felt the blade of his success cut through my skin. And I wasn't exactly squeamish; in middle school my favorite movie was *Kill Bill*. Even more nauseating was that, judging by blood, I had no choice but to identify with the narrator: Iranian father, Indian mother.

While I was so low that you had to assume there was nowhere to go but up, my mother's early work was her most brilliant.

In the mid-nineties, as my father stumbled back down the prover-bial ladder and I jumped double rope on public school asphalt, my mother began to rescue snippets of time for herself. For her work. She snatched long mute minutes from the blue-black night, and hours clut-tered with birdsong from the thin of morning. She tackled PMLA's revise-and-resubmit request and reread her sources. She felt the rush of picking a prestigious quarterly from the Recent rack at the library and reading her own words on page twenty-two. In 1997 her erstwhile dissertation was picked up by a respectable academic press, emerging from the tortured chrysalis of the untenured mind into the world as her first book. It was that book that won her an assistant professorship, that finally got her foot in the door.

As with any scholarly tome, you didn't need to read past page two. In a gripping opening anecdote she argues—present tense, by academic convention—that the inflection point in *Pride and Prejudice* (orig. 1813) comes not, as commonly thought, when Mr. Darcy saves the reputation of Elizabeth Bennet's "fallen" (i.e., fornicating) sister, and thus of the entire Bennet family, but rather, when Elizabeth tours Darcy's estate with her aunt and uncle. There, alone amidst brushed walnut and gilded frames, our heroine meets Darcy's eyes—in the form of his portrait. Elizabeth and Darcy gaze at each other, real and representation. The painting contains the truth of Darcy's person. His honesty, his sense of justice. Elizabeth has already realized her mistake about Darcy's character, but it is here at Pemberley that she begins to earnestly shed her prejudice. (Though cinematic, I'll take the liberty of adding, it is a scene that film adaptations consistently miss.)

That art should contain the truth of life is old news. My mother's genius lay in focusing on the gaze itself. It is, she claims, this refracted, metonymized union of the lovers' gazes, rather than crude, direct eye contact, that leads to knowledge—and, eventually, consequently, to love. At once reflecting and reinforcing Victorian mores, the portrait protects the feminized seer from the force of truth as a camera obscura protects the eye from an eclipse.

Maybe my mother's research did mirror her experience, but in the way of any household mirror over the bathroom sink: in reverse. In contrast to her heroine, she and my father fell in love eye to eye, and that crass collision had only led to disappointment.

That was the problem with love stories: they ended with the beginning. Of my parents' marriage, I'd only witnessed carnage.

TWENTY-EIGHT MINUTES LATER I was back at the edge of the neigh-borhood and the end of three miles. Tingling with serotonin, practically sauntering from the high of the cooldown, I headed home. Out front, I put a hand on the pomegranate tree to stretch. I hadn't taken much notice of it since my photo shoot for the apps, and now the red flow-ers winked in the sunlight. In the fall, when I aimed to be someone's fiancée, the same low branches would bear full, fleshy fruit. At least in theory. My father kept a pomegranate tree in the courtyard of his house in Tehran, a much grander one. Visiting him there in 2015 months after his heart attack, right around this time of year, I was happy to catch it flowering, but he'd only bemoaned that summer blooms boded an unproductive fall.

I sensed my quad pinch and release. On my phone, an email noti-fication hovered: the nondescript subject line of a customary rejection, from the very same postdoc my mother had called about. Her timing was no coincidence. She knew it was coming. In my inbox, an "FYI" from my mother sent just minutes prior claimed that she'd recused herself from the committee. I didn't believe her. She had no reason to; we didn't share a last name.

I plucked a flower from the pomegranate tree. A thick pink skin was swallowing the flower into the budding fruit, forcing the stigmata closer together and the petals to close. Their lips were papery, the flower at the end of its bloom. It was dying. And that was good.

My body fizzed with heat and exhaustion and the blind confidence of prey. I'd once overheard a student athlete say that the body wants to quit after only 40 percent of "what's in the tank." To the tune of pop songs I'd never publicly admit I liked, I went back out the gate and kept running.

Past the laundromat around the corner and across Vermont. Past the seedy hotel parking and through the swarm of flies feeding on shit.

My body and the plastics that encased it—the soles of my shoes, the stretch in my sports bra—formed a collection of pliant vectors whose orientation shifted by the split second. The cracked sidewalk buoyed me forward, reflecting my force to shoot up up up up my calves knees quads hips abs and into my brain.

My project was changing, from writing about marriage to securing one. From mind to body, theory to practice.

Date #13: Queer Vernacular

EVEN IN LA, CITY of long lunches and floating weekends, Monday is not a good day for a date. Sex is another matter.

On Monday the white-collar worker feels the week's weight around her neck. The rich man whose riches she has been entrusted to grow guilts her for the past weekend, that forced pause on infinite growth. (Except the service worker who serves them both kept working. Even on Sundays the blue-and-gray trucks bludgeon by, delivering boxes as big as children of toilet paper to wipe your ass.)

Monday morning passes in a spin. "Catching up" on emails and calls whose nature is to outrun her, she morphs into a gray-blue spiral ready to empty with centrifugal force. Tuesday waits, and Wednesday and Thursday and and and all the way to next Monday. For now, there's this Monday afternoon. The clock becomes a countdown.

After work she tries to fill the void. She hits the gym, she eats her vegetables, she texts a friend. Nothing does the trick—she's cored.

For a body such as this, another body's just the thing.

Explode, and let the fallout fill you.

MONDAY NIGHT I WAS fucked by a butch producer perched high in the Hollywood Hills, terrified all the while that the emergency brake on my faded Ford Focus wouldn't hold.

Around nine o'clock, parked above a red Porsche Cayenne Coupé, I'd found the back gate ajar. On the tiles just inside, someone I took to be a gay guy lay shirtless, idly flipping through an architectural digest, with nails gel-manicured to perfection. Moonbathing, maybe, except the moon had already set.

"Hey?" I said, unsure how to get around him.

He propped his head up on an elbow and turned to one side, odalisque-esque. Then he lifted himself into a side plank, kilt pleats fanning.

"Just go, sweetheart," he said in a Southern drawl, waving me over with his free hand.

I managed to clear him despite my espadrilles and minidress. The skirt was so tight it limited my stride.

Now squarely on the property, I could see the living room past the pool, lit up behind floor-to-ceiling windows. On the L-sofa floating at the center of the room like an anchored yacht, a whole group was huddled over the coffee table—over, presumably, a mirrored tray. She hadn't said anything about a party.

I felt a splash on my toes (electric pink, my handiwork).

A body had surfaced from the pool, a lean line of leopard-print surf suit. They stretched their arms overhead and shook off, wringing out long brown locks limpened by water. Our eyes met. I smiled stupidly, wondering if I'd dressed too femme for a ciswoman, given the crowd.

"She's inside."

The swimmer broke out into a smile. They took a sharp breath and dove back in.

By now my date had spotted me through the glass curtain. She pointed and cupped her hands to her mouth, but I couldn't hear what she was saying. The glass was first-rate, entirely soundproof.

"Backdoor," the kilt translated. He was still in plank.

OUR COLLECTIVE HOST OCCUPIED the corner of the sofa like a throne, legs spread, arms out.

"Hey there, welcome," she called over the din of chatter as I entered through the galley kitchen. "Beers in the fridge."

Broad-shouldered and big-bellied, she had on black jeans and a black tee. Her salt-and-pepper hair was cropped and gelled. Against the young bright things set up outside like pride-edition garden gnomes, the folks inside looked drab and dated. Just a bunch of old-school gays and lesbians who'd gotten rich and fat to rebel against their younger selves.

Back from the kitchen, armed with a glass of screw-top wine, I settled in beside her only to realize, to my great horror, that what sat on the coffee table—what these white people were crooked over in cold filtered air, while just beyond the glass, warm stars shone over a private infinity pool—wasn't a mound of coke, but a Monopoly board.

SEVERAL HOURS AND MY personal bottle of pinot later, the room finally emptied, board folded, custom pieces packed, including the miniature model "Porsh-uh"—two syllables—whose replica sat parked outside.

The producer and I conducted our business on the short prick of the L. She set the terms, my compliance my contribution. Tongue, then straight to the strap-on according to the grammar of the queer vernacular, a grammar that allows for conjunctions, for desire not curtailed by fillers and politesse.

As I climaxed on my back, pumiced feet pressing into the firm cushions, I gazed out the glass wall. Light, man-made and otherwise, seeped out the city's pores and out the sky's, touching here, reaching there. I lay, a finger drowned in the eye of my own silver skin, every surface humming.

5

Tuesday, July 2

TUESDAY MORNING—MUCH TO MY confusion, I'd been invited to "crash" on her bed, and rather cordially supplied with a hotel-branded toothbrush—I snuck out early to take a dip in the pool. Two weeks into my experiment, and finally I was getting somewhere. This wasn't exactly U-Hauling, but it was promising.

No one was awake, the water cold, the sun low. The move, I knew, would be to go nude. I settled for my bra and briefs. I swam a few laps. I surfaced to a yard soaked in sun, all of Los Angeles unraveled under me like a rug. Water fell from my skin as a dog's pelt, drumming blithely against the poolside. So this was how the other half lived. And by "half" I meant a fraction of the 1 percent.

One flat white and two goodbye kisses later, I was back on the graying asphalt of the public road, fresh as a daisy. But my car wasn't where I'd left it. It was in fact two feet downhill, ass to lips with the Porsche. There was a ticket on the windshield for failing to turn my wheels, as if this weren't in evidence. Fortune was fastidious when she wanted to be.

The slutty red pucker of the Cayenne Coupé's exaggerated nose was smacked flat, and who knew what garish scratches would be exposed as soon as I managed to peel out. Why couldn't people with garages use them?—then again maybe the garage was for the weekender.

I got into my car, trying to keep quiet as I eased forward. The bumpers made an awful sound as they unstuck. But the hillside air remained still, the street undisturbed. A bomb could go off and these folks wouldn't know any better inside their sealed glass boxes. In my mirror I could now see the Porsche's freshly skewed front vanity plate, which referenced some very valuable lowbrow IP. The same IP, I assumed, that had paid for the infinity pool and midcentury Danish coffee table, and, I hoped, some damned good car insurance. I made the daintiest three-point turn American manufacturing would allow and rolled me and my Ford, unnoticed, back downhill to plebes' quarters.

The parking ticket fluttered away behind me.

BACK IN MY (AT best) middle-class neighborhood that evening, I went to grab a taco around the corner. I'd snuck in a day-date while descending from the Hills in my damp underwear. Next on the lineup was post-dinner drinks.

This particular taco truck had little to recommend it but proximity. While it monopolized the meters outside the laundromat, half my wardrobe spun in the machines inside. Asada grease dripping down my arm, I opened the spreadsheet on my phone. Dutifully I recorded numbers 12 (lawyer, junior associate) through 14 (PA who just made agent). Eugene Kim's independent wealth aside, #13, the capital-P (as listed in the credits) Producer, made the most money. My note from #4, "in production," barked at me: "Life is good!" Had he actually said that? The same motto that was printed on the Nalgene the freckled Section 8–housed quarterback used to carry around my high school? It was an unlikely coincidence. I had no choice but to ask myself whether I was a classist stereotyping bitch who'd fashioned a font of happy-go-lucky wisdom out of the only working-class guy who'd dripped through my filter. Moreover, did the algorithm know that what we bougie assholes wanted out of the wage worker was a man at peace with his exploitation?

Somewhere in this run of Shia-style self-flagellation, my phone dinged. And dinged, and dinged, all app notifications.

The Producer had discovered the dent. In other words, I'd finally landed a genuine prospect last night only to fuck it up this morning by hitting-and-running her bisyllabically-pronounced Porsche.

I deleted the match and ordered another taco. Sweet silence. Thanks to queerness, we hadn't exchanged phone numbers.

The thing was, when it came to the picket line in the next inevitable IATSE strike, I'd always support the folks in production over the producers—I'd looked up *LA Times* clippings, and evidently Hollywood was overdue for a shakedown. Number 4 catered kale Caesar salads for B-listers, while I catered my classes to a generation who thought that *The Philadelphia Story* was about cream cheese and *Waiting to Exhale* was a mindfulness app. Between teaching and grad studenting, I'd been a union member myself for years. Hands dirty with taco fixings, I realized that to marry rich I'd have to put aside my politics. To stay married I'd have to quash them.

With a plop, stark white bird shit landed on my remaining bite. I tossed the plate, and the meat landed softly in the trash. Maybe I couldn't kill my conscience in a day. But there was always tomorrow.

Date #24: Dada

ON A WEEKDAY AFTERNOON I found myself circling forty minutes to find parking in Hollywood at rush hour, which is Angelenese for "hell." On the docket: a willowy blonde who'd evaded all my attempts at assessing what she did for work, meaning she was either broke or uber-rich.

Now tête-à-tête with this assemblage of found material from Goodwill—i.e., über-rich—I discovered that I'd been led to the foot of Runyon Canyon, rather than a bar. First she'd pulled me to her front door through peak traffic with a blonde's presumption, and now this.

"Feel like a stroll?"

I was in kitten heels, to say nothing of sweat's toll on suede. Whereas the medium for Untitled #24 constituted little-boys'-section jorts, City of Commerce-based mom-and-pop mechanic-shop decennial-celebration hoodie, graying Crocs. Either she was testing me, or punishing me for being femme.

"Absolutely," I said, stepping through the gates.

In all my years in LA I'd never done Runyon. Chalk it up to intuition. As I now experienced, far from the dusty trails that hung from Griffith Park like gold chains and the shaded groves at its foot that enabled a rather productive type of navel-gazing if not downright epiphanies, this hiking path was paved and more crowded than the Grove on a Saturday afternoon.

She chain-smoked as we took the hill, attracting the ire of the school of human fish we'd invaded, a slow upstream flow of Lululemon-wrapped Instagram models and freelancers who used *creative* as a noun. Inquiries into her age, profession, marital status, etc., went artfully unanswered. Even her name came hedged: "My friends call me Aspen." Asking about my sign, scandalized that I didn't know my rising, she then steered us into the cosmos. My every yen, every fault and fancy, virtue and tendency, was dictated by the stars. It was an interpretation of the world more damning than anything I'd experienced in organized religion. No room for merit or random beauty.

"Nice to meet you, Aspen," I said, finally back on level ground.

"Ibsen," she corrected.

She smoothed a hand through her hair, and I saw a flash of silver at her wrist, peeking over the tired elastic of her cuff.

"Ibsen?"

I tried to catch a glimpse of her watch face.

"Yeah, Aspen."

"Okay, Aspen—"

"No, Ibsen."

"So, Ibsen."

"*Aspen*. Names are a sign of respect."

As our exchange slid into Dada, or whatever avant-garde school of performance art she was practicing on me, I fished for my car keys. Maybe the self is a construct, but this was rapist-murderer material.

Still, I had to know what she was hiding under all this dirty laundry. I offered a handshake, and, smirking rather understandably at the foolishness, she took it. Holding her in a stiff grip, I could finally read the watch face.

Rolex.

Back to the independently wealthy. I was getting warmer.

6

Friday, July 12

ANOTHER WEEK CAME AND went. July lurched into puberty. People populated the spreadsheet, but my affections remained unattached.

After Date #35 I got a text from Adam.

What you up to this weekend?

It was a Friday night. Just a few minutes prior I'd shaken off my date—a twiggy oncology resident who'd been too good on paper to give up until, as dessert menus arrived on date three, the prospect of fucking him came too close for comfort—and now I was out in the Valley, drunk alone, without a car. My options were a two-hour bus-to-bus journey home, given the red-line was down, or a seventeen-minute straight shot to a birthday party in Mar Vista for someone in my old cohort, every one of whom was still stuck in limbo, in school. I'd missed the cohort's last sorry shindig, and if I didn't show up to something soon, they'd think I thought I was better than them. I did, but that wasn't the point.

I checked the price of cars. Getting home would cost more than an entire tank of gas, but Mar Vista was within reach for the cost of drugstore mascara. Except then, in a few hours when even the two-buck chuck was drained, I'd have to trek home from west of the 405. I was only delaying the inevitable.

Any chance you're free tonight?

Double-texting meant Adam was desperate to make up. This was forgiveness. "Supportive" wasn't exactly my forte, he knew as well as I.

"Heyy," he picked up.

His voice was soft and gruff all at once, and the chord plucked at something in my chest.

"Hi, friend!"

My awkwardness expressed as enthusiasm.

"One sec," he said. "Just finishing something up."

I could hear the click-clack of a keyboard. Was he still at work? My geriatric dinner had wrapped up by seven, but still. I thought he'd be out drinking, or at Julia's, or—I don't know, just doing something sexier than meeting the requirements of a nine-to-five. I imagined him in one of his collared shirts, phone cradled between shoulder and ear, fingers ferrying from keys to mouse. I was happy to listen, almost hoping he'd forget I was on the other end—maybe then I could think of how to proceed. Seemingly he did. A minute or two passed.

"Sorry about that."

"I guess they really make you work for that 401k."

"Nah." I could hear his smile. "I'm not at the office. I was working on the book."

My image readjusted: Adam in that moth-eaten cashmere sweater he always wore at home, lying on the couch with the manuscript on his stomach and a red pen. He was staying home on a Friday night to write about that long lost love, his Juliette before Julia; to write to the one who got away. So I'd been doing him a favor by not checking in. To be a poet in the year 2019, you had to get off on being ignored.

"Look—" I paused. "I know it's been a minute, but—well—"

Why was a simple "sorry" so hard for me to say?

"Can we hang out?" Adam spoke into the silence. "I'll come to you."

"I'm on the hook for a thing in Mar Vista later."

"Okay."

Okay?

"Can't I come with you?"

One month and we were already strangers.

"I'm not going. Actually."

I wasn't sure why I was testing him, but I was. I started down the block in search for a cup of coffee. Softening, I went on.

"I'm wandering the nether reaches of LA county, and my car's at home."

"Long Beach? Pomona? You're gonna have to be more specific."

"Ventura Blvd. The two blocks that're suddenly fancy."

"Drop me a pin, and I'll head out in five."

A beat passed when I should've said "thanks."

"Sherman Oaks is within city limits, just FYI," Adam said, before hanging up.

BY THE MIRACLE THAT's the 101, Adam's red two-door first-gen Insight was crawling up to the café curb twenty-three minutes later. Another eleven, and we were bathed in the cool air of the Armenian grocery store in Van Nuys, the metal gate swinging behind us. With the delicious prospect of spending Saturday morning solo in the comfort of my own middle-class bed, it had occurred to me that I had nothing for breakfast.

We ambled through the aisles, quiet in each other's company. Cans of beets and tuna and ready-made dolmas. Jars of olives both green and black. I usually did my grocery shopping at the outpost of the same local chain that was near my place, on Vermont, and I felt at ease here. The place flickered with Third World patina, the fluorescents softer than at American-American supermarkets, the floors less mercilessly shined.

I paused before the spices. There was an entire section with Farsi labels. Powdered lime rind and sumac, the likes of which had stocked the spice drawer when I was growing up.

According to the heteropatriarchal imperialism that structured my family, my mother had learned to cook Iranian food for the sake of my father. He had an old friend from grad school send the packets from Potomac, Maryland, second only to LA in the FOB factor of Iranian expats. When he first got to this country, my father liked to say, they didn't sell turmeric outside of Dearborn and San Francisco. As for my mother, she was all too happy to give up on her roots. She said curry powder seeped through the pores, and your sweat gave you away. (As what?—I only thought to ask myself later.)

Every morning from June 2014, when I advanced to Candidacy, to June 2017, when I finished my PhD, I packed my backpack in time for the 7:02 shuttle to campus, the top shelf of my fridge stacked with single-size portions of rice and khoresht in cheap plasticware that would endure the apocalypse, prepped the Sunday prior just like my mother used to do for my father when she was around my age. (And for herself, nothing but uncut fruit.) Except, in my own pathetic rebellion, sometimes curry took the place of khoresht. Palak paneer and daal and korma, generic fare I achieved via Americanized recipes sourced from the internet. Sunday afternoons, eyes glazed over at the research library, I had only to float down Westwood Blvd to the "Persian" grocery to restock on dehydrated sabzi, or catch the green bus to Culver West for curry powder and masala mix.

Now, as Adam studied the branding of competing Moroccan olive oils an aisle over, I weighed a bag of whole dry limes in my hand. But the idea that I'd have time to stand over the stove stirring a pot of grass green ghormeh sabzi or rusty gheimeh was a joke. Practically all my meals next week were promised to strangers. Adam and me aside, even my normal friendships were suffering.

How's the sexcapade? a friend had texted the other day. *Don't wear her out.* I supposed the "she" didn't merit explanation.

"Let me see"—a skirt-aproned employee reached around me for the za'atar that had been lumped in with the Iranian stuff. Adam was just behind her. Gaze lingering on the biceps bared under his tee, she left him with the spice mix and a wide grin.

"I see you're back at those pushups," I said.

"Huh?"

Adam blushed. He didn't go for big boobs. (That made one of us.)

Settling for a packet of cardamom for my tea, I steered over to produce. Raw bananas and overripe tomatoes. Sharp arugula sold in big plastic boxes. Stone fruit you could smell from where you were standing—I didn't even have to bend my back. Adam followed me with the cart, bowing to my silence. I didn't want to talk about Julia, and his muscle definition was proof enough. The honeymoon phase always left him with too much energy.

"So," I said as I bagged some peaches. "You owe me one."

This was my version of an olive branch.

"For what?"

"Last month. That night in Ktown."

I forced a teasing tone, hoping to make light of the situation. His idiocy in going back to her, and my idiocy in pointing that out.

"You issue this big press release on being single, then don't even last the night alone."

"Isn't that what friends are for?"

He said the word "friends" as though in air quotes. We made our way to the bakery. I grabbed a seeded loaf and, succumbing to strategic product placement, a jar of the sour cherry marmalade that stood in a neat row above. Adam took the items from me and set them in the cart.

"A secondhand bouquet is cruel," I said, taking the jam back out to read the label, though I couldn't care less.

"That's not how I meant it."

I met his eyes. They looked genuinely pained. We moved to check-out, beading ourselves at the end of a long line. Friday night and every worker was stuck either finding something to eat or selling it. "Anahit to the register," an announcement came over the loudspeaker. The MILF who'd helped find the za'atar sauntered by, winking at Adam, who pretended not to notice.

"How *is* your girlfriend by the way?"

"Ex. Ex-girlfriend—"

Well, that was news. And what about that dot in Silver Lake?

"How's your book?" he asked, meeting my sarcasm with sincerity.

"Nonexistent."

We shifted to the new register, still at the back, but of a shorter line.

"Okay then, what's the new article on?"

He was shamelessly changing the subject. In all these years I'd only managed to place one journal article. Given the asinine banalities I saw published by authors with "Professor" titles according to this same process of blind peer review, I suspected the process wasn't as blind as "blind" claimed.

"Chimeric Cumming?" he went on. "That's c-u-, by the way, not c-o."

I stepped out of line to see what the holdup was—we hadn't moved an inch. An old Armenian man was counting out change for a six-pack of beers.

"You're not happy when you're not working," Adam said after a silence long enough to near us to the register.

"I *am* working."

Adam loaded the groceries onto the belt.

"On what."

"Marrying rich."

I folded my arms, moving my gaze elsewhere. I could feel his.

"It was your idea," I said.

"Operation Golddigger? You've got to be kidding me."

"I'll settle for silver."

"If all you want is silver—"

"Cash or credit?"

Anahit had rung us up together, and Adam waved away my card. She gave me the up and down, and frowned.

"Or wait," Adam said, bagging the heaviest of the groceries first. "I've got one better: Rehearsing Bi-privilege, Resisting Biphobia." He bumped my elbow. "That's good, you should use that."

"Très amusant."

Outside, the desert night glistered, cold and dry as black diamonds. Across the lot someone took out a phone, and the screen shone against the darkness like a dot on a map.

"I've got it," I said, refusing to let him help me load the trunk.

We never lied to each other. Or at least not like that.

FOR MY FIRST SIX years in LA, the closest thing I'd had to home was my university-owned rental in Mar Vista, a neighborhood whose vista had in fact never been available to me. Whether in singles or family housing, the graduate colony was relegated to the lowlands, while professors floated from room to sunlit room to pool to porch in hilltop houses mortgaged, according to a faculty incentives program, not by a private bank but by our public university at favorable rates, their property values ever increasing due to gentrification. It was almost as absurd as the satellite campuses popping up every season in places like Florence and Mexico City. Moneylender, real estate developer, global franchiser; there was nothing the twenty-first-century university couldn't do.

Within a week of receiving my doctorate, before the diploma had arrived in the mail, I was kicked out of grad student housing. Forced to forego the cool temperatures and uncool vibes of the Westside, but also perhaps ready, besides, to enter the phase of my adulthood in which I didn't cross the street whenever I caught sight of my (now newly former) advisor—I, sweaty in spandex at the climax of a run, betraying an investment in the body ill-suited to a scholar; she, herding preteens into an SUV, i.e., the offspring into its armor, betraying an equally embarrassing level of hope verging on climate denial (to say nothing of the eight-cylinder engine)—I abandoned the beach side of the 405 to head east. East along the 10 until I hit still more articled numbers hitherto only familiar to me on weekends: the 101, the 110, the 5.

My spot in Little Armenia was what I could afford. Empty wrappers collected inside the low gate to my building, fluttering through black iron bars to get lodged in the fly-infested rosemary bush, a graveyard, as it was, for flashy business cards offering to give you a ride or adjust the pH of your water. I often arrived at my car at 7:45 a.m., avoiding the 8:00 ticket I could otherwise expect for interrupting street sweeping, to confront the fresh offense of a *WE BUY JUNK* flyer on the windshield. Meantime, gleaming white Mercedeses (pl. Mercedi?) hogged the parking on the narrow street, shiny white phalluses protected from theft and scuffing by no more than their owners' reputations—clear indication, as far as my suburban-bred brain could tell, that the block was still run by the mob. Like the citations that trail a social science paper, the tattoos that flowered on my neighbors' backs, catching some SoCal sun alongside the rosebushes and pomegranate trees, only proved what was common sense. In short, when I passed someone walking his dog, I made sure to smile.

THERE IN MY STUDIO, my queen bed now beckoned, the mute slab of direct-to-consumer foam silently mouthing my name—we could be basking in the blue light of my computer right this moment, I, curled atop the summer sheets in my pajamas, Adam, leaning back in my office chair (no outside clothes on the bed, please), a happy ending playing out tranquilly on screen.

Instead I was loitering by a plastic slide, stilettos sinking into Astroturf in the Mar Vista family housing complex, as Adam finished off a joint.

It had taken two stiff pours and a game of chess at a twee saloon in the valley to thaw our suspicions of each other. (Though admittedly, I held on to one.) Bubbling with some kind of manic makeup energy—in love and friendship, the same logic applies—Adam had insisted on staying out. All the more so when I finally admitted to him, and thus to myself, that in truth I was avoiding my cohort. Just being here in Mar Vista was enough to profess failure, my failure to exceed my past.

"You can just feel the anxiety," I said, rechecking the invite for the building and unit number. "It's in the air. Poisoning us as we speak."

"You need to get your swagger back." Adam took a drag. "Immersion therapy."

He held out the burning butt.

"Might soothe your trauma?"

I shook my head and lit a cigarette from a fresh pack. Downers weren't really my thing. Life was bad enough.

The family housing compound was eerily quiet, most windows dark—and on a Saturday, no less. When I'd lived in singles housing down the road, the occasional noise-complaint-worthy fête had created at least some semblance of normalcy in nerdland.

"Last call." I held out the cigarette.

Adam glowered. We both knew I was trolling him. Social smoking was a vice Adam couldn't abide. When I'd rerouted the GPS to stop at a cigarette kiosk, he'd demanded a family-size bag of chips I knew he wouldn't eat, just to punish me. Now, he picked it out of the bucket swing where I'd left it.

"Let's get this party started."

"Whatever you say."

I blew the smoke in his direction.

The building was clear on the other end. I started us toward the pee-filled kiddie pool, navigating the maze of playgrounds that apparently constituted *family*. The birthday boy was ignoring my calls, and we'd slithered in on foot behind a beat-up Civic. I assumed a friend of his was hosting. Last I'd checked, he was as sad and single as any Foucauldian can rightly expect.

Only on the third knock did someone open the door. It wasn't my cohort mate. Adam introduced himself with a suspiciously genuine smile, and we entered. The tiny open-plan kitchen doubled as a foyer, and we set the chips on the counter, a sorry offering. I could see four or five disheveled approximations of men lined up on the sofa. Autogenerated psychedelic music trickled out of a laptop on the peeling Ikea coffee table. A baby sat upright, quiet but fully alert, caged in a crib in the corner. There wasn't a woman in sight and the men were too unkempt to be gay—where was its mother?

"I'm gonna kill you," I whispered to Adam a moment later, our heads crooked into an open fridge.

Only the reject beers were left. Or maybe these folks actually preferred passion-fruit-crème-brûlée-flavored IPAs.

"This is your world," he said.

Peeling two bottles from the dehydrated goo that covered the shelf, he handed me one with a shrug.

Reluctantly I followed him to join the circle. My cohort mate was nowhere to be found.

I recognized the sofa set from our coursework days, in particular an intensive yearlong seminar on critical theory in which these folks—theory bros, they were called, a genus my cohort mate belonged to without really belonging—postured about Derridean deconstruction and Frankfurt School classics without accurately comprehending a word of what we read. Either they'd skimmed the Wiki or were illiterate. Unfortunately for them, our black-jeans-black-tee-wearing white-man full professor didn't have time for bullshit, and instead took a shine to me.

In theory, the theory bro is not a misogynist—is indeed, he swears, a feminist; that he regularly quotes Donna Haraway proves as much. In practice, encountering women not on the page but in the physical realm, he cannot countenance brains trapped in a woman's body. Seated on the couch, shoulders touching—and thighs, the wily erotics of straight masculinity—the bros offered Adam warm fist bumps and me, at best, a nod. So they still hadn't forgiven me for garnering daddy's approval. Marveling at the paucity of the male spirit, I took a seat on the carpeted floor.

All too late I realized that I'd placed myself dangerously close to the child. Common courtesy—that is, an oppressive and widespread natalism—dictated that I interact with it. The kid was getting restless, pushing against the mesh wall of its playpen. Bored, evidently, of the movie that flickered on a second laptop positioned on a bookshelf nearby for its benefit. I poked at the hand that bulged against the mesh. The tiny pink hand pushed back. Adam was across the room, sitting cross-legged by the sofa, nodding meditatively as another man talked. He was obviously stoned.

"Hey, there!" The birthday boy settled down next to me, speaking through a mouthful of my chips. "It's been forever."

"About a year, yeah," I said. "Happy birthday."

I'd always had a soft spot for this particular bro—though I was now searching for why. Did you deserve a medal for not being sexist? I took a handful of chips when he offered, and we munched together for a moment.

It was then that I registered the movie screening in front of the playpen: *When Harry Met Sally*. Classic Nora Ephron. Why anyone had thought a rom-com, iconic as this one was, could sustain the attention of a human light years away from romancing anyone was unclear. But for better or worse, Harry and Sally's banter was currently the most stimulating conversation in the room.

"Can't believe you made it."

I couldn't agree more.

He brushed the salt from his hands. "Have you seen this before?"

"Too many times to count." He smiled, and I went on. "The first time was at school, actually. Valentine's Day. So much for AP Gov."

As the child clumsily managed to get on his feet and babble for attention, my bro demanded mine. He'd never heard of Nora Ephron. I found myself reciting my long-held prejudice against the friends-to-lovers plot, which I considered the most unimaginative of all the rom-com subgenres. As though, to find love, you had to choose from a list of all the losers you already knew.

"It's a slap in the face of realism," I said, glancing across the room.

Adam was gesticulating, elbows deep in some anecdote, and the sofa bros laughed.

"Friendzoning," I said. "Now that's real."

Now my bro laughed.

"Maybe, I mean, maybe—" he ventured with all the timidity of a grad student who still raises their hand in seminar.

It was dawning on me that this was what I had come for, to preen in the glow of his admiration and respect, the worthless respect of another peon.

"Maybe that's what people like about it, right. Like, it's pure fantasy, right?"

He popped another beer, taking a sip after I'd waved off the offer. I still had half of mine to go.

"Yes, of course," I said, hearing myself rather too clearly. One of those inexplicable lulls that plague even good parties had befallen us, and my voice carried. "Still, the question is what fuels the fantasy. The desire to collapse the friend and lover stems from the same confusion as the Oedipal complex, or Electra or whatnot. If we take a Freudian tack."

"Falling in love with someone you already love?" He took a second to consider it, then nodded, lips pursed in approval. "Yeah, that's good."

On the sofa, the theory bros were one man down. Adam was in his spot, head lolling, asleep.

"Honestly, it's all Lacan," I said, a consequence of the passion-fruit-crème-brûlée already souring in my stomach. "Screw Freud. It's about that lack we feel in our cores, that sense that there's always something missing. That's what it is to want your friend."

I got up. One hand around my beer and the other on my heart, I said, "The figure of the friend-lover is the objet petit à—"

This was just what I was after, this thrill. I could hear a whole series of lectures shaping up, an entire fall syllabus on chick flicks, just what I needed to save me. I saw myself in my most punishing vintage skirt suit (the waist was so tight I'd better stay standing), saw the smiling Gen-Z faces of my most intractable students, felt my heart swelling with the rare ecstasy of a humanist talking about material that other people actually read and watched. Unit I, "From Making Friends to Making Love." Start at home in LA with *Love & Basketball* then hop in the car with Harry and Sally in Chicago and drive east to New York. (By now, in fact, the credits were rolling.)

"Therein," I said, swinging my beer to drive my point, "lies an attempt to complete the self."

Just then the monotone and genderless call characteristic to human nestlings ripped through the apartment, drawing our collective attention to the playpen—toppled now on its side, baby limbs spilling out. Adam roused from his slumber, rubbing his eyes. A woman genied into existence.

"Oh honey, that's okay," my cohort mate scooped up the screaming child and passed it to the woman. Large drops of my beer saturated the child's white onesie like piss.

Adam joined me at my side as the woman sniffed at the stained onesie. While I wondered at the nouns that were being thrown around—"wife," "baby," "job"—Adam smiled and asked follow-up questions with a genial yet not overpowering level of enthusiasm. The nap had sobered him.

"Wow, and TT, too?" Adam said to her in academic argot. (I'd trained him well.) "Congrats, landing a UC is no joke."

The woman beamed. My cohort mate beamed. Together they fussed over the child.

"Yeah, thanks," she said, stripping the infant to its diaper. "Such a relief we don't have to leave California."

"It's just fantastic," my cohort mate said over his shoulder. "I'm so proud of her."

He was whisking the beer-soaked onesie to the laundry, and I was grateful that his guilt meant he wouldn't dare incriminate me. Getting a kid a little wet was nothing compared to the sin of neglect. It wasn't my baby who'd manage to topple his own playpen.

"You're both gonna love Merced," Adam said. "Definitely."

I forced a smile.

"What field did you say you're in?"

"English," she said.

My breath caught. I felt the brush of a finger against my palm. It was Adam attempting to calm me.

"Black lit. I did my dissertation on—"

But I'd stopped listening. So this white girl had scored a job in the UC system—never mind that I didn't know where in the bumfuck Republican farmlands Merced even was—was, in fact, on her way to tenure and a pension for having something to say about—and what's more, teaching other people about—the Black experience. I could see why Black feminists were angry.

Catching my eye, Adam let out an exaggerated yawn and placed a hand on my arm.

"Let's get out of here before I'm too tired to drive?"

He looked more alert than a homing missile.

Turning to our hosts, he offered thanks, apologies, excuses. Weakly echoing the thank you, I salvaged my purse from under the wrecked playpen, and we slipped out.

ON THE SIDEWALK, SAFELY on the other side of the black iron bars, Adam offered to get the car. Earlier he'd dropped me off before parking, in deference to my heels.

"Nah," I said. "I could use the walk."

"Wait, before we go." He flicked his lighter. "Should we torch the place?"

I laughed.

Adam offered me his arm. I took it. A tingle went up my own.

We walked for a few blocks like that. I felt hot, as though the stars had descended. Then we walked a few more. The balls of my feet chirped, overburdened for several hours by now, and sore. No matter how comfortable the stilettos or stoic the wearer, at some point, it caught up to you.

"Did you park in Palms?"

Adam laughed.

"It's just around the corner."

At the car, I pulled out a cigarette. To my surprise he leaned in to light it for me. Even with my extra four inches he was half a head taller, and I had to crane my neck to look at him, like I was waiting for a kiss.

But by definition, I never got the chance to finish, *the objet petit à can't be had*. That was Lacan, straight up, and the logic of the real world was more Lacanian than Ephronian. Friends-to-lovers was a sham.

Adam leaned back against the butt of his Insight.

"But seriously. You want to die in Merced?"

I didn't.

"That child's going to grow up to be a new wave fascist," I said.

"Well no, that's more like Silicon Valley."

My cigarette tapered in silence. When I was done, I put it out with my shoe, then picked the butt up so as not to litter. It was a stupid tic, but it made me feel better.

"Can I ask you something."

I felt my body stiffen, but Adam's voice was soft. My own question for him reared its head.

"You can make that kind of money in Merced doing any range of foolishness. My job, for example. Selling things to help people sell things. What do you really want?"

I wanted to get an explanation for what he was doing at Julia's that morning two weeks ago.

"Respect," I said.

"Sure." Adam narrowed his eyes. "But what is it you're after?"

His gaze bore into me. It melted the edge off my voice.

"Justice, I guess."

"Who for? You act like everything's zero-sum. Power. Freedom."

My research, put in academic terms, existed at the intersection of queer theory, feminist histories, and Iranian studies to analyze the ways the modern, Western-inflected institution of companionate marriage— which defined marriage as a union between two individuals rather than two families or even communities, eventually introducing the affective language of "love" into the equation as the basis for any relationship, and thus occulting marriage's legal ramifications and obscuring its power dynamics—helped structure and reinforce the codependent systems of binary gender and heterosexuality in pre- and post-Revolutionary Iran via international literature and film, arguing that the twentieth-century concepts of World Literature and World Cinema served to institutionalize Euro-American constructs of gender and sexuality as "universal" in postcolonial contexts.

In human terms, this amounted to calling out the bullshit that made life so insufferable, including but not limited to: how everyone wanted you to be straight; how you got assigned "male" or "female" at birth then had to follow an arbitrary set of rules; how being Iranian—or, in my case, half-Iranian—was probably more fun a hundred and fifty years ago, at least in terms of fucking and falling in love; and last but not least, how the US and Europe pretty much got to decide everything for all of us. The idea, I supposed, was that if you screamed and waved your hands alongside—"in conversation with"—other dorks who were doing the same, eventually, maybe, things would get better.

"I know I can't make a difference," I finally said to Adam. "But it just seems sad not to try." I kept my gaze trained on the dark road. "To live a whole life that way, giving up on the world. That's hard, too."

A car passed, another errant soul barreling into the night.

"I forgot to say love," Adam said. "Love is not zero-sum."

He opened the car door for me. I climbed in. Fingers wrapped over the door frame, he leaned in to look at me.

Some green sentiment swam there. Some sweetness, or pain—I couldn't tell.

The air grew stale with the unsaid, and he shut me in.

7

Saturday, July 13

JEALOUSY MAKES A QUICK catalyst. The next day I started to draft my syllabus. Pushing through a cloud of brain fog—I was convinced it was the crème brûlée beer that did me in—I went on a (very slow) run and made myself brunch. I downed a tall glass of Alka-Seltzer. Like all good academics, I started my inquiry with what I most despised. Unit I, Friends to Lovers. Except my field's conventions in nomenclature dictated cheap poeticisms and tinny sound devices; in short, being as cheesy as possible.

Notepad out, feet up on my desk, I drafted alternative titles.

From Making Friends to Making Love
From Hey-You to I-Do

More to the point were the PG-13 translations:

From Friendship to Fucking
From Bitch to Boo

I had to be in the Palisades by cocktail hour, my interlocuter (#34, B2B COO) excited about some new mall that fancied itself a "village." With just enough time to rewatch a couple contenders before heading west to the cliffs, I popped a bag of popcorn and propped my laptop on a stack of books. What was that do-gooder saying, "We teach what we need to learn"?

I kicked off my double feature with *When Harry Met Sally*, rewatching it in full, free of infantile distractions. I still wanted to start with Sanaa Lathan, but after witnessing a woman of color actually make something of herself, students could catch Meg Ryan faking an orgasm. Here I myself got distracted, detouring into metanarrative for some time—an actor acting like she's acting, it was bait for anyone who'd ever even flirted with poststructuralism.[1] But I did, eventually, manage to move on, pulling up an old favorite of mine that I considered cruelly underrated, the Barbra Streisand classic, *The Mirror Has Two Faces*.

In this rather strange lost gem from the nineties, Barbra plays English professor Rose Morgan. Via a personal ad placed by her married sister, this old maid scholar meets a conveniently handsome colleague from the math department. The two hit it off as nerd friends, and soon willingly enter a companionate marriage in the most literal sense: all talk, no sex. Until, rather inconveniently, the professor falls for her mathematician.

I began to develop a working thesis that the friends-to-lovers plot mirrored a typical arranged marriage. In both, mutual understanding and experience serve as the soil for true love. While Sally falls in love with ertswhile frenemy, now friend, Harry, Professor Morgan platonically marries—in a courthouse ensemble drab as an abaya, I was then

---

1   Building on last night's fantasy, I could feel the electricity in the room as I led my students, step by step, turn by turn, through the corridors of my mind. First I replayed the clip. Notice how Sally's performance at the diner—a scene since enshrined in the annals of chick-flickdom—both horrifies and impresses Harry. Notice an old lady at a table nearby provides the scene's punchline: "I'll have what she's having." The old lady (played by director Rob Reiner's mother) is among the most desexed of American identities—but even she's turned on. As in, Sally's that convincing; the performance is that good. This performance within the film—this intradiegetic performance, to introduce a little film-studies vocab—then draws attention to the film as a performance. That is to say, Meg Ryan's performance is that good. She's acting like Sally acting, and we're all eating it up. The scene becomes an extradiegetic joke, Hollywood congratulating itself on its superior skill. Genuine, masturbatory self-satisfaction.

noting afresh—her colleague. As in any ideal arranged marriage, each couple starts with companionship and, soon enough, opens its eyes to love. The platonic thus sexualized, a suitable, practical match turns into a desirable one.

Americans recoiled at the very idea of arranged marriage. Yet any lay anthropologist could see that it was in fact common practice. Somewhere like Iran or India, such introductions came formalized, out in the open, while in America the blind date operated alongside more subtle forms of vetting. Harry meets Sally because they went to college together, boasting degrees from the Ivy-adjacent University of Chicago. Professors Morgan and Larkin both teach at the bloodsucking actual Ivy in Manhattan where, incidentally, Adam and I also met. Alumni groups and algorithms, what were these but forms of social engineering? But ways to ensure endogamy? To prevent, in brief, not only race mixing but, just as crucially for the social order, class mixing.

Good breeding must not be polluted. That was the lesson, from the all-American hottie Sally/Meg, to the supposed freak, Rose/Barbra, who's too smart, too "ugly," and too Jewish. By Hollywood standards— they had Julia Roberts playing a "Portugee" pizza-slinger in the eighties and J.Lo an Italian wedding planner all the way in 2001—this little bit of difference was diversity.

As if to say to hyphenated America: If Barbra can manage to get hitched, so can you.

Date #51: Open or Closed

THIS THESIS WAS CONSISTENTLY undermined.

Then on a weekday in late July I had new hope: a first date with an engineer who could actually hold a conversation. It was a rare breed. Plus he drove a Z4.

We met for a late-night tea, his suggestion. Address set to the café-bar, my phone routed me to a nondescript office building at the edge of Mid-City, a plain gray cube I might've passed a thousand and one times without noticing. Pulling past the posted rates into the underground parking, praying to God that they validated, I descended down down down before I could find a spot—nose to nose, it turned out, with his car, according to the profile photos. Its body gleamed with a fresh wax, while my old Ford whimpered with abuse. An air freshener hung from the rearview mirror in the form of a black fist. The car was black. The owner was Black. It was a Black-power Beamer—weren't the Panthers socialists?

At any rate I wasn't one to quibble. I needed tonight to work. On the stairs, foregoing the elevator to calm my jitters, I played with buttoning and unbuttoning my men's dress shirt: one button undone came too close to a teaching day, and two turned positively slutty. I decided to consult my notes, i.e., our messaging history, for a clue. It was mercifully short, given my battery was on its dying gasp.

At this point in the project, I'd learned the rule on chatting was get in and get out. Make a date if there's potential, and wait. Better leave us to nurse our fantasies than to juice each other before we'd had a go at it. Afforded all the time it took to surface from Hades—my glutes were on fire—I read the entirety of our archive. Highlights included where to find the best chelo kabob in LA, and who killed Malcolm X. (The FBI, obviously.)

Buttoned all the way up, battery sacrificed, I emerged from the fluorescent staircase into the staid warmth of millennial décor. Swimming in pale pinks and grays, I passed through this empty coworking space into a vestibule, and from there, via a dedicated elevator, to my destination.

The lofted space was so vast that for a moment I thought I was back outside, maybe even on the roof. Vines ran up the walls. Whole trees stood trapped indoors, fig leaves reaching for the glass ceiling like dark hands. Between the plants, wicker sofas accompanied coffee tables with ebony figurines for legs, the sort that might be sold or exhibited under the generic title "African art." The place had been made out to look like a jungle outpost: colonial chic, haute ironic.

Dressed in a collared shirt, dreads pulled back in a ponytail, my date sat reading a tablet in one of the many tall rattan armchairs that populated the room. A potted tree stretched on either side, narrow trunks tall as staffs. There was a snakeskin woven through one as though slithering through the leaves. It was a strange play on an iconic image.

AN HOUR LATER, PLEASANTRIES skipped thanks to the *Financial Times*, we sat over a second pot of cooling saffron tea (his pick). I'd opened by asking what he was reading, and getting into the weeds of a story on the efficiencies of 3D-printed architecture led serendipitously to his family contracting business. His middling engineering career hung on the green screen of family wealth, just a click away from a change in scene.

"Father," as it were, thought it high time he quit his job and join the team, which was based in the Bay. The son's role would be to penetrate the LA market. I thought back to the guarded opulence of the Kim estate, also owed to contracting. Evidently there were only two ways to make money in this town: houses or Hollywood. At any rate, the very prospect of inheriting a multimillion-dollar company was stressful, and he had been practicing meditation.

"Why put off the inevitable," I said. "I'm sure you'll end up working for—with—him sooner or later."

"Okay, I see you." He leaned forward, elbows on knees, with a wry smile. "How's your quarter-life crisis shaping up?"

I'd presented myself as a lit PhD looking to land a stable position. Which I was, in my own way.

"Ask me in September," I said. "I'm on vacation."

Flashes of white pierced through the vines behind me. I peered through the window. There were strobe lights installed along the sidewalk, shattering the night's peace. Inside, Billie Holiday pressed through the speakers, almost too hushed to make out. (Also offed by the FBI. When it comes to crediting conspiracy, don't mess with a Muslim.)

"I hope you're not subject to seizures," I said. "This light's awful."

"They do it to deter the homeless."

"Is that legal?"

Who did I expect to save the day, LAPD?

"Yeah, it's unconscionable."

His tablet lit up with a notification, brightening a lock screen photo. A family of five was staged on the hearth of a grand, garlanded fireplace. Matriarch at the center, seated; patriarch, standing; three adult children at the flanks—two boys and one girl in providenced balance. Skirt suits for the women, jackets for the men. They looked like Kennedys with more curves.

He took his teacup and saucer in his hands and leaned back.

"I always wanted to learn Farsi," he said.

"Why? It's useless."

"Don't tell my ex." He half smiled. "The Iranians have got to count for something?"

He pronounced "Iranian" with a long "ah," the right way. But I hadn't said anything about my dissertation. He'd clocked my name, my looks.

"Not since about 1747," I said.

"What about Afghans?" he asked, smiling. "Tajiks?"

I kept shaking my head no.

"Those old-guard Pakistanis who read too much Iqbal?"

I laughed. He leaned forward to top off my tea. This nearness, though slight, sent a spark in the air.

I held the teacup to my lips and met the iron smell of stale tea leaves and nothing else. Whatever this was, it certainly wasn't saffron.

"So are you CIA or what?" I asked.

"I studied Arabic in college."

"Again . . ."

He laughed.

"Convert? Military? Just plain old Muslim?"

"Christian at least as far back as the arrivants."

"Well then?" I tapped my foot, a ticking clock. "You have an Iranian ex and you speak Arabic. That deserves an explanation."

"I was just interested. Nine-eleven, the Iraq War. Figured I may as well know what's actually going on."

I flagged a waiter down to ask for more hot water. Mind on my parents' failure of a mixed marriage, I wondered what happened to the ex.

"So what do you teach?"

"Right now, I'm working on a chick flick syllabus."

"Yeah? I've seen *You've Got Mail* about a hundred times."

"That film is capitalist propaganda. A guy inherits his father's corporation, proceeds to demolish a quaint woman-owned business beloved by the community—and somehow he's the hero."

He put his hands up as if to plead innocence.

"My mother puts it on every year around the holidays."

Had his mother disapproved, his sister? Race aside, we were talking about a Christian and a Muslim. You couldn't always expect some Malcolm–Martin peace accord.

"Excuse me, I have to get this."

The tablet had woken to an incoming call routed from his phone, last year's Christmas card illuminated once more.

"Hey baby."

He rose to take the call, popping in an earbud. It was only then that I noticed the tattoo. A black band around his ring finger, rebellion gone trad. He was married.

Just open.

Indignance foamed inside me and just as quickly flattened into exhaustion. Had I missed something on his profile? But my phone was dead. Desire and promise and just the wondrous incongruity of two strangers connecting—all that had danced on the surface of my evening sea now sank.

He returned, check in hand.

"Sorry, that was just my wife. Let's pick this up soon?"

His family's dignified small smiles again shone through the face of the tablet, and I realized my mistake about the Christmas card. The young woman wasn't his sister but his wife.

He handed me the bill. "We can split."

My credit card felt like lead in my hand, and yet the bright, thin plastic looked like a toy next to his Amex Black. He was standing by the tree draped with the snakeskin. It flared gold with each flash of the strobe light. Hollow, bodiless, ready to be filled. Any old body would do. I wondered whether his ex and I looked anything alike.

"I'll get it," I said, returning his card.

Each pot of liquorless, saffronless "saffron" tea had cost thirty-seven dollars. With tax and tip, I was out a hundred. But at least I hadn't been reduced to a fetish.

Pride can drive a person to idiocy. Dignity can be bought.

8

July, contd.

I BECAME AN EXPERT in want.

The feeling of that first look, the ache of possibility. A line skewing to laughter. A brush of skin. Small confidences.

Outside in the streets of Los Angeles, gray skies gave way definitively to a white heat as blank as the boxes of my spreadsheet. When filled—and they did fill—they only begged for more.

I collected others' wants. I set them before my bathroom mirror on the sill of the sink I scoured twice weekly with bleach, and studied them. A bonus, a baby, a six-thousand dollar espresso machine—these petty curiosities were someone else's way to shape a life. With the care of a colonial archaeologist, I felt the contours of these dreams, judged their weight. I brushed them clean and burned the tarnish that had settled into their crevices and corners. My care was sincere.

Gripping the hilt of my mascara, I considered what life would be, to want what others wanted. I considered, leaning into the mirror to apply lipstick I'd soon eat off, what I would be, to be what others wanted.

I shoved a hand down my throat and searched my wet blue insides for anything as hard and dense as these manufactured desires. I came up short.

Instead I watched the larva birthed from the friction of two people crashing into each other squirm in my palm. Cell after cell darkened with language as the chrysalis formed. Red under my fingernails, I held hands. Clutched necks. Scratched backs. Touched where the current ran. Metamorphosis complete, I let this creature go to pass its last gasp in peace, out of sight.

Just as often, the creature met a more violent end. I watched it bloom only to watch it die.

Summersessionsinecure.xlsx (Abridged)

	A	B
1	Clara	Model/actress. Dad owns copper mines. Needs a green card (Australian).
2	Coleman	Heir to major oil and gas fortune that fomented war in the Middle East and extincted an otter species recently turned angel investor. Decent sense of humor.
3	Christian	Serial entrepreneur, a.k.a. professional failure. Attentive in bed.
4	Rory	Healthcare consultant. Didn't know Whitney Houston was Black.
5	Steph	Second-gen screenwriter, keeps great aunt's acting Emmy on toilet tank. Negs.
6	Manuel	Wealth manager. Commissioned self portrait installed on bedroom ceiling; nude sketch à la Pontormo in red chalk, exaggerated musculature.
7	Maxwell	Dog psychic, clients include Taye Diggs, Hugh Grant, the Sacklers, and Cher. Loves dogs.
8	Navid	Maxillofacial surgeon joining family practice in Orange County. Bad breath.
9	Bryan	Tax attorney with self-published coffee table-book of Mapplethorpe rip-offs. Lousy lay.
10	Connie	Self-described "entrepreneuse."
11	Kendrick	PR at Raytheon. Snores.
12	Ana	"Socialist" trust fund babe. Venmo requested after paying.
13	Cary	Socialite/yachtsman with drinking problem.
14	Bryan	Some kind of junta money. Risk of extradition.

15	Zinzi	Crypto-queen (early bitcoin). Fridge devoted to White Zinfandel in basement bunker.
16	Frank	Flipped half of Highland Park. Charming, but Burner.
17	Hiro	Family foundation board member. Loves show tunes.
18	Bob	Movie financing. Very funny, impossible to google, probably canceled.
19	Morgan	Three grandparents dead in six months, inherited two houses. Pet rabbits.
20	Bryan	Artist/writer/aspiring slumlord. Unpublished.
21	Tran	Santa Monica divorcé at twenty-nine. Now lives south of Montana.
22	Marie	Biotech. Homesick for Austria, cried.
23	Phillip	Gramps invented mall kiosks. Pronounces karate "KA-RA-TEY."
24	Bryan	Licensed architect camped out in Park City parents' DTLA pied-à-terre. Mom packs his lunch when in town.
25	Rahul	Hedge fund manager. Overbearing professor mother. Too close to home.
26	Bryan	Sold tech company early. Excellent cook. Ghosted.

TWO

1

Some Spring Weekday in 1994

AS A SCHOOLGIRL MY mother allowed me personal days. Three per year. School was a kind of work, and I, a worker like any other.

A worker works but there are mornings when a worker cannot work anymore. She must rest. What lets her relax is not idleness but rather the knowledge that there is more work waiting, that there is a doing meant for her to do. In this case, speaking the colonizer's tongue better than the colonizer, plus actually learning how to do mental math.

Work, in my family, began well before dawn.

My father's habit was to poke into my bedroom and kiss me good-bye on his way to work—when he had work—just after fajr, as the white thread of dawn drew across the sky. So early in the morning that Americans still considered it night. I was a restless sleeper and the brush on the cheek never failed to wake me. To know that he'd disturbed me, his only child, before dawn would have upset him, and knowing this, I lay there, corpselike, keeping my breaths long and flat, to receive the kiss. But in fact I could sense every soul, every footstep. Those of a fly walking on the kitchen window, those of my mother walking under the weight of her books.

My mother's habit was to spend the morning working alone. Depending on the season, she had a span of an hour or two between fajr and seven o'clock, when my alarm sounded. She woke at the same hallowed hour as my father but, unable to leave—to leave me—set herself up at the kitchen table, books open, notebook out. There was always something to read or write: the dissertation, the book, other people's books. Peeking from the shadows at the top of the stairs, I'd look for her. Though quick to chide me for my bad posture, alone, she bent over her notebook; she bowed. Maybe the work, unlike the world, deserved it.

Soon the sun would rise, and I would rise, and she would have to dress me, feed me, drive me. But not now, not just yet. It was at this ungodly holy hour that she did her best work. I could tell it was her best work by the stillness of her face. Nostrils unflared, lips unpursed. Skin, cartilage, fat—all was at rest, a dark and placid galaxy through which her eyes shone as suns, fires that fed on their flesh, burning from the inside out. When seven o'clock arrived and I, her only child, with it, her forehead would neatly pleat, her eyes darken.

For now I went back to bed. Sometimes sleep came.

ON WHAT TURNED OUT to be my first personal day in first grade, I ignored my alarm. I stretched a child-sized arm and pulled the blinds. I looked out at the gray driveway and let the light invade my adult-sized eyes—usually that did the trick. It was officially spring. But the yard was spotted with stale snow, and the yellowed grass was a sorry sight. The numbers on the digital clockface read 7:10. I didn't get up.

7:30.

7:40.

When the room was white with light, she finally came for me. The door swung open.

"Chalo, you'll miss the bus."

A catchphrase or two aside, my mother spoke to me strictly in English, a language she herself had learned as a schoolgirl, the detritus of decades of direct rule. (Or perhaps its spoils.) In contrast, my father's

ESL so discomfited him that he took it off as soon as he got home, hanging English on the back of my parents' bedroom door along with his outside clothes. Of course, it was only with me that he enjoyed the luxury. Farsi served as our secret code: my mother never learned. She had no use for it.

Standing in the doorway of my bedroom at 7:41, she cut a mean figure. Tall and broad-shouldered, already dressed. It was the usual pairing: dark jeans she creased with an iron and an oversized button-up from the men's section at Macy's, worn untucked like a kameez. To teach, to leave the house, there would be one final touch: a sheer white dupatta that hung at her neck. Always at the neck, never on her head, and white, invariably white. White, she said, matched with anything.

"Do you plan to go to school?" she said from the doorway. Neither of us had moved.

Her tone was not sarcastic.

"Yeah—yes."

"Indeed."

This was as close as my mother got to agreeing with you.

"May I?" she said, as though the room were truly mine.

She stepped a bare, pedicured foot across the threshold. Her jeans, hemmed to accommodate a high heel, caught underfoot.

"Do you feel well?"

She crouched by my bed and put a hand to my forehead.

"Sore throat? Chills?"

Each time I shook my head no. There was nothing my mother hated more than a lie.

"Just not in the mood?"

I held still, suspicious. Moods were not to be countenanced. My mother stood back up and gazed out the window. The gray grass lay there, starved of sun.

"It's a strange landscape, no. All this snow, and yet it looks so unclean."

"Indeed," I said. Her little parrot.

She let out a laugh. Pinched my chin, which made me smile.

"Learning is hard work. Like teaching." She smoothed my hair. "If you want to take a personal day, that's your prerogative."

Purr-ogg-a-tiv—I spun the word around my mouth, trying to memorize its contours so I could look it up later. I knew better than to ask; that's what dictionaries were for.

"Do you know what that means?" my mother said. "A personal day?"

I didn't, and yet I was disappointed that in her generosity she'd chosen the wrong word to define.

"No," I said.

"It means that you can take a day off. You're not sick and there's nothing truly wrong but—" This time her gaze reached around the room. "Just because. Because you want a day to yourself. It's *personal*."

These were still the early days of my father's descent down the ladder. He'd found a part-time gig a couple hours away and my mother was adjuncting overtime for our healthcare.

"That said," she said, taking a look at her watch, "under the circumstances, you'll have to spend your personal day with me, learning about the Romantics."

My mother made a woman of me that day, though I didn't know it. Brushing my teeth before the medicine cabinet as she fetched her dupatta and heels, purring with satisfaction, I rehearsed my new word. *Prerogative*: I was now someone with agency, and enough power to exercise it. (The former without the latter means nothing, goes limp.) I spit and rinsed. Looked up. It was a woman's eyes I met in the mirror, rather than those of a girl of five or six.

Purr—

She said I was—

—*ogg*—

so I was:

—*a*—

A speech act

—*tiv.*

à la Austin via Butler, to whose work my mother would never refer, though she made me live it.

Only later did I realize how much I'd lost. Childhood was a birthright. How eagerly I'd cast it away, how hungrily she'd snatched it.

That day, the "p-r-" in "prerogative" was what did me in. Waiting in the department library for my mother's day to quiet—for her lecture to finish, for her office hours to dwindle, for the light outside the windows to dim—I endured long hours before I could pull her to the reference shelf and ask for help. As dusk settled, we stood side by side over a volume of the *Oxford English Dictionary*, my feet on a chair, our gazes level.

2

Wednesday, July 31

ON WEDNESDAY, JULY 31, eighty-nine dates achieved, I decided that I'd accrued a personal day. My first day off since beginning my project in June. I called Adam's landline at work.

"Hello?"

"It's me," I said. "Your midweek savior. Here to rescue you from the dregs of American life."

Earbuds in, I was studying the contents of my fridge. The shelves were again depressingly sparse, a casualty of my unforgiving schedule.

"One," Adam said, "please don't use this line. And two, what exactly does being rescued entail?"

"I want to go to the beach," I said to the second shelf, as if Adam's head sat there on a silver platter, behind an old carton of eggs. (White, grade A; I couldn't afford brown.)

A low voice came over the line: "I want to remain employed."

My own work was steady, if the ladder yet unclear. Forty-five days and eighty-nine dates, each entered on its own tidy line. Granted, twenty were good old-fashioned speed-dates, first at an event hosted by Beverly Hills Persian Moms for Marriage—I, drawn not by "my" people but by the zip code—and second, an LGBT redux at a vaguely Orientalist gay bar in Silver Lake that was now letting in women. Both yielded deplorable results. I wasn't promonarchist enough for the first crowd or gay enough for the second.

Such fraudulent accounting notwithstanding, this morning I stood eighteen days and eleven dates away from my goal of a hundred dates by August 17. Back from a milestone ten-mile run an hour ago, waking up to my exhaustion in body and spirit alike, I'd been tempted to push through: Art for art's sake.

But that was just it. My project was being reduced to a practice. The texting, the toggling, the eyelining; the tacos and coffees and smiles and drinks, and drinks, and drinks—I'd even gone bowling.

That was the other problem: I was surrounded by whiteness. White masculinity, in particular. No one else could afford to squander their resources. Between teatime with the heir to the Black Kennedy fortune and getting sloshed on martinis with the returning king of Echo Park, I'd learned an important lesson about America: people liked to keep the money in the family. And since you couldn't marry your cousin (in most states), settling for someone in the community was the next best thing.

Sex was different. Sex, eo ipso, served some purpose. It was one of few activities in life whose motives you didn't need to account for. At the start of my inquiry, I'd hypothesized that sex was a necessary and even sufficient condition to marriage: enough of it could sustain the most lackluster of communions; any orthodox religious community was proof. But it had quickly become clear that a proper phenomenology of sex must exceed such limits. Sex could be instrumental, a path to pleasure, or race propagation, or a new bag—and yet, there was a more perfect logic at play. Producing the togetherness that it reflected, sex was an argument that satisfied its own terms. Sex was tautology. Simple, comprehensible, universally understood. Meaningless, but— and—significant all the same.

Adam's line had gone muffled, his palm over the mic. Now the pitch of a cheery "sorry" cut through.

"Sorry, one sec," Adam said, seemingly to me.

If I bowed half as often as he, I would've been flattened before I hit my fifteenth birthday. "Sorry" when his manager mismanaged so that the team he managed missed a deadline. "Sorry" when Julia—otherwise so punctual—was so late for dinner my saag began to sag. "Sorry" when she ashed her cigarette in my cactus. "Sorry" when she shredded his last shred of self-respect and fed it to her gender-fluid greyhound.

"K, sorry, still there?"

I supposed you didn't need to get self-righteous when the world was built to make you feel right.

"Yeah."

The line went dead. Grabbing the eggs to check the expiration— four days past—I called back. Voicemail.

A text floated to the top of my screen from his cell.

Sincere regrets. Already underwater without the waves.

A few emojis followed turning on the theme of water, the last one, sadistically, a tiny, serene beach flagged with a beach umbrella.

Eggs beaten, I had my fingers in a bag of dry parsley. I wiped them on a dishtowel.

Call me.

I needed to see him. Partly from guilt—though I wondered whether I really had it in me for a confession—partly for pleasure. He was my friend and we were almost back to normal. By the time Adam called, I'd finished my French omelet. I picked up.

"So you'd forego a day in the sun to work for the man? You're no native Angeleno."

"On the contrary," he said. "Surf's up at sunrise."

"But the beauty's in the sunset."

I toggled to my weather app. Over ninety, and not yet noon. Was he really going to make me beg?

"Please?" I said. "I'll drive and you can content-produce in the car. You'll hit your word count before we cross Lincoln."

"I got promoted, remember? About five years ago."

I could hear his smile through the phone.

"Exactly. What's the point of power you can't abuse?"

As middle manager, Adam had a habit of showing up to work after ten—at which point he left a cardigan on the chair to signal his presence and went to grab a coffee around the corner. No one would notice he was gone until well after lunch, and by then, they'd all be too focused on making it to happy hour to bother tracking him down.

Now all I could hear was background noise, including a flush punctuated by "sure, absolutely." The boss-boss had found him on the hole: one knows no peace in corporate America.

My toaster dinged with a nub of bread I'd fished from the freezer. I buttered it and bit in. Not bad for stuff dating back to December. Over the phone, the swish of a revolving door gave way to street sounds.

"Fuck it."

I could hardly make him out. For some reason he was still whispering, like we were a couple of high school kids playing hooky on twenty bucks' allowance. "What was that?" I teased, but Adam went on whispering—he'd be at home and ready in fifteen.

"Don't forget your sunscreen," I said, already wrist deep in my swimsuit drawer.

IN A CITY DISCIPLINED by commuter traffic, driving midday on a weekday is nirvana.

Fourteen minutes later I headed south on Vermont in my sunfaded Focus, cruising, green after green, further south. Past the LACC campus that had once seated the city's UC, now home to the community college. (How different the urban geography would've been had the UC stayed put, professors emeritus sizzling in the Eastside heat while the poor cooled under the cliffsides.) Past the Braille Institute, and past strip mall signs in still more scripts I couldn't read.

I rolled the windows down to let the pollution-filled breeze ruffle my hair. My pixie cut stuck to my scalp, but it was a nice idea. At the intersection of Vermont and Wilshire, I swung a right on red without slowing, the boulevard free for the taking.

Adam was waiting outside when I pulled up at The Gaylord a minute before my announced ETA. He was perched on the sidewalk atop his signature mini-cooler, looking like he was about to take a shit on a squat toilet. The travesty of a car behind me, a BMW hybrid hatchback, swerved by with a long press of the horn. Adam didn't even flinch. Renting on Wilshire had washed him of life instinct.

Leaning back in the passenger seat, he unfurled a brown paper bag marked with a gorgeous grease stain, anonymity undone.

"Tribute for the emperor."

The donut is to LA as the bagel is to New York: cheap, excellent, ubiquitous, and a performance of Americana.

I opened the bag to take my plain glazed twist.

Early in my LA tenure, Adam had told me that the donut shops once served as a foothold for refugees from the Khmer Rouge. Minor gains on much work, that was the immigrant's way. What I liked about the place on Sixth, in particular, was that it had missed the memo on American taste: alongside vanilla, that colonial spice, notes of orange and lemongrass were assimilated into the glaze. In a city where "minorities" form the majority but still, somehow, weren't the ones in power, this donut was giving the finger to whiteness. Its bouquet lingered on my fingers and on the nose, scoring the air with a perfume heady and oriental.

"Eh?" Adam broke the silence, holding up the golden butt of his maple stick to offer it to me. A touch of cream spurted invitingly over the biteline.

I waved it off.

"Your taste in romance is as bad as your taste in donuts."

"As in?"

"Saccharine. To the point of pain."

"Wow."

Adam crumpled the empty paper bag and stuffed it in his tote.

"I'm gonna try to nap. Wake me up when your blood sugar rises."

DESPITE THE PROMISE OF the hour, the 10 was backed up from Crenshaw to Culver. Someone had offended the gods. As we slowed, I raised my window against the exhaust. My practical father had always advised manual windows: you could roll them down and swim to the surface if you drove off a cliff. (The assumption being, you did it on accident.) But Adam was already asleep, his peace as undisturbed by the dust as by the light penetrating his eyelids, that tenuous veil of skin.

AT ROBERTSON, AS FORETOLD by the map on my screen, the road began to clear. I let my foot weigh on the gas, and we blazed past National, signs herding the OC-bound into the turnoff for the 405 South. A truck beat by, my day made briefly night by its shadow, light flickering in the rearview mirror like a camera flash. No, in fact, I didn't want to go to Venice Beach. With a glance at my blind spot, barreling through a wall of justifiable honks, I abandoned the 10 for the 405 South.

"Whither we go, O Captain?" Adam asked, eyes closed, his body registering the unexpected turn.

"Trust."

"Ends of the earth with you."

We took flight. Up the ramp into the sun, and soon back down, the Ford gliding by my old exit, Mar Vista tucked in its sleepy corner behind us.

AT FIRST IT'S NOTHING much.

Abandon the 405 for Inglewood Ave once you hit Redondo.	The usual strip malls and car lots, gas stations pumping black gold from halfway around the globe.
Snake through Torrance, down Anza, Del Amo, and Prospect.	A strip of greenery trying to spruce up another drab thoroughfare, a ribbon in unwashed hair.
Right at the juncture to Palos Verdes Boulevard.	Stucco condos and modest homes that now cost a fortune, though once made for the middle class—the windows are the giveaway, small and square.
Go straight. Keep to the coast.	The trees start just before the church, a canopy of eucalyptus and birch, trunks tall and white, draped in bark that weathers but does not bruise. Through this paradisical curtain, the residences peek, veiled, guarded.

Welcome to the Estates.

THERE WAS A CROWD at the beach, weekday notwithstanding. Children too young or rich for daycare, in sunsuits that protected their paleness. Middle-aged residents on lawn chairs for whom the water had lost its mystery, come down from the cliffside in the odd hour between calls.

The midday sun beat against my skin with a heavy hand. Unfurling a Turkish towel I situated myself, body exposed, face cloaked by the shadow of Adam's umbrella. I covered my face with my hat for good measure and closed my eyes. The hiss of spray-bottle sunscreen layered atop the water's hush.

"Lather up."

A kiss of cold metal brushed my stomach. I flicked away the can without unveiling.

"I'm so white I could pass," I said into the crown of my straw hat.

"Come on, you'll burn."

I lifted my hat. Adam had a corkscrew dug into the mouth of a bottle of cloudy rosé. I propped myself up, accepting a glass tumbler and a healthy pour. Against the pink his skin looked bluer, mine greener. It was a matter of undertone, my middle school art teacher had taught me. That's what made me "olive."

Adam and I drank and watched the water. Sweat beaded on my skin—I could feel it pushing through my pores, the body struggling to cool, to regulate. The wetness started at my armpits and under my breasts, at the crease of my bikini line; everywhere the skin runs thin. We'd been here, what, fifteen minutes, and already I glistened like off-color tourmaline in the workshop of some lesser Mughal king, too brown to pass for ruby and yet too valuable for the court artisans to discard.

Adam rose and went for a swim. I lay there, waiting to be carved.

SUN RESISTANCE, I'D ONCE read, was developed either young or never. Skin hidden from the sun in adolescence burned easily forever, meaning, till death.

The story behind why I was so sensitive—in some sense, the story of my skin, tout court—traced back to Tuesday, September 11, 2001. Around 8:45 that morning, I was in computer lab in my Michigan hometown. The teacher was demonstrating how to use the sum function in Excel on a fat desktop, jabbing at plastic number keys yellowed with sebum as we took note. At 8:50, the bell rang. Some of us eighth graders filtered into Advanced English, others left behind. At 8:57, there was a knock on the door. Frowns, whispers. We crowded around the tabletop television the English teacher kept at her desk to catch the lunchtime soaps.

No one had been to New York City, including Ms. White. The name "Wall Street" meant nothing to us. When the newscaster described this foreign land as the "global financial capital" an hour later—then captured on screen in psychedelic color, a phoenician cycle of self-immolation and reconstruction that was on every channel repeating ad infinitum—that meant still less. Even so, Ms. White began to cry. Big fat tears that cleared runways through her blush.

That evening, my mother excused herself from dinner to get some grading done.

"Didn't you notice that the Pentagon was practically an after-thought?" my father said, free to speak Farsi. "So which is the true seat of power, Wall Street or Washington?"

He cut into the roast my mother had prepared in a rare show of Americana I was beginning to suspect was not without its ironies. Speaking more or less between bites, he went on, talking about the CIA backing the Taliban in Afghanistan in the eighties; and the CIA overthrowing the first Iranian democracy back in '53; and the CIA sponsoring, whether secretly or openly, dictators and tyrants in Cuba, and Iraq, and Egypt, and Chile, and Jordan, and—well, pretty much everywhere at some point in the twentieth century.

"They sprouted like mint after the rains," he said, back on Afghanistan and the global network of men who called themselves jihadis. "American guns, American dollars. You can't water the weeds then act surprised when the garden's overrun."

Meat and potatoes stuck between my molars, I wondered about the "you." I was the true American.

BEFORE 9/11 THE NATURE of my discomfort had been vague, devi-ance marked but not delineated. At school, I was one of few Muslims.

Perhaps intuiting that sticking together would only do us in, we each found our own clique. Mine was the not-dumb not-quite jocks. I ran track, ranking in the middle on middle distance, and my smarts could be forgiven on account of my Asiatic roots.

Of course, on occasion I grazed against the hard edge of difference. It was America, after all.

That very year, during the summer of 2001, my best friend had "gifted" me a silver cross on a delicate chain, her regard for my soul too kind and misguided to reject—I wore it like a friendship necklace. On our first day back from break, my secret crush had expressed his surprise that "even" my skin could tan. (This frosted-tipped braid of straw and sinew would soon, at sixteen, achieve his destiny as an Abercrombie & Fitch greeter, at once vindicating my preteen taste and proving my second-gen lack of imagination.) But most hours, most days, I was, as the Social Studies teacher liked to put it, just another "citizen" of our humble community.

In homeroom on September 12, 2001, my friend asked for her silver cross back. I snapped the chain from my neck, then still visible. By the following week my crush no longer turned to grin at me when passing back papers; he crooked an elbow over his head and let me reach for them. At Sunday school later that month, we, Muslims, scrubbed graffiti off the side of the mosque. When the bullets hit early October—warning shots fired in the dead of night—an adult would do the spackling.

Around Thanksgiving strangers came to the mosque and said even stranger things. Beards dyed with henna, dishdashas as bleached as their skin, they milled about the parking lot sermonizing about jihad— not the soulful kind of jihad we were used to, which meant fighting your worst self, but a much more literal interpretation. That Sunday I'd spent the midday prayer taking stock of my future, my mind on paltry desires I calculated as questions: How far from home could a perfect PSAT score fling you? Had Sana Aunty also prepared spinach pakoras or only aloo? God immediately let me down (aloo), and it was difficult to see how joining a global army would help.

On the car ride home my mother, who rarely came in but often picked me up, explained our position vis-à-vis the American justice system. Key takeaways included:

1) Innocence doesn't mean you're not guilty.
2) The phones are tapped.
3) White guys who correctly pronounce the Arabic letter 'ayn are FBI agents, at best. Worse, informants.
4) That brown guy with the fancy new cellphone whose face is suddenly popping up in every corner of the masjid at all hours of the day including at 3 a.m. at Salatul Layl (or so says Tarik, or was it Ali, via Sarah or Tabinda), is also an informant.
5) Smile.

January 2002, on our first day back from Christmas break, I wore hijab to school. Cast out, why not become an outcast.

"IT'S LIKE TRAINING WHEELS, but backwards," Adam said, body dripping in the shade of the beach umbrella. "I mean, eight years. It's like unlearning how to ride a bike."

Reclined flat on his back, voice set against the drum of the waves, he was talking about Julia. About the breakup—or what he still insisted was a "breakup," though I had evidence to the contrary. Separated by a bar of sand, our legs drew lines like a double-edged ruler, taking measure of the world in such different ways.

"It's her bike, that was the problem, you know, with Julia it was always her, hers, everything her, there was no space for me—"

The actual shrink, their couples' therapist, had reportedly lasted one single session before recommending a permanent dissolution of ties. I turned to my side, studying Adam as he kept his gaze trained upward. He was frowning into the ambient light floating through the umbrella. Its underside was pocked white with salt.

"—I was on my bike the other day, like my actual bike—

The wine, the heat—it had unraveled his tongue. Mine, less so. I couldn't confront him without incriminating myself.

"—just kind of noodling around after work to stretch my legs, and I ended up over by the Reservoir, and 'Lovefool' comes on—it was on shuffle—"

Plus I knew for a fact that he'd texted her as recently as Sunday. As in, three days ago. To say nothing of finding him at Julia's on the tracker back in June. So they were, what, fucking but not together?—as a dot hovering over Julia's address, it all looked the same.

"—and 'member how Julia had a thing for that song, that was her go-to at karaoke—I started crying—I mean I'm pumping up Silver Lake, sweat dripping off my chin strap, tears streaming down my face, sobbing, actually sobbing, because of the Cardigans—I started laughing so hard I had to stop—"

He looked at me and grinned. I tried to smile then looked away.

"That's when I knew I was over her."

The waters were graying with evening clouds, and I caught glimpse of something scuttling out of the algae that had washed up on shore. Who was to say this wouldn't end like it always did? Nine chances out of ten, Adam's faith in their "us" still survived, a morsel of soft white meat lying dormant under red pain and chitinous lust.

I pressed my hand into the sand and lifted it. Adam put his own on the impression, widening it, lengthening it.

"I mean, it's a start, right?"

His voice was now soft as the water's. I stood up.

"I should dip my toes in before it gets too cold."

Ducking out of the shade of the umbrella, Adam joined me. We locked eyes. His, warm with sorrow and contrition and a million answers for questions I wasn't ready to ask. Mine, still steeled against the winter that blew at the bounds of our friendship, marking where not to go.

"Three, two—" I whispered.

We raced to the water. Neither of us won. Or as Adam might say, we both did.

Date #85: Date with the Devil

JUST THE OTHER DAY I'd run into Julia. Saturday night; technically, Sunday morning. We were both waiting for the bathroom at a warehouse party downtown, each alone, spun off from friends still sweating on the dance floor. I could imagine the sort she was with: Julia, like most aristocrats, clung to friends from high school, where there were fewer scholarships to contaminate the pool. In her case, that translated to LA art kids who wore all white at night and smelled of self-assurance. Not their money but the liberty it purchased was their true asset. Their careers took off precisely because nothing was riding on that success.

Julia's high-gloss lips gleamed in the lavender glow of the fluorescent tube light that had been installed on the warehouse wall. Breakup or no breakup, I knew that Adam wouldn't be with her. He'd given up uppers at thirty and could hardly stay ticking past midnight, let alone till sunrise. Like some kind of off-kilter Flavin, the fluorescent tube was hung at an angle, raking light and shadow in pleasing geometric shapes. Within them still more lines—Julia's cheekbones, and clavicle, and the bridge of her nose—glistened with sweat and shimmer. Flimsy thighs peered out from the screen of her mesh basketball shorts, while her white tee announced that tonight she'd gone braless.

She gave me an up-down. Despite the heat off-gassing from hundreds of bodies, I was in an eighties blazer and leather shorts. My harlequin sequins, my shoulder pads fit for an NFL quarterback, my short shorts and high high-tops—under her gaze, against the logic of her aesthetic, I found myself reinterpreting the joy written on my body as excess.

Julia slipped her phone into the fanny pack slung at her disappearing hips, her pockets evidently decorative. She'd had acrylics done. Graduated stripes, from gray to white.

"How's your night, babe?" she asked.

The "babe" was of course merely idiomatic, and still, it was not customary for Julia to devote her full attention to me. I figured she must be high on something good and expensive.

"No complaints," I said.

"Do you feel as good as you look?"

She'd left the zipper undone on her fanny pack, and her phone blinked with incoming messages.

"Someone's gonna steal your stuff."

I reached over to pull the zipper shut—but first, slid a finger in to tilt her phone face up. Julia didn't stop me. Adam's name was among those on her lockscreen. I could read it, our bodies were now that close. I felt a blue heat swell inside my chest—how could he?

"Nothing's irreplaceable," Julia said.

"Nothing?"

"Huh-uh."

She held my gaze and shook her head. I tugged on the zipper. Its teeth clamped.

I leaned against the cinder block wall. No matter how queer the party or underground the venue, the bathroom lines remained gender-segregated—this would be a while.

Julia was now swaying to the music drifting down the hall, either oblivious or indifferent to my gaze. Acrylics aside, she'd done her eyes up in a signature geisha red, black liner long and flat. It was an

Orientalist gesture, a self-Orientalizing gesture staked by a body desperate to secure its claim to otherness. Here was a poverty from which I did not suffer.

The last two people in the men's line went in together, the women's unmoving. On a whim, I stepped over to take the guys' place. Julia followed. You could smell the piss from the doorway.

In the strategic red glow of the bathroom, I could make out a shirtless guy at the urinal and four feet in the only stall. Julia stepped closer. Done, the guy at the urinal turned and left. The twosome in the stall was taking their time.

Julia was taller than I, had several inches on me, in fact, and I could feel her breath against my ear, long and thin and cool somehow, which made me think it must be hot, I must be hot, for human breath to feel cool by comparison.

"Fuck it, I'm sick of waiting."

Ten pointy plastic nails pressed into my shoulders like acupuncture needles, pushing me forward. We passed into the bathroom. The duo in the stall were still hard at work. Julia pounded on the door, soliciting a rather fair "fuck off." She giggled and toed at the doorstop under the main door. It slammed shut.

"First things first."

She opened the mouth of her fanny pack to flaunt a glass vial on a silver chain. For a moment I took the vial for her artwork, and thus the flecks of white inside for her skin, before my own less-than-sober brain computed what was in it. The vial was still a third full, though the night, inevitably, nearly done. The elixir hovered behind the glass like snow in a snow globe, never graying and never melting. Until it hit the tongue, lifting those it touched in defiance of the laws of physics, from the inside out.

As Julia fiddled with the open vial, attempting to extract a doll-sized spoon without spilling any of the precious powder, I played with the freed chain. It ran through my fingers like water. It danced like a snake. Treacherous fluidity; movement I couldn't predict. I strung it round my neck with the excess at my back like a noose.

Silver spoon secured, Julia offered me the first bump.

"Quite the gentleman," I said, leaning in.

Julia laughed. Head bowed, she helped herself, then flung her long head back. She swiped her nostrils with the pads of her fingers and reached to clean mine with the back of a nail. The acrylic slid against my skin, tepid and frictionless. Dipping into the vial again, she took another bump and offered me the same.

"No thanks." I shook my head.

Everything in moderation, as my grandmother used to say (or so said my father). Plus, eventually, in an hour or two, I needed to drive myself home.

Julia hooked a fingernail under the chain pressed to the base of my neck—her chain—and pulled so that the necklace hung down my chest like normal. The vial cap settled between my breasts. She screwed the vial back on, turn by turn. A shadow of pleasure sparked on my skin.

Then she pressed the vial into my chest. Hard. Metal and glass against bone. I didn't step back. I inhaled, pushing my chest out, pushing back. Into the glass, the metal, the pain. She kissed me. I kissed back. She pegged her tongue into my mouth.

The men stepped out of the stall.

"All yours, ladies—" one of them cooed.

I broke away.

"Fuck off," Julia said, stepping into the stall. She turned to look at me. "Coming?"

I looked at her.

"Did you have to pee or what?"

"See you out there," I said.

"Suit yourself."

The stall lock clicked. I stepped around a new man swaying by the urinal to gaze into the cracked mirror over the sink. But I couldn't make much out in the lurid light. I took Julia's necklace off, dropped it in my purse, and left.

In bed later that morning, when neither sun nor sobriety could any longer be staved off, I wondered who was the worse liar, me or Adam. The necklace lay coiled in the cupholder of my car, a silver sleeping cobra waiting for someone else's flute.

3

Wednesday, July 31, ctd: That Evening

IT WAS ONE OF those days that never ends. The sun stretched time as rainwater does a thread, heaviest just before heaving the next drop. Dusk fell definitively, and the white picket fences off Abbot Kinney clung to what little luminescence remained.

You could tell something was amiss at Adam's childhood home before stepping through the gate. Sharon—into whose Venetian existence I'd peered all too often during grad school, given Adam's habit of casually stopping by Mar Vista for coffee on his way west to his mother's, only to then beg me, fully sober on a Sunday morning, to get in the car, just as he had an hour ago, on our way back from Palos Verdes, convinced me to detour here via the 90 for dinner—was not one for maintenance. Once the sorry exception on an otherwise refurbished block, her bungalow now glittered like the neighbors'. White, sterile, landscaped. It looked so different from the old version, you'd think it had been flipped. I lifted the gate latch. No creak.

Our entrance roused the mini electric tiki torches that now led to the front door, the path between freshly laid with slate stepping stones as though lily pads on a swamp. I watched Adam take in the crisp coat of paint on the siding. Last I'd been here, patches of bare wood shone like flesh through skinned knees.

Neglecting the house and loving Adam had been Sharon's greatest revenge—on whom, was unclear—for the indignity she'd been made to suffer when Adam's biological grandparents had paid her off. The house's face had hung in shambles so that her own could be met in the mirror. It was her picture of Dorian Gray. Or, had been.

Adam's silence steeped the air like tea left too long. Thickening, embittering.

"It looks good," I said.

Adam looked at me.

"This is a fucking disaster. Cutout cute."

The brown bag from our pit stop at the butcher's hung at Adam's side, sagging under the weight of raw meat. I started on a tour of the small yard. Adam stayed stuck to his lily pad.

The balding grass Sharon had tried to maintain with such misplaced tenacity drought after drought had been stripped back, down to the dirt. A broad ribbon of pebbles ran along the front of the house with the occasional succulent poking out of the stormy gray. This framing then effected to give the bare and pale dirt a purpose, redefining lack as an aesthetics of withholding.

It was a palette and brushstroke characteristic of Sharon's work. A paid, professional landscaper would have used more mature plants—moreover, would never have settled for plain, pale dirt. Even the most minimalist craftsman had to justify their cost.

I heard it before I saw it, the sound of Adam kicking the pebbles, tearing the clean line that Sharon had painstakingly drawn. I flinched. The pebbles he'd kicked out of place shone against the pale sand like a bruise. I had the impulse to mend the tear, to collect each tiny rock and put it back in its place—to be the woman, in short. I stopped myself.

"Are you going to fix that?"

"Fix what?"

Adam and I stood there eye to eye, two animals circling a fight. And yet still, completely still, the thick air like gasoline waiting for a match. He/she, it was a bind that exceeded us, and in that moment I identified with his mother as much as I would with any other "she" out there, a sorry sisterhood of signifiers put into relief by this bubbling over of masculinity, this minor violence.

The fake tiki torches flickered off; we'd been motionless for that long.

Adam's shoulders slumped. His chest deflated.

"I don't know what's wrong with me," he said.

"Try testosterone."

Adam handed me the butcher's bag, and I cradled it in my arms, suddenly aware of flesh wrapped neatly inside, the sentience snuffed out for the sake of our pleasure. Back bent low, he did the work with his hands. Palm and fingers tensed like a scalpel, he pushed and scraped the pebbles into place, trying to achieve the same uniform edge as his mother. I stood there, waiting. When he was finally done, the clean line glinted against the night.

"OH, IT'S JUST YOU, doll." Sharon said from the shadowy hallway well after we'd let ourselves in. "What a relief, I thought he was giving it another go with the Empress of Toluca Lake."

I let out a laugh, though to best Julia was not really any compliment at all. I was standing by the coffee table—now shiny polycarbonate, formerly brushed walnut—leafing through a glossy. I'd found it open to an ad for three-hundred-dollar rejuvenating cream. Down the hall behind Sharon, the door to Adam's boyhood bedroom remained ajar just a crack, casting a slab of light onto the blanched floor. I couldn't see in given the angle, but historically, the room had remained as dark and dusty as a crypt.

Sharon's dress swept the refinished floorboards as she neared. The oppressive drape of the thick white linen was at odds with a neckline that sank so low as to expose half her breasts, freckled and relaxed with many years under too much sun. She went in for a pro forma hug.

"Adam hasn't brought you around in so long, I thought you got married or something."

"No," I said. "Just working."

"Good for you. I guess he's also been busy. I haven't seen him since Mother's Day."

While she'd outright declared war on Julia, with me, historically, Sharon was hot and cold. Tonight, for example, it was hard to say whether the marriage comment was the usual dig at my intimacy with Adam, or veiled racism that assumed I'd be married off at some point. (That my father did, in fact, want to marry me off was my business.)

We stood in silence. Sweet smells wafted from the kitchen, courtesy of Adam. Bread warming, butter browning. He'd headed straight to work on dinner, no comment. I'd heard him rummage around the (evidently reorganized) cupboards for a decent knife. Now he was chopping with the zeal of a convert.

"Adam's in the kitchen," I said stupidly.

Sharon's nose wrinkled. "I could smell it from my room."

With company—a category that excluded me—Sharon went on about hot new restaurants, about grades of cold-pressed olive oil, about the best croissant in Los Angeles lying tragically as far away as Atwater. But among family, comfortably in her own skin, food repulsed her. The typical Sunday brunch consisted of not-dressed greens and filaments of low-salt seitan; about as much substance, in short, as a mesh thong. Furthermore, she demanded that the grill be used to prep the protein and the picnic table for consumption—anything to keep the smell outside the house. Adam, of course, knew this perfectly well; that's why we were still inside.

Sharon floated to the kitchen and back, summoning a bottle of piquette and two wine glasses as wide as fishbowls—so she hadn't gotten rid of all her nineties holdovers. She stopped short of me by a stretch, standing in the no-man's-land beyond the seating area.

"I like what you've done out front," I said, crossing to her.

Based on the sizzling that sounded through the closed door, Adam had won the argument to keep his little theater indoors. I watched her pour the piquette. It was a marvelous color, and I wouldn't have been surprised to learn that she'd picked it for that reason. Coral in the ocean, the red breathed life into an icy room.

"The palette," I said, "especially."

Inside the house had proved as foreign as outside. Like the coffee table, the reflectiveness of every surface had been inverted. Walls that once shone with a wipeable, writeable blue-white paint—an artifact from Adam's too-free toddlerhood in which he'd had license to express himself anytime, anywhere—now stood a muted gray, while the waxed floorboards had been brushed back to a natural finish that struck me as affected, a greasy nose blotted too late in the night for such pretenses.

"What about the palette?"

She offered me the glass by the stem, and I took it by the bowl.

"It's bold," I said, unsure whether I was messing with her or myself.

"Bold? The white or the gray?"

Sharon gave a wry smile. Her own glass now weighted with red, she set the bottle on the wood floor. Surely the new finish rendered it more susceptible to stains.

"Well, I'd argue," I went on, "that here, they function as nudes. The pale, naked dirt, of course, but then also the gray pebbles, the white fencing. Those lines function like shadow and light. Almost like the cracks and crevices of a body, the bulges. It's a deconstructed nude."

"That's not half bad."

"Maybe even"—I was enjoying this—"less so a deconstruction than a closeup. A self-portrait—a selfie, zoomed in so close we lose track of the body part."

Sharon took a dainty sip of piquette.

"You know, that's always been my problem with academic criticism. It's too abstract. Art is about *feeling* something. Going wild. Falling head over heels. Thinking with your heart." She cocked her head in the direction of the kitchen. "Honey," she called, "would you like a glass of wine?"

Without waiting for a response, Sharon swooped up the bottle of piquette—it hadn't left a ring on the wood—and pushed through the kitchen door.

Sweat rolled down my chest under my caftan, a white-lady look I wouldn't be caught dead in, had we not come straight from the beach. I wondered whether Adam had lit the oven in the middle of summer just to punish us.

Finally I sat down. A lone white leather loveseat had replaced the old family set of pink florals, and I had the awkward sensation of being called in at the gynecologist's, a peculiarly chichi one. I was tired and hungry, my runner's muscles especially sore.

Back from tending to Adam, Sharon poured herself another half-pour.

"I could eat a horse," she said.

I stood to cede my seat—personal feelings aside, she was my elder—but Sharon didn't take it. She stood sipping in the same spot as before, setting the bottle down beside her. Minutes crept by.

Why all this change now? You had to wonder. Menopause? Mid-life crisis? Sharon certainly wasn't above a cliché. Thinking with your heart must be a little easier with a multi-million-dollar property appreciating underfoot.

Emptying the bottle into her glass, Sharon swept over to the sofa. She settled in next to me.

"I'm so glad he's moving on," she said in a hoarse whisper. "What that girl put him through—"

She shook her head.

"I mean . . ." I said, confused by this sudden intimacy.

Sharon and I rarely went beyond the pleasantries without Adam there to translate. Her imperiousness irked me, while my—well, I wasn't sure what her problem was with me. Probably the same thing.

"It takes two," I said.

"No no no," Sharon said, no longer whispering. "That was absolutely beyond the pale. A mother worries, you know. What if I died, or moved to Bali, or got married? I won't always be able to be there for him like that."

Considering Adam could hardly bear to see her without me there as a buffer, this seemed a rosy view to take.

"He'll find someone else, I'm sure."

I meant this as a closer, but Sharon kept going.

"He gets so hung up on things, that's his problem. His life has to be just how he imagined it'd be at eighteen. Same job, same hobbies, same girl. But people grow up. Things change."

"I don't think he was dreaming about 'project management' our freshman year," I said.

Sharon had definitely passed menopause, and it wasn't just the white couch. She was over mothering Adam.

"Oh sweetie." She looked at me, face overridden with pity. "That's not the part of the dream that matters."

The door whooshed open. Adam held a broad cutting board laid with bread and steak and asparagus, caramelized onion scattered like confetti. Our eyes met and he smiled.

"Let's eat."

"Oops, we haven't even set the table," Sharon said, getting up. She leaned down to me as she passed. "For the record, his poetry's his real job, and all that's just a hobby."

But I hadn't said anything to the contrary. I was more interested in the "girl."

Walking the bottle to the recycling on my way to the bathroom, I was pleased to see, there on the floor where she'd last set it, a wine stain on the natural wood. Throughout the night it would darken, a perfect circle radiating out from the edge like an early photo of a solar eclipse. A strange scar on pale skin.

AN HOUR OR TWO later—dessert served and what would be eaten, eaten; a second bottle of abysmally low-ABV piquette emptied; and the dishwasher running—the night came to its natural conclusion. Adam had even successfully forced himself to compliment the renovations as Sharon detailed each decision, each cost, each workaround, his kind words warring with his eyes.

"Okay, Mom," he said as he wiped his hands on a dish towel. "We've got a long drive back."

He tossed the towel in the stacked washer-dryer that occupied the pantry, leaving no space for food. My back hurt from the backless steel stools, my bra line was drenched with sweat, and the skin on my shoulders tingled. I made for the exit.

Sharon was back on the sofa, having sat out cleanup, tucked under a wide-weave throw. She did not rise to see us out.

"Just leave the gate unlocked, honey," she said, receiving Adam's hug. "My friend will be here any minute."

Adam withdrew.

"Friend?"

Truly, in all these years I'd never known Sharon to have any. Curators, colleagues, nemeses, neighbors, even boyfriends, yes—but no friends.

"Oh you know, friend, lover—at a certain age it's all the same." This was a marked departure from the relish with which she'd said "boyfriend" doing introductions just a couple Passovers ago. Looking at me, she added in a stage whisper: "I think it's getting serious." Her laugh was tinny as a schoolgirl's.

Adam cleared his throat. All dinner we'd been rehearsing banalities—he had a point. But I didn't have it in me to broach Sharon's feelings. And if we stayed here any longer, Adam might see what she'd done to his room. It was now an artist's studio, canvases leaning against the wall, tarp laid on the floor. I'd poked around on my way to the bathroom, shutting the bedroom door on my way out.

"Shall we?" I said.

"Yeah, okay," Adam said. He pecked Sharon on the cheek. "Have fun."

At the door I handed Adam the keys. I was too tired to get us home. We left the bungalow, tiki lights brightening in our wake, only to blacken soon enough.

Someday Sharon would be gone, and this house would be his. Inside, an aging Adam would sit at his desk, pen to paper (oh, a poet's twee luxuries), in a room whose past lives collected like change in one's pocket, so that most days, he'd hardly remember that it once contained the petty blows and sunny ignorance of his childhood and the flexed anxieties of adolescence; and when he did, one cold, gray morning before the marine layer had had a chance to burn off, he'd work the image into the poem he was working by hand for the book dedicated to that same girl, the long-lost Y who was now, at long last, his wife; and when she wrested her gaze from her laptop to look at him from the desk across the room, she'd see wrinkles that wavered as beautifully as his sloppy hand, and sense without his saying that the work was going well, so all was well, as it was with hers—Sharon's final abandonment would make space for that.

A man passed us on the sidewalk. I turned to watch him. He stopped at Sharon's, adjusted his bulge, and walked across the nude yard. Beneath his tee, a mass of muscles—I knew, I recognized—stretched, dense and disciplined, judging. He entered without knocking, and Sharon's front door shut behind him. Adam was already in the car when I turned back.

"Hey?" He rolled down the window. "Wanna get out of here?"

Quiet as a secret, I got in.

4

Moments Later

I ONLY HAD TO lean against the seat to realize how wholly I'd screwed myself over at the beach. I felt needles on my skin, a thousand and one needles straight through my back.

"Are you okay?" Adam said. "Seriously. You're grimacing."

I forced my face to relax. Lifting my caftan to my belly button, I turned on the car light.

"Jesus," he whispered.

My stomach was raw and red over my bikini. Tender as anger. I flipped the visor mirror down and pulled on my collar to reveal my chest. I touched the skin, ever so gingerly, with one finger. My body tensed with pain. I closed my eyes and breathed.

"Just don't say I told you so," I said. He didn't.

Soon—or maybe later, my eyes shut, my pain at once compacting and slackening time—I felt the car slow and turn. Pull to a stop.

"I'm getting you some aloe. Want anything else?"

I shook my head.

"Text me if you think of anything."

"Thanks."

Adam came back with the aloe and some painkillers, plus a pint of vanilla ice cream and a couple of nips. He screwed the tiny top off a miniature whiskey, and handed it to me. I washed down the pills with a swig. Sharon had managed to recreate herself in two months flat, and I'd spent all day with Adam without the courage to confront him, or myself.

Digging a well in the unforgiving ice cream—a triumph to which one of our spoons was sacrificed—Adam handed me the remaining, overfull spoon. The ice cream felt rich on my tongue. Cooling.

"Talk about First World problems," I said. "You definitely told me so."

A smile tickled Adam's eyes.

"Nah, you're perfect." He held up the second miniature whiskey bottle. "Will you do the honors?"

I tipped the bottle over the pint and watched the amber liquid fill the well, muddying with cream. Flourishing his fingers like an amateur magician Adam reached into the drugstore bag to reveal the puniest kind of California contraband: two single-use plastic straws. I clapped. Under the heat of the whiskey and Adam's hands, the ice cream softened, warmed inside and out. Adam stirred it with the single spoon that remained to us and sunk the straws in.

We bent our heads together, lips locked over the straws. It was easy to imagine a life like this. Aspirin and parking lots and stupid pain: all the usual ugliness, but under it, through it—this. Whatever this was.

I pulled back. I reached into the cup holder, and Julia's chain slithered through my fingers. It was a Chekhov's gun that had managed not to go off, and here I was pointing it at my own chest.

"See this?"

"Yeah?"

Adam looked at me blankly. I wondered at him. What was this subjectivity so softly handled that it could afford such trust?

"You don't recognize it?"

The parking lot fluorescence crashed through the windshield, cold, precise.

"It's not mine," I said.

Breathing heavier now, Adam stuffed the pint into the cup holder, forcing it to fit. The waxed cardboard crumpled, the melted brown sludge threatening to overflow.

"What are you saying to me."

"I ran into her the other night. Saturday, when I was out. We kind of—" I bit my lip.

He'd drawn as far back as the cramped car allowed, arms crossed.

"Something happened," I went on.

"Something."

I grimaced.

"What the fuck is something?"

"It wasn't a big deal—I mean it was really fucked up. But—I don't know, she started it—"

"She started it?"

He had every right to seethe, and I was sorry, so sorry—I wanted to reach out and put a hand on his, I wanted tears to alchemize my sorrows into contrition and relief. And yet my eyes remained dry, my face steeled against his censure. This was what the world had cost me; I was so used to defending myself against no wrong that when I was wrong, I grew defensive.

"It's not like you told me you were still together," I said. "You were texting her that same night, I saw."

Admittedly, when it came to messing around with your best friend's girlfriend, other people managed just fine.

Adam turned away from me and gripped the wheel. Thin blue veins strained against his skin.

"That's right. I texted her."

His voice was placid. Dead, like water in a reservoir.

"I was with someone for eight years, and then we broke up, and when I got low one night, I broke down and texted her."

His reserve fueled my anger.

"And what does one ask for at four in the morning on a Saturday?" I said.

"Where did it stop?" Adam said quietly.

I pushed on.

"You kept seeing her back in June. You talked to her basically yesterday. You've been lying to me this whole time."

"Don't say that," Adam said. "I didn't lie to you. We went to therapy once, and I saw her once to pick up my shit." Now he had a warning tone. "And I wasn't expecting anything from her on Saturday. I was clearing my photos, if you must know. That text was from before I went to bed." He looked at me, eyes narrowed. "So now you tell me. Where did it stop?"

"Adam."

It came out in a whisper, all I could muster.

The silver chain screamed in the harsh light. I moved it through my fingers like a rosary. *Know thyself*—the world was no excuse. I took a deep breath and regained my voice.

"Just a kiss."

"*Just?*"—I could hear his rejoinder as I said it. But Adam didn't say a thing—he pounded his head against the steering wheel. By impulse I grabbed his shoulder. The touch shocked me as much as him. For one long second my arm was a rope that bound our two bodies, soaked with pain and pleasure and swelling with the fact of existence. Just being there, still being there. Staying there. What if this was what I was after?—a life overwritten with this.

Adam shrugged me off and started the engine. We tunneled through the city suspended in midnight ink, LA inert outside the window. I squeezed the vial in my fist, the glass more unforgiving than the metal, mashing against the fine tendons buried in my palm. I willed it to break—willed Adam to see my pain and soften. But the glass didn't break, and Adam didn't speak, and the space between us stayed vast and hot.

Adam parked at the end of my block and popped the trunk and grabbed his stuff and called a car, and I walked the dark quiet street home alone.

5

Thursday, August 1

THE MORNING AFTER MY evening at Sharon's, my own mother texted.

Your father's had another heart attack.

I was at my desk, double-tasking, a rom-com streaming on my laptop, my spreadsheet open on my phone. Clarity to the point of cruelty, her signature.

I tried calling, only to be shot straight to voicemail.

My eyes fell on the little aloe plant that lived at the corner of my desk. Years ago, noticing it paling in the shadowy grad student lounge, I'd brought it home. Now I pressed a tendril between two fingers while heeding the spikes.

It gave way far too easily, dry from neglect.

IN SECOND OR THIRD grade I'd gotten off the bus after school to see my mother waiting for me on the front porch. She was sitting on the step.

"Your grandmother has died," she said as I slid in next to her. "Maternal grandmother."

Muttering the Fatiha, I sensed my throat constrict. Like when my mother denied me some bauble I wanted at the store, not by telling me no, but by generally making herself so well understood that I never asked.

I had never met my mother's mother, had never seen where my mother grew up. And yet I'd fantasized about the sweet sting of her pinching my cheeks, about the laddu she'd have slipped into my pockets at Eid. They were scenes I'd lifted from Bollywood movies. The one grandmother I had met—my father's mother—did nothing of the sort.

My mother stared straight ahead, hands clasped around her knees, eyes dry. When the neighbor waved many minutes later, she didn't see.

Finally the phone rang and we went inside. It was a telemarketer.

She did not go back for the burial.

AS I WAITED FOR my mother to call me back, I carried my aloe to the kitchen and set the pot soaking in a bowl of water. The squeeze-top aloe vera gel Adam had bought me for my sunburn lay on the counter. I had to reapply every forty or fifty minutes, whenever I got up for a glass of water, and now I did the same. My skin stung at my touch.

God willing, my father didn't need bypass surgery. It wasn't the surgery that killed you in a place like Iran, but the post-op—that much was common knowledge. The surgeons were skilled, but aftercare was stretched thin, and there was a high risk of infection, among other problems. If something more mysterious went wrong, you were really fucked. Good luck getting a CT scan; there were about two machines in the entire country.

Literally only five hundred-some, as of two years ago, when my father had tried to help a much richer expat-retiree donate a couple used CT scanners to a public hospital. The US, apparently, had almost fourteen thousand—three times as many, per person. But my father and his friend had become ensnared in a web of noxious politics and sanctions, and the medical devices had stayed comfortably in the First World, collecting dust in storage.

A CALENDAR ALERT CHIMED from my phone a full fifteen minutes later: my mother had shared her itinerary. She was flying in a few hours. I was to follow her that night, she messaged, booking whatever I could. I hearted her text and slipped my phone back into my pocket.

Lifting the aloe, I watched it piss into the sink.

I already knew one thing: she considered him good as dead. It was the only reason she'd go.

تهران

TEHRAN

یک

YEK

ONE

١

Saturday, August 3

LIKE ANY THIRD WORLD airport worth its salt, Imam Khomeini International feigned a First World sheen. Jumpsuited janitors, gray-suited businessmen, and women attired in everything from red lipstick to black chadors staged the terminal like an architectural model. Light crashed through wide windows onto waxed floors. Suitcases slipped through the exiting X-ray machine, uncensored. Families kissed in cool filtered air. No sign of the dirt and dysfunction swirling just beyond the doors. For foreigners, one must put on a good face.

I looked up at the arrivals and departures board: it was almost two in the afternoon on Saturday.

The heart attack had happened all the way back on Thursday. Thursday night, local time; Thursday morning, LA time, not long before my mother messaged me. Due to US-imposed sanctions, there weren't any direct flights from LA to Tehran. Between two stopovers (Atlanta, Doha) and a ten-and-a-half-hour time difference, I'd lost two days.

My mother had fared a little better. Routed through New York and Moscow on Aeroflot—the things you had to do to get here—she'd gotten in around three last night. Straight to the hospital, according to the texts I got while pacing the Doha airport on my layover. My father's condition was stable. She was with him. I couldn't get through in real time, but my father had sent a voice memo asking for "those fancy chocolate-dipped dates the Gulfies like," plus a selfie that cut off one ear.

DRAGGING MY CARRY-ON BEHIND me now, wheels heaving as the smooth tiles gave way to cement, I stepped outside. It smelled like exhaust. Here Saturday was Monday, the first day of the work week, and yet the curb was crowded with people picking up or dropping off their loved ones. The cabs stood all the way at the other end of the lot, an afterthought.

Before landing, prompted by the chiming seatbelt signs, I and all the other bareheaded women had risen like synchronized swimmers to fish in our carry-ons for our own versions of manteau and rusari. In my case, a drab black shirtdress and the black shawl I'd bought last time.

As I made my way across the lot, I scanned the women for the state of hijab law. Like tax evasion in the US, what you could get away with depended on who was president. More rather than less, apparently, these days. I'd overcorrected. Everyone else looked like sixties stars in convertibles, bright silk scarves knotted under-chin, ponytails spilling out the back.

I rehearsed how to order a cab. Don't make eye contact, and give the name of the main road, not the side street, by way of address. This was the problem with being here. For me, even breathing took work.

"Sohrevardi South, please," I said.

The cabbie put out his cigarette on the hood of his car and slipped the half-used smoke back into the pack.

"Ticket?"

He sighed exaggeratedly when he realized I hadn't prepaid at the taxi stand, like you were supposed to, and directed me back inside.

At the kiosk in the terminal, Departures winking invitingly overhead, I realized I was really screwed. Stateside, I'd checked and rechecked to make sure I had both my passports, but money, toman—I'd forgotten all about that. My American debit card was useless, thanks again to the sanctions, and I didn't have any cash.

Wallet, backpack, laptop sleeve, pockets—I tore into my stuff, praying to catch glimpse of the toman's peaches and pinks. Iranian currency came in the colors of a bridal bouquet.

While I searched I took tally of my father's health. Four years ago marked heart attack number one. That had prompted my second trip to Iran. This was my third. The man was pushing seventy and hadn't exercised a day in his life; you could only ask for so much. But that still didn't amount to a death sentence—I refused to give in to my mother's cynicism ("realism," she said).

At long last I felt the velvet skin of worn bills under my fingertips. Yuan, tucked into the back flap of my Iranian passport case: in 2015 I'd had a layover in Shanghai. Hopefully the Chinese economy was doing as well as they said.

There was a line at the exchange composed of a couple adventurous Europeans and a bunch of businessmen local to Asia. Only a foreigner would give up dollars at the official government rate. With all the delusions of a self-help bestseller, the government tried to "manifest" a strong toman by simply stating that it was worth more than it was. Any real Iranian, anyone with family here, would wait to get into the city for the black-market rate—otherwise known as the global exchange rate. But here I was, standing in line a full hour after landing, tapping a foot against the polished floor as I tried to tether my phone to the feeble free Wi-Fi.

At LAX the other day, my less censored but surveilled data connection still available to me, I'd opened the apps and contended with my calendar.

a) First date spritzes with a semi-professional ballerina: gone. Femme-femme, where would that have gotten us?—frictionless, a fantasy.

b) Second date with the entertainment lawyer who'd dribbled cashew cheese on her collar on date one but was up for partner: postponed.

c) Barcade beers with the bro in the Dodgers' cap: absolutely not. What kind of manic optimism had led me to consent to beer in the first place?

d) Third date with the dermatologist who hadn't finished a book since *White Fang*: status change to Let's Be In Touch.

I expected to be back in America in a week; two, tops. Last heart attack he'd been in and out of the state hospital quicker than an oil change. The news had reached us only ex post facto. By the time I visited Tehran months later, courtesy of a summer research grant, he was back to ordering fried chicken every night. The only development was that a bottle of blood thinners lived by the ketchup.

Finally I got through on the Wi-Fi. In my email, the subject line "Re: 2019–20 Appointments" caught my gaze. My body buzzed with giddy relief. So they'd just been running behind on scheduling, after all. Maybe I could even pitch the chick flick syllabus.

I clicked. "I regret to inform you," the email began. The department was breaking up with me. And so graciously, it was offensive. Words like "unfortunately" and "sadly" peppered the body of the email, false and redundant, until a final coup of condescension: "grateful for your service."

Allegedly they had "no need" for the courses, but I knew, and the secretary who sent the email knew, that the move was just the latest tactic in the war against the "contingent faculty" union. I was only a minor casualty. The same Marxist anti-imperialist scholars who'd earned our department its good name came out of faculty meetings, undereyes bloated with pod-pumped coffee, determined to let the serfs starve.

In fact the writers I taught would not be read. The history I taught would not be represented. The "diversity" I introduced would not be encountered. At least not in our small corner of the university. Profit over knowledge, knowledge over understanding—that was culture under capitalism.

There was only one person left in front of me in line at the exchange. I gazed at the posted rates, willing my mind, unsuccessfully, to do the math. Instead, an image of my studio back in LA pressed on me like heartache. The volumes piled atop already stuffed bookcases. The sticky-notes jostling for space on their dormant pages. The aloe I'd left leaking on the kitchen counter. I was officially out of a job. If only I didn't have books or a body, I wouldn't need to pay rent.

The clerk at the exchange sent me away with 23,800 toman, after fees, and a smile. Service here didn't require it, and I smiled back. For a 25,000 toman ride, this should suffice. The guy at the taxi stand would take pity on me—I was a woman after all.

٢

An Hour or So Later

I ARRIVED AT MY father's house to find my mother crouched on the low stone ledge of the garden bed out front, under the scant shade of the pomegranate tree, steam rising from a fresh glass of tea.

My father's house, like all houses, was surrounded by high walls, with heavy double doors of steel that were kept shut all day. Inside the gate, before the door to the house, lay the yawning open-air courtyard in which I now stood with my carry-on, having let myself in.

Catching my eyes, my mother smiled.

"Our sole successor."

She rose, coming to greet me. Her heels clicked against the dusty tiles that covered the courtyard from wall to wall to wall, interrupted only by the garden bed built into the corner, which my father tended himself. Pomegranate tree roots ran shallow, and this foot or so of soil was enough.

We traded cheek kisses. It was the opposite of intimacy. Hugs required more surface area.

"I thought you'd still be at the hospital," I said, finally dumping my backpack.

"I came home to freshen up."

She was dressed in the usual uniform: dark jeans, high heels, an oversized men's shirt that must have passed for a manteau in public. Her white dupatta had fallen to her shoulders, wrinkling under the weight of her graying waves.

She took a long look at me, and reached to ruffle my hair.

"You look well."

I hadn't showered since Thursday. Or seen her since Thanksgiving.

"You look better," I said.

I considered confiding in her, showing her the email from my department. Admitting my failure.

I didn't have the balls.

"Come, let's sit."

She led the way. A short way, to the spot on the garden ledge where she'd left her tea. Next to it, there was a plastic card table and folding chair my father had repurposed for the courtyard. Place for one.

"Your father's well. They were switching his room when I left, out of the ICU."

"That's great."

Relief washed over me, and guilt. I'd arrived too late to do anything for him.

My mother offered me her tea. I took a sip, both of us still standing.

"Catch your breath," she said. "We'll go soon."

I tossed my keys on the table and sank into the chair. In 2015, my father had pressed a set of house keys to my palm, "just in case." They were brass skeleton keys that I assumed were as old as the house, maybe eighty. Not much older than my father.

My mother remained standing. Behind her, hard, unripe pomegranates hovered between the leaves, green on green, light against dark.

When I was a kid, we took exactly one family trip to Iran. "That Indian girl" was how my paternal grandmother referred to my mother, as soon as my father was out of earshot. But I could hear. The moment we left Iranian airspace, as the Dutch flight attendants on KLM shed their rusaris, my mother had foresworn future visits. She was a woman of her word, and that first trip had been her last.

Until now. Words, too, had their hierarchies, and a contract trumped a promise. He was in need. She was his wife.

She was here.

Fingering my keys, she cracked a wry smile.

"The rightful heir comes home."

THE PUBLIC HOSPITAL WAS busy as the airport without its light or lightness of step. Bodies sat slumped in wheelchairs, while other bodies stood pushing them. Bodies sat erect behind the reception desk. Bodies creased head over knees on waiting room benches.

I led us through the swarm of beseechers hovering by the desk. My father had texted my mother his new room number soon after she'd left that morning.

"Excuse me," I said in Farsi.

As in the taxi I'd called to get here, I had to do the talking. I could feel the eyes on my mother behind my back.

"Excuse me?"

I couldn't get anyone's attention. The women at the desk were all busy, working with the efficiency of the understaffed. They rebuffed a guy who was trying to get his wife prematurely released, directed a wizened chadori to the pharmacy, and cooed at a little girl held in her father's arms—all while receiving calls and clicking on their keyboards and collecting payments that seemed to my American sensibilities shockingly, depressingly small.

"Excuse me—" I said loudly. "Could you tell me how to get to twelve thirty-seven?"

Without looking up from her monitor, one of the receptionists addressed me.

"Patient name?"

I gave the last name my father had given me.

"But I just want to get to twelve thirty-seven."

"There is no twelve thirty-seven," she said as she typed. "Ah. Two hundred thirty-seven. Left-hand corridor, turn right, all the way to the end."

I led us through the room, aware of the eyes that followed my mother. She'd changed into a green shalwar kameez with a matching dupatta as I showered. My mother never wore shalwar kameez. She was actively trying to stick out, as though Iranians couldn't already read her difference on her skin, and I resented her for it. I could pass, at least before I opened my mouth.

I touched her arm.

"Where did you get this from?"

"It's just an old thing."

"Sure. But where from?"

"Back home."

She never used proper nouns when talking about her life before the US. Once, years after her mother died, she'd taken me to India, but limited our travels to the Tourist Triangle: Agra, Delhi, Jaipur. Even there my mother didn't deign speak a word that wasn't English. I could tell she understood Hindi, via Urdu. As could the bellhops and ticket takers, the cabbies she complained smelled of sweat and curry. (And as did the aunties at home in America, when she dropped me off at a sleepover or picked me up from Sunday School.) But my mother always responded in English, acting like any other tourist or American, when everyone knew she was not. Though, really, what did I know. Maybe in those cities she was.

Now she paused at a fork in the hallway.

"Which way?"

The room numbers were anglicized, but I hadn't repeated the directions.

"Left," I said.

Here in Iran, she was helpless without me.

IN ROOM 237, MY father lay sleeping under anonymous white cotton. Sheets so plain and pristine they could have doubled as shrouds.

My mother took what looked like a school chair from the opposite bedside and turned it toward him. Offering me the seat—I declined, as expected of me now that we were in public—she sat down.

"Don't disturb him," she whispered.

She set her bag on the bed by my father's feet, and it creaked—what did she have in there, the collected works of Dickens? My father didn't stir. He'd always been a luxurious sleeper.

I hadn't seen him since 2015, and I couldn't even remember the last time all three of us had been in the same room. He'd thinned in that old-man kind of way, muscles melting from the bone, limbs like winter branches, bare down to the fingers. He had both hands on top of the sheet. Neither my father nor my mother wore their wedding rings. But they were not divorced. Not technically.

Her lips were moving, and I realized she was reciting dua. It was ridiculous. Neither of us fasted or prayed anymore.

I took my father's hand. Loosely, gently. It felt far too light. Too small. He'd loomed over my childhood like a god. Deferred to and yet irrelevant to the workings of the everyday. Now he lay there, a leaf of paper. Shuddering with the labor of his own breath.

We watched him breathe.

A NURSE CAME TO tend to the patient in bed next to him within the hour. I asked when we could take my father home.

"I'd have to check his chart."

"If you could—"

She was already on her way out.

She returned with a wheelchair. Back to the other man's bedside.

"Khanum," I addressed her formally. "It would be such a help—"

"Can't you see I'm occupied?"

She shimmied behind the now loaded wheelchair.

"Just a little patience," she said when she'd reached the doorway. "I'll be back."

I translated the interaction for my mother.

"Leave her alone," she said. "They're sure to keep him another night."

By then it was around five.

AN HOUR PASSED, THEN another.

I grew hungry. Tired.

Bored.

Around 7:15 the jet lag hit me like cheap cocaine. Jittery mock energy that passed as quickly as it came. Back in LA it was still morning.

I wanted to text Adam, I hadn't told him I'd left. But I was sure I was the last person he wanted to hear from.

My mother was still on her dua, or Donne or whatever. I took out my phone. There wasn't any public Wi-Fi.

I hadn't thought of what it would actually be like to linger by a sickbed. The mute waiting. The useless passing of time.

MY MOTHER WAS THE first to notice. A slight dew had formed on my father's forehead. He has a fever, she said, and a fever in his condition was a dangerous thing.

She sent me to get the nurse. I practically pulled someone into my father's room to examine the sweat my mother told me not to wipe away as evidence. This time she spoke and I translated.

Not bothering to wake him, the nurse slipped an electric thermometer under my father's tongue. It didn't twitch in reflex. Inert as the tongue he'd once scooped and skinned for me from a pot of sheep's head stew. The thermometer beeped. His temperature, though higher than the last reading according to his chart, remained within the normal range.

My mother demanded a doctor. When was the last reading? No one had taken his vitals since we'd been there.

The nurse talked about rounds, other patients, priorities. My mother repeated herself. Slowly, sternly, without raising her voice. Again, I translated. But it was my mother's imperiousness that made things move, her dignity that finally summoned the doctor.

THE DOCTOR ARRIVED. SHE stayed in the doorway, and we were forced to rise to meet her. My mother introduced herself as a professor. They shook hands. I stood a step behind my mother, like the interpreter to an ambassador.

"This isn't my floor," the doctor said. "But please, go on."

Again, my mother talked, and I translated, just to be sure. Even an educated person like the doctor could scarcely be expected to understand English at this clip.

The heart attack, the ICU, supposedly a smooth transfer this morning—but my mother was sure something had gone wrong. Under the spell of my mother's voice the doctor's brows furrowed. Her eyes softened. She was relatively young, and a little alt, despite the anonymizing white doctor's coat and navy maghnaeh, her uniform hijab not unlike a nun's habit. It was in the way she stood, feet planted wide, shoulders back; and it was in the mustache she'd refused to tweeze.

"I try to find his doctor," she said in English. "I am hope."

With a subtle bow of the head, she left.

SHE RETURNED WITHIN THE minute. My mother and I were still standing, lingering nervously.

"How's his speech?" the doctor asked, looking at my mother.

I translated. My mother frowned.

"Truthfully we don't know," I said of my own accord. "He's been resting."

"His responsiveness?"

I was silent.

"Did they do a CT scan this morning?"

My mother made out the phrase "see tee e-scan" without my translating.

"Why does he need a CT scan?" she said to me, exasperated. "He was fully himself when I left."

"No, khanum doctor," I said to the doctor. "It seems he was lively this morning."

I lowered my eyes. This was an exam, and we were failing.

"They don't have enough machines over in Radiology," she said wearily, the borrowed term "rādiolozhē" again echoing English. "Or they would've taken the precaution, at his age especially."

"She thinks they should've done a scan to be safe," I told my mother.

The doctor swept past us to my father's bedside.

"Sir?"

My father didn't respond.

"Sir!" This time she was louder.

She put a hand on his shoulder. Nothing happened. She pinched him. Nothing happened. Gripping with both hands she shook the body that lay on my father's bed. The body was still.

The doctor ran out, loafers beating against the floor like a war drum. My mother and I looked on, impotent. Still.

ALL MORNING, AS MY mother took a taxi from the hospital back to the house, and showered and redressed and took her tea in the courtyard; and all afternoon, as I deboarded the flight, and tried to take a taxi, and double backed to the exchange, and begged the guy at the taxi stand to take pity on me for the sake of my sick father though I was short by over a thousand toman, and spent an hour in midday traffic while contemplating how pathetic it was that I didn't know these streets and couldn't direct the cabbie except to repeat the name of the main road by my father's house, Sohrevardi South; and that next hour at the house, as I sipped two sips of tea and showered and redressed and called a car via the neighborhood taxi service whose number was inscribed on the phone cradle in neat ESL cursive in my father's hand; and every minute my mother and I waited for the car and rode in the car; and every second we waited for the receptionist and waited for the nurse and waited for the doctor and waited for them to transport my father to Imaging and for the CT scanner to free up and for the surgeons to scrub in—all this time, two nascent brain bleeds born of my father's heart attack had been left to their natural vocation: to grow, to spread, working uninterrupted and aided by blood thinners coated in ketchup, hacking away at my father's consciousness until they threatened his soul.

MY FATHER CAME OUT of surgery alive. I was sent home just after midnight. My mother stayed with her husband.

۳

That Night

THE NIGHT OPENED ANOTHER world to me. My father's newfound life coursed through me like a contact high. Fingers, nose, and toes—I tingled, electric with possibility.

Inside his house, I drew back the blinds. I opened all the windows. They side-hinged like doors, and I stepped through, barefoot, into the courtyard.

Outside, mosquitos floated alongside the neighbor's music. Soft percussion and double bass, solo female vocals. The kind of stuff that was theoretically banned and, in practice, everywhere. Half the units on the block still had their lights on. Summer in the semidesert: night was when you did your living.

My father's was the only house on the block that still had a full courtyard, fit with a traditional garden: who but a foreigner would bother to maintain the old ways? All the other houses had been knocked down to build lucrative four-story apartments, their courtyards swallowed into parking or more square footage—meterage, rather. As my uncle had put it to me in 2015, life in Tehran came down to high rent, whether paying or charging it.

Now my gaze followed the music over the high brick wall of my father's courtyard, and over the iron arrows that trimmed the wall, to dissuade thieves. Up the pale apartment building next door, up to the top-floor balcony. Through the open curtains that fluttered with a passing breeze, and into an empty bedroom. Of course. Wherever the party was, it was tucked inside, at a safe distance from the windows.

I jumped up and down, the tiles cool against the soles of my feet. I stepped onto the garden ledge, and the stones were so cold it sent a shiver up my spine. I remembered the punishing heat in Palm Springs, its tenacious grip on the courtyard bricks at the Kim estate. This desert was more forgiving. I walked the L of the garden perimeter like a kid tracing the painted lines of a parking spot, heel to toe. Hopped down and ran the length of the courtyard, from the gate to the house door. Lapping once, twice, thrice.

Out of breath absurdly quick, I stopped.

"Khasteh nabāshīd," a woman's voice called from above.

May you not be tired. As in, good work. If not for racism, it was a wonder my mother didn't fit in here: sarcasm was the national pastime.

A lone woman now leaned over the balcony, the tip of her cigarette a mole on the face of the night. Her breasts pushed against a tight, embroidered velvet vest, vague village drag. Except she wore nothing underneath. I imagined undoing the toggles, and the thought turned liquid between my legs. It seemed fast, even for me. Maybe there was some truth to the cliché that the smell of death makes you horny.

A man entered the stage with a jar of what looked like river water— moonshine, surely—and two waisted tea glasses. He passed one off to the woman and, pouring first for her then himself, took a shot.

By now every other apartment on the block hung dark and quiet, and at the neighbor's, someone inside had turned the music down to a trickle.

"We have company," the woman said. "Down there."

"Khūbī?" he called, a familiar *hey*.

He poured two more shots, but she passed hers back.

"What about you, thirsty?"—and suddenly a glass was gliding

through the air and over the spiked courtyard wall, wet and winking in the night sky, and I could already hear the awful commotion it'd make, breaking like a bomb against the courtyard floor.

Instead I felt the lick of glass against my skin. It had landed in my palm.

Laughing, she clapped for me, while her friend shook his hand like it hurt.

"Who the fuck is this?" he said.

Drunk on unearned success, I felt a man's confidence. I turned the glass upside down.

"It's empty."

"So come up," she called, "and I'll sort you out."

The man whistled. He passed her the jar of moonshine and spun inside, but not without first filling his glass to the brim.

In a handful of hours at dawn, a thin oriental light would wash the courtyard. My mother, I knew, would stay at the hospital for at least an hour or two after that, waiting for a stronger sun to dismiss her.

I fetched my keys and my shawl from inside the house, and soon eased back out the window and into my father's slippers. The court-yard doors sighed shut behind me, moaning and quivering before they finally fell silent, conjoined.

Date #90: The Girl Next Door

MAKING A TIGHT TURN, I buzzed the top unit at the neighbor's. The laughter and music tumbling off her balcony had picked up again, and I held down the buzzer. Though I hadn't had the guts to step into the street without some semblance of hijab, throwing my shawl over whatever I had on, I'd foregone the manteau. I was now out in public, in jeans and a wifebeater. I wished she'd hurry.

Instead of the pedestrian door, the car gate yawned open. I walked over. The tiles sloped down, into the gaping mouth of basement parking. The building was set back, flush with my father's, and the ramp was in the open air. To the right—where the pedestrian door would've led me—lay the vestige of the old courtyard. The edge that dropped off to the ramp had no safety railing, just a scrim of potted plants.

She was standing there, moonshine in hand. Big curls, red lipstick, Kahlo-esque eyebrows. Finding a gap between two plants, she lowered herself to the ramp, then retrieved the whiskey from the ledge.

"Come, come."

"Such a nice night," I said, pulling off my shawl as we stepped toward each other.

Up close I saw her eyes were drawn in thick black kohl. Not eyeliner but kohl, an indie affectation to match the vest. The kohl had migrated into her undereye wrinkles, and I figured she was about forty.

It was then that I remembered that I hadn't redone my makeup after my shower. Between going au naturale and my wifebeater, this constituted false advertising.

"Let's stay down here awhile," she said, starting down the ramp and waving a hand up toward the balcony. "My friends are trash. They're gonna get us all arrested."

I followed, trying not to trip down the steep slope in my father's shoes. At the bottom, beyond the usual Asian-make sedans, an open-topped shed occupied the last parking spot. The bricks closest to the cars—tan, like the building—were black with exhaust. A simple wood bench stood on one side.

"It's nice and quiet here," she said, taking a seat. "We can talk."

We didn't talk; we drank, sipping straight from the jar. The air sparked, and yet we sat without touching. I realized I'd never flirted in Farsi, and I wondered when this shit would kick in.

"What's in here?" I knocked on the shed.

"See for yourself."

Inside, the shed was lined with shelves. Ceramics in various states of undress sat in disarray. Unglazed, half-glazed. A silver kiln gleaned in the far corner, vented to the outside—outside outside, by the looks of it, probably into an open airshaft like that behind my father's house—via an umbilical cord that ran straight through the back wall. In other words, it was an expensive setup. Custom, and the kiln was so shiny it looked new.

"Is this your work?" I asked.

"Yes, sir."

"You just started?"

She raised her eyebrows.

"No, my dear, I've been working for a long time."

"But your—" I didn't know the word for *kiln* "—machine? It doesn't have a scratch."

"Fresh from Europe. I gave the old one to a friend."

My back to her, I heard the flicker of a lighter—the sweet toxicity of a cigarette filled the small space. There was a row of finished work. Sculptures, sort of, each the size of a dinner plate, except ovular and with the center punched out. The outer rims were bulbous, the inner edges raw and toothy. Vaginas, clearly. Or rather, mangled vaginas.

"Feel free," she said, taking a drag as I turned to look at her. "If you have any critiques."

She almost sounded sincere.

My first thought was that the work was derivative, stuck in the Second Wave. Judy Chicago came to mind, of course; during undergrad I'd made a pilgrimage to Brooklyn to view *The Dinner Party*, that icon of seventies American feminism. But then again, these works were much more visceral, less ornate: there were real holes in the middle, holes the artist had cut from her own creation. From, in a sense, her own flesh.

"It's about violence against women?" I said.

"In a way."

The only finished work was unequivocally gorgeous. Dark rich hues like navy and black in a high shine glaze that still looked wet.

"Is it easy to show this stuff here?" I asked, knowing that I'd already given myself away. Clearly I wasn't from here.

She smiled wryly.

"There's a difference between seeing and comprehending. You can show people what they won't see without getting into trouble."

She came and toyed with a figurine on another shelf. A big-bellied nude that fit in her palm.

"Or you can always just show the work to certain people."

"You do a lot of private viewings?"

Still stuck on the plates, I wanted to finger the hole. Without asking permission, I touched the gash of an unfinished work.

I felt a prick, blood beading on my fingertip.

"What happened?"

She took my finger and sucked it clean. A shiver crawled through me.

Our breaths sounded against the still basement air. She leaned in to kiss me. Long but not hard. Long enough that by the time I felt her below, her touch was solace, the easing of an ache.

Several minutes later, as I came, her fingers deep within me, my back against the cool kiln, I heard a car—very close, just outside the shed. The spit of the engine, the shush of tires. Her downstairs neighbors—her tenants, I'd soon discover—heading out before dawn to beat traffic. I straightened myself out.

It was then that she told me her name.

Leili. After the star-crossed lovers, Leyli and Majnun. In the poem, the tragic heroine drives her beloved "crazy," or "majnūn," while she's called after the Arabic word for *night*, "layl." The more common name *Leila* came from the same root, but this version insisted on the classical reference, a mark of high culture. It was a matter of the final vowel, which sighed itself into oblivion.

"Layl-ī," meaning, *of the night*.

۴

Sunday, August 4

ONCE UPON A TIME, two youths, a Sunni and a Shia, met at the university MSA and got married. Joining two sects, meeting without an introduction from family; it was what some called a "love marriage." The love quickly faded. The marriage survived. Islam—that is, the day's blinkered interpretation of Islam—kept the couple together, plus structures of self-policing that were just as effective. Respectability politics came cloaked as religion, just as religion so often stands in for faith.

As their child, more an inevitability than an accident, I'd long served as the medium for their marriage, at once a product of their contract and its manifestation. But like any overwrought symbol, I eventually folded under the weight of too much meaning.

Case in point: all the sexing and the spreadsheeting I'd gotten up to this summer, most recently just last night. They say religion skips a generation. Respectability was probably the same.

THE NEXT MORNING, I woke to the sound of the shower running. Downstairs, where I was sleeping, though there was another bathroom upstairs. My mother was home.

Lest her passive aggression lose its passivity, I willed myself upright. The hard Japanese-style futon I'd laid out in the living room, the jet lag, the sex, and perhaps, too, the adrenaline ride from witnessing my father cheating death—put together, I felt like lead. Admittedly the moonshine was not helping.

With a cursory knock, I went in to brush my teeth.

"Morning," I said.

"Good afternoon," my mother said from behind the curtain. It wasn't yet ten. "Don't use the hot water," she added.

Two could play at this game. I splashed my face with hot water.

In the mirror I faced my father's eyes. Smallish, almost entirely black, nothing to give a person pause. You have our eyes, my grandmother once said to me. My mother had camel eyes the likes of which could've been elegized by Omar Khayyam. Genetics could be cruel.

"How is he?" I asked.

"Your father? Unwell."

"Right," I said. "But how is he, all things considered?"

Watching the water rush down the drain, I again considered admitting my unemployment to my mother. It was Sunday, August 4, and I'd managed to pay late rent from my only-when-downright-destitute account.

"They put him through bloody brain surgery and they still haven't managed to reduce his fever."

The scream of the shower stopped. My mother's hand reached out from behind the curtain, blindly searching for a towel. I handed her mine.

"As soon as they tamp it," my mother said, voice climbing a minor scale, "it shoots back up."

The "curtain" was really just a liner, a bachelor's touch. Her silhouette arced behind the flimsy plastic like a willow bent to breaking point.

"I'll put the kettle on."

I shut the door behind me.

AT BREAKFAST, OVER STALE bread dug out of my father's freezer and butter that wouldn't spread, my mother announced her intention to get my father, in her words, "out of the periphery of the periphery of empire and back to the center."

"Have you called the insurance?" I asked.

"I haven't had the chance."

I checked the clock ticking by the built-in china cabinet. Just after ten here in Tehran, it was the middle of the night in Michigan, where my father was covered under my mother's insurance. (Much to his objection—he despised private healthcare.)

I assumed that medical evacuations weren't exactly cheap. Plus, this was Iran we were talking about. Could American insurance really help you here? There wasn't even an embassy. The Swiss looked after the rare American tourist, or spy, or journalist (each as likely to get screwed)—and when hyphens got involved, it was unclear who counted as American. We were all three here on Iranian passports.

"Did you try the Swiss Embassy?"

"Not yet."

"Well it's Sunday. So that's promising."

What if they kept to the Western workweek? My mother started rifling through a folder she drew from her bag.

"How is this supposed to work?" I said. "The Islamic Republic of Iran and the US of A aren't exactly friendly?"

"Don't patronize your mother."

She was right of course. I wondered for what crime I was punishing her. His absence? Her difference? For showering in "my" bathroom? She'd leaned on me for one day and I'd already tired of it. Maybe this was what motherhood felt like.

TECHNICALLY MY MOTHER WAS also Iranian, at least according to the Iranian state. My father had gotten us both passports back in the nineties, before that big family trip, and a passport meant you were a citizen. As the child of an Iranian father, I didn't have a choice—you couldn't apply for a tourist visa. "See this color?" my father had said when the barberry red passports arrived via DHL, twenty-seven summers ago. "That's the color of civilization. Two and a half millennia of forks and spoons."

Decade after decade, he'd kept our documents up to date. Hoping against hope that one of these years when he flocked home to see his maman and the budding spring of Nouruz, we might join him, steeping at his side in the drunken stupor of a million blooming hyacinths carried through city streets.

All I smelled now was his own sour wilting.

MY MOTHER PLACED A shiny plastic card on the table, customer service number up, and handed me the cordless phone. I balked.

"That call will bankrupt him."

Given the exchange rate, perhaps not strictly true, but I went and got my laptop. Miraculously I remembered to go through the university VPN before running my card for calling credit; the last thing I needed was sanctions-flagging on my accounts.

I dialed the insurance company. The system hung up on me. Once, twice—on the third try, against all logic, the call went through. After an obstacle course of failed voice recognition followed by manual inputs, I was mercifully placed on hold.

I crossed the adjoining rooms to the windows. The courtyard was cast like an overexposed photo, tiles paling under the summer sun. What was my father doing here anyway? He'd come "back home." Naturally. But what about his wife, his child?

AN ETERNITY LATER, I finally had a live human on the other end. In a time zone, her accent suggested, even further east than here.

"I'm calling about the policy's international coverage," I explained, back at the table with another round of tea. "My father isn't in the US—"

"May I ask where you are located at present?"

I hesitated. To ask for a medical evacuation from Iran to America—you'd have to have been born yesterday. I set the tea tray down, serving my mother first, and took a seat. My mother nodded in acknowledgment but didn't look at me.

She sat at the head of the table, uncharacteristically blank, staring vacantly down the grand varnished dining table that my grandmother had brought to her husband's house as a young bride—along with the stiff baroque chairs under our bony asses, and the delicate tea glass that now pressed hot against my fingers, and the dirty porcelain I hadn't yet cleaned up from breakfast that my mother was absently drumming with long rounded fingernails, and all the other furnishings big or small, heavy or light; outfitting the house was the bride's responsibility by custom, as was the reproductive labor that resulted in my father, whose aged body now lay in a nearby hospital, an indistinguishable braid of these two women's labors, the mother and the wife.

"Madam? Are you with me?"

"Tehran," I finally said.

"Tehran, Iran, madam? Have I heard you correctly?"

The goodbye kisses my father had given me as a child before dawn each morning as I feigned sleep—I saw the scene now as if I'd been the one watching from the doorway rather than the one in bed. How hard my mother had worked to provide for us, and how easily he'd stolen my affection.

My father was always absent, I realized, sitting there in that house in Tehran that was only his. Even when he was right there in the foreground, lying napping in the living room in Michigan, limbs loose as a corpse, he existed as a fixture, breathing and unmoving, like the nameless plants my mother had me water when she remembered them.

But I remembered this, too: when he cracked a smile, just looking at me over a serving dish of rice. When he took me to the park after dinner as a kid, and I flew through the monkey bars in the long light of summer till my hands blistered, made fearless by his refusal to watch me, to fuss.

I wondered whether there was for my mother some similar worm wriggling beneath the hard shell of duty, naked and soft.

Her eyes were dry. Mine were slick with unshed tears.

"Yes, Tehran," I said. "I'd like a medical evacuation from Tehran."

Love was a form of idiocy. And this thing I had with my father was probably some kind of love.

AN HOUR AND ANOTHER round of credit later, I was told that there was little that could or would be done for us. Though should we wish to submit hospital bills for reimbursement, they might be honored, pending review, if filed within six weeks of the date of service, along with notarized translations of any documentation not in English from one of the following approved vendors.

I shut my laptop. My mother left the room. In a few minutes, I heard her stomping around upstairs in her heels, readying to leave.

I called the same taxi service as yesterday. The attendant recognized me, and when again I asked to go to the hospital, he apologized that a driver wouldn't be free for twenty, thirty minutes.

"That's fine," I said, too worn to call around. "We'll wait."

"Sure thing, khanum, khodā bad nadeh," he said all in one breath. *May God not give you troubles*, mechanized kindness.

"Salāmat bāshīd."

I bid him good health in return and hung up.

By now it was almost noon, and the parlor was hot from the sun. Before heading to don my manteau-rusari—and to admit the delay to my mother—I drew the blinds dark. Embraced by shadow, I imagined the thread of life as a thin silk thread held against the dusk, catching the moonlight. My parents believed that God took us when our time came. Perhaps my father's thread was not to be cut short, but had, more simply, come into view, end to end. The thought didn't flush the bitterness and tenderness and loss that swam within me, but rather, floated on top like a leaf.

And yet even if a person's time on this earth were so neatly apportioned, who were we to guess its sum?

◊

That Afternoon

POST-OP AT THE STATE hospital, my father stayed stuck in sleep. His responsiveness, as they called it, had not improved. The doctor who'd so helped us yesterday—who'd saved him—was gone. It was her day off.

My mother was visibly upset. "Disturbed," in the parlance of the novels she'd once taught and studied, before giving them up for a corner office and her own dedicated Keurig. She paced the hallway, arms crossed, lips pursed, prayer and poetry alike abandoned to her nerves. Soon she tired of that and got online, pulling from her bag a portable hotspot I wish I'd known about yesterday.

An evacuation to the First World rendered impossible, my mother settled on making a fuss in the Third. She set her sights on moving my father to a private hospital uptown, choosing the one with the nicest website. Beside her, on a bed of punishingly white sheets, a tempest raged inside my father's body. If only he would open his eyes.

Today's doctor advised against moving him. There was the ambulance ride, and if he woke up, the strangeness of a new space—a comatose patient was fragile, why add to the risk?

"Fragile?" my mother scoffed as I translated. "And pray tell, how will these incompetent nurses, this overrun institution, handle that fragility?"

I stared at my father's body, now so tubed and wired that I could hardly believe it had ever been able to move of its own accord. I thought about the authority we wielded over his body. Over him.

"But this is what he wants," I said to my mother. "He brought himself here. To the public hospital."

My father believed in this society, in the principles of the social welfare state. He had trusted himself to its care.

"This is neither the time nor place for ideology," my mother said. "We're talking about life and death, you do understand that?"

I did and I didn't. I was starting to suspect that neither did she.

When I visited four years ago, my father and I walked the neighborhood each night to the same juice stand. He drank blended honeydew or wheatgrass sharbat, summer drinks that slipped their cool down your throat. I insisted—unseasonably, he scolded me—on pomegranate juice. Winter fruit, pomegranate was least fresh when the days went long.

We never spoke much. Just sipped our juice and walked home.

۶

One Day in 1990

MY FATHER'S HOUSE WAS once his father's.

The old patriarch died decades ago, soon after the Iran-Iraq War, in 1990 by the Gregorian calendar. The house was his only asset, and he had not left a will.

As dictated by law, upon his death, the house was professionally appraised and parceled into shares. Sons received twice as much as daughters. His wife, my paternal grandmother, a flat 12.5 percent.

According to family lore, my grandparents' marriage was true love. Notes passed through interlocutors (his friend and her friend were brother and sister). Maybe even a date or two or ten (chaperoned, certainly).

Still, when the time came to legitimize the relationship, he'd come calling the usual way, asking her father whether he might stop by for tea, and arriving with the requisite bouquet and box from the bakery. Fifteen and eleven months old, she was as eager for the wedding—and wedding night—as her mother was to have one less mouth crowding her sofra the next day at breakfast. On the girl's sixteenth birthday, the first day it was legally permissible—back then, that is; now the marriage age is lower—she was happily married off. (Meaning, even my grandmother got laid younger than I did.)

Love aside, the marriage made sense. She was an attractive girl from a respectable family. He was a widower still trim enough to make use of a belt. And he owned a house. This house.

While her husband was alive, the house was her dominion. To furnish and clean and fill with scents of tarragon and saffron. To service, but also to rule.

But now he was dead, and twelve and a half percent of a house meant you couldn't live there. The house she'd lived in since her teens was, one day in 1990, suddenly no longer hers. Instead her sons claimed the majority share.

Of her four sons, one had been martyred—hardly an event, everyone had given up someone—and another was in America. The two who remained lived in the neighborhood with their families, working as plastics engineers at the same shoe company.

For a few months the old lady was left alone. To lay her sofra on the floor next to the Western-style dining table. (Chairs gave her indigestion.) To prune the pomegranate tree in the courtyard. To puncture the striped plastic balls the neighbor kids kicked over the courtyard wall. But her sons had dreams, and this peace was not fated to last.

SEVERAL MONTHS PRIOR, MY uncle had been sent to the corner store by his wife. He was to top up on yogurt for mast-o-khiar.

The War was over. And with it, the milk ration. Plain yogurt and strained yogurt and soft cheese—once more, stores were stocked with the staples.

Bucket of semi-firm, slightly sour yogurt in hand, my uncle reached for a bag of chips. Now here was a strange overabundance. Chips came in clear plastic bags that were knotted on top and stuck with a white label. But why hadn't anyone touched them? Nearby, a new imported brand in sealed, bright blue pouches danced under the fluorescent lights. There were only a handful left.

He bought one, and on the walk home realized he'd wasted the extra fifty toman. They were just as oily, maybe a little less stale.

The next day, picking up a pack of cigarettes, the stuff was sold out. And the day after that. And the day after that.

He inquired with the shopkeeper, who dismissed him with a hand wave: you, too, my good man? It's the same old junk. I shelve what they give me, and it goes like the wind.

That night he went straight to his younger brother's, chain-smoking until he got there. The domestic food industry was industrializing. But what was missing was the look and feel of foreign manufacturing. They'd get in on packaging. An empire of trash to wrap trash: low margins, high volume. Except they needed seed money.

Their father died a month later. Went to bed one night and simply never woke up, no sickness, no groveling with God—it was grace itself. They could sell the house and take their share of the cash.

Except for one wrinkle. Their mother clung to the house like crow to carrion, claiming that the minute they moved her she'd die. They half-believed her; she might manage it out of spite.

Their sister urged compassion: how many days could the old lady really have left? And what would come of a business built without a mother's blessing? But they wouldn't hear reason. They had their own wives to worry about, their own sons and daughters. Finally their sister phoned abroad for an intercessor, appealing to the brother sainted by the dollar.

My father bought them all out, his two brothers, his sister, his mother. She was welcome to live out her days there, and use the cash for her expenses. The house became his.

WITHIN A YEAR HIS brothers had built the factory that now produced the plurality of Iranian food packaging, a deal with an aspiring dairy outfit struck late in '91 fated to become their flagship cooperation.

In short, they got rich.

V

Sunday Evening

THE PRIVATE HOSPITAL WAS considerably further uptown, in a chichi neighborhood I recognized as my uncle's. On a map Tehran looked more like a circle, but my father and his siblings lived along a single axis: the richer you were, the further north.

Precisely at sunset, my father's adhan app went off for maghreb. My mother had uncovered his phone in the bundle of clothes reissued upon his release as though from prison. His new nurse had lent us a charger.

But Shias didn't pray maghreb at sunset; they waited for the sky to saturate. Fifteen, twenty minutes, till you could—as the hadith went, according to my father—distinguish a white thread from the dark night. Outside in the streets of Tehran, the mosques sat quiet, but here at my father's bedside, the American prayer app on his American phone was calling the adhan. I knew this recording. My first real Ramadan, in fall 2001, he used to rewind and replay a cassette of the same reedy Egyptian muezzin at random times throughout the day. Now the Sunni muezzin strained against the phone speaker, issuing the adhan into my father's right ear, as for the newly born or newly dead.

Paying no heed, the nurse tested my father's responsiveness. She asked him how he was feeling, lips painted in a tasteful shade of nude. My father's mouth hung slightly open to breathe, his nose now occupied by a feeding tube.

The nursed touched my father's shoulders with French-manicured fingers. The grand Cairene muezzin called to the believers.

The nurse took his vitals. His temperature was nearly as high as yesterday, the new normal; no one was alarmed. Lofty and effeminate, the call cut to the soul.

The nurse took a cloth to the bedside table—not a tray in this five-star hospital but an actual table, with a lamp for bedtime reading—and, with the precision of a hotel maid, straightened the few objects we'd set there. Silence fell.

In the kind glow of expensive lighting, my mother smiled small at the nurse in thanks, pleased with her success. I took my father's hand, and its heat took me aback. He didn't register my touch, face lax, lids heavy, lips ajar in a meaningless frown.

Whatever lay inside lay dormant. Unmoving, unmoved.

Λ

Monday, August 5–Wednesday, August 7: Days

FOR THREE DAYS AND three nights my mother sat wake at my father's bedside, coming home early each morning to nap and shower. I joined her from nine to five, like I was reporting for work.

The roles we'd assumed our first morning ossified. As she showered, I laid out breakfast. Bread and butter and sour cherry marmalade, whatever my father had around. But the milk my mother required for tea, I had to buy. In America she drank black tea and black coffee, no milk, no sugar, yet here she refused to take her tea like a local. She sent me out Monday morning for fresh milk, shouting from behind the shower curtain and specifying that shelf-stable wouldn't do. Scanning the corner store fridge, I recognized my uncles' packaging and went for the other brand.

At the hospital I was idle. Between the ten-pound Shia dua book and his outdated textbooks from grad school, there was little by way of leisure reading on my father's shelves. The big book in my mother's tote, it turned out, was yet another Quran, hauled all the way from Michigan. She certainly couldn't have tracked one down in the Islamic Republic.

According to my mother, who took a break from God every now and then to check her work email, the Wi-Fi was solid. But to sit in a grid of sick people, clicking on a laptop, seemed somehow cynical; padding at a phone, simply grotesque.

So I paced, passed time.

SOMETIMES I THOUGHT ABOUT Adam.

The first time I saw him, even before that donors' reception, was during orientation. Our assigned groups had crossed each other on a campus tour. I saw him as I edged the lawn, saw his nose, his jaw, his kohl-black curls. His fingers fine and cypresslike, not unlike mine. That evening in the grand foyer of the old library, a knot formed inside me as Adam approached. I wanted to touch him. Be touched. That night, lying in the too-long twin bed of my dorm room, the knot unraveled to reveal a pit. I was a good Muslim girl and good girls didn't date. Especially not white boys.

We became friends. We snuck muffins into vaulted rooms and ate breakfast among gold-embossed leather spines. We skipped lecture and flew down to midtown on the express to get the best halal cart. We talked till the dining hall staff kicked us out. By the time I'd given up on hijab and moved to LA for grad school, by the time I'd gone bad, Julia had entered the picture.

I looked at my father shriveled under the sheets. I looked at my mother not looking at him, her sudden turn to scripture at once sincere and an excuse. To look at him would be to admit the failure of our family life.

My father's hands lay atop his blanket. Wide, hairy. What strength the world had endowed them. A godgiven body manipulated by a thousand human forces, by myriad violences big and small and of unmistakable cruelty—that was what manliness was.

How cruelly it had served him. I thought back to my childhood, listening for their fights, searching for when the "you" grew accusatory. I was young, very young, a child by any fair definition. Maybe five or six when tensions started. By my teens their laughs had turned acid. In fact, of the happy times I had only a few hazy snapshots fading at the bottom of my shoebox of memories.

I sensed the riddle of their marriage unknot—the nail in the coffin, I now saw, was when they switched roles, when she became the breadwinner. He had fallen out of love with her from pride. It was his dependency that drove him away.

Now he lay there, eyes shut to the world and his own existence, my mother within reach. So close that as a younger self he could have woken up to touch her, pull her close.

٩

Monday, August 5–Wednesday, August 7: Nights

EVENINGS, I WENT HOME alone.

I had the desk nurses call me a car at five sharp, when the trip back downtown was still easy; everyone else in Tehran worked till six or seven. In the back of a rundown sedan, chauffeured through streets and thoroughfares whose names I didn't bother to learn, I soaked in the silver summer light. Tehran was almost at the same latitude as Los Angeles. The same sun slapped against my skin.

At home I showered, first thing, trying to wash away the aura of death. And I did, the magic of ritual.

Clean, I ate a snack. Nuts or dried fruit my father had out on the sill of the kitchen cut-out window, picking the almonds and dried mulberries from the ajil, leaving the chalky chickpeas. That first night, sunset cherries I found rotting at the bottom of a fridge drawer, what I could salvage of the bunch, yellow skins blushing.

Fed, I scoured YouTube via VPN for free aerobics videos. This wasn't a city where you could double-knot your laces and hop outside for a jog. Like some eighties housewife I knee-lifted and butt-kicked and jumping-jacked until I sweat.

Outside, over the courtyard walls, the sky came to match the cherry skin. I showered a third shower.

The sky slid to dusk, and the adhan from the mosque at the edge of the neighborhood could be heard in the courtyard, if you knew to listen for it. I listened.

The sky darkened. From the depths of my father's freezer and the backs of his cabinets, I found enough for dinner.

One handful of kidney beans and a bag of dried herbs, plus a cube of dehydrated bone broth and a few hours on the stove, made ghormeh sabzi. I made ghormeh sabzi on night one, and alone, I ate for three days.

The dark deepened. I slept.

Date #91: Neighborly

THE SECOND TIME I saw Leili, it was she who came to me.

I heard the buzzer ring around nine. My mother, I assumed, tired of proving her good-wifeliness and come home for dinner; too tired even to search for her key. It was our fourth full day at the private hospital.

"Salaam, khūbī? It's Leili."

She had the sort of deep rasp that made me swoon, in a woman. (Men were so accustomed to hearing themselves speak that their voices circulated like Monopoly money.)

"Look have you had any dinner?" she went on. "I'm going around the corner—"

I buzzed her into the courtyard.

"Be out in just a sec."

At home in LA, I might have enjoyed agonizing for ten luxurious minutes over what to wear. As it was, everything I'd packed felt like a kind of drag: XL tees and boxer shorts long enough to appease my father; billowy blouses and pleated slacks for bending before his callers, serving tea on a silver tray. Bent over my carryon, I flipped through the folded clothes like the pages of a book, growing more hopeless by the second. Until I reached my underwear. I never skimped on lingerie. It was an insurance policy against suicide.

I unfolded the silk travel organizer to reveal a series of matching sets. Leafy laces in peony pink and fresh pine green. Black mesh and white satin. High waist, hip-slung. Full coverage or plunge, but either way, underwire. This was femininity in its most honest form: structured, constructed.

I stripped, selecting an orange set rife with cutouts. The color of California poppies, of a superbloom after winter rains. I couldn't remember what set I'd been wearing our first hookup, but I knew it wasn't this.

Leili was stooped over the garden when I finally entered the courtyard. She brushed her hands off at the sound of my footsteps, and the soil hovered in the air, dry as dust. A breeze blew by, and I got a whiff of the night-blooms my father had planted. Debutantes, offering themselves to the night as prey.

She gave me the up-and-down.

"So you're not coming?"

I'd come out in jeans and a tee, but had left my manteau and shawl hooked in the hallway.

"Forty years ago," she went on, "there was a revolution here . . ."

I rolled my eyes. Between her short tunic and narrow scarf, curls spilling out both sides, she was hardly the paragon of modesty.

"And what about you," I said. "That's not hijab, it's a gesture."

She laughed.

"You've got the hang of it. Around here we're all semioticians."

AT THE SANDWICH SHOP a few blocks over—I'd let her lead the way only to end up somewhere I already knew—I ordered two specials, two Cokes.

"So you know your way around the neighborhood?" Leili asked as the boy behind the counter eased a bottle opener under the Coke caps.

"Something like that."

The shopkeeper's son called our order out to the back. He rang us up without a calculator, quoting a nothing number. But when I reached for my wallet, Leili stopped me.

"My treat."

My income, no matter how nonexistent, came in dollars, and letting her spend her toman on me was unseemly.

But so was every mating call. She paid.

WE ATE OUTSIDE ON red plastic stools. Soujouk that burst against our teeth, parsley that got stuck in between. Our Cokes sat on the sidewalk, straws sticking out from the bottle lips like tongues.

My father had grown up spending his pocket money on these sandwiches. My father's father had occasionally snuck one in as a predinner snack.

I'd had my first taste as a kid. We'd strolled over one evening on a lazy night out, just the three of us, my mother and father and me—it hadn't occurred to me then to ask why we would've been left alone for a meal. Had my mother demanded a break from the in-laws, or had my grandmother refused to cook for us? My father had made a point of referring to us as his family. "My wife will have—." "For my daughter—." It was a way of quieting the stares.

On my summer fellowship in 2015 I'd come back alone. My father wouldn't go near the place anymore. He said it was because the owners were Armenian (code for Christian) and their meat wasn't halal. But according to local clerical rulings, it was. American Islam had ruined him, I thought then. The freedom of deferring to authority was about the only benefit of being Shia, and instead he was acting like some fundamentalist, insisting on the most punishing path.

Now I wondered whether all that piety hadn't been a cover for his pain. "My wife will have—." It was a line he never had the chance to repeat.

"IF YOUR FAMILY'S WAY uptown, how'd you end up in this neighborhood?" I asked Leili.

She was telling me about her family, cheeks flush from the raw onion, palms wet with grease. She'd grown up with two dogs and one sister in Zafaraniyeh. I didn't really know Tehran, but I knew enough to know that was somewhere by the mountains, and posh.

"Oh come on," she said, unraveling the soaked sandwich paper to reveal the bottom nub of baguette. "It's full of yuppies up there. I'd suffocate. When my dad wanted to find me a place, I told him, please just not north of Seyyed Khandan. Anything with a pulse lives around here or even further downtown."

Last trip I'd done some exploring. Setting out from my father's house in any direction, you were bound to come across a trendy gallery or bookstore or café in under a mile, practically next door for a car-centric city like LA or Tehran. Now I gathered it was no coincidence. Here, as elsewhere, forces of gentrification were remapping the city. What was affordable became desirable until it was no longer affordable. At least for most.

"Honestly I was hoping for something closer to—" she started to go on but stopped herself. Her lips curled into a smile, red lipstick reduced to a stain. "What's it to you anyway, Miss America. The point is, my dad worked it out. He even found the first tenants."

I was struck by how casually she'd laid it all out, unabashed by her naked wealth. The American artists I'd met—Julia, when sober, but also that serial killer with the Rolex (#24)—kept their independent wealth as closeted as gays under the Third Reich.

Leili finished off the baguette, the last of her lipstick going with it.

"What about your sister?" I asked. "Where does she live in town?"

"Oh she betrayed me a while ago. She moved to Frankfurt when she got married." Crumpling her sandwich paper, she went on: "Everyone leaves. Friend or foe, lover and fling."

She was giving me a line.

"Then why'd you stay?"

Few did, given the means to leave.

Leili set down her Coke and began rummaging in her bag. She lit a cigarette. A horn honked in the distance, followed by shouting men. You couldn't see Sohrevardi from here, but every now and then, the thoroughfare announced itself, waiting beyond the maze of skinny streets and one-way alleys.

"Leaving only makes you small."

As Leili smoked, I focused on eating. Despite my hunger, I'd hardly made a dent in my sandwich. I pulled a piece of soujouk out of the baguette with a plastic fork. On its own, the sausage took me back to LA, to my neighborhood, and I was stung with homesickness. How many bowls of soujouk had I eaten at that staple white tablecloth restaurant in Little Armenia, whether alone or with Adam, rolling each piece in a tear of pita, scooping tabouli with my fork between bites. That spot was Armenian-Lebanese, and American, this place Armenian-Iranian—it suddenly seemed strange that my father should be rooted in one Little Armenia and I ended up in another. Stranger still that these two worlds existed in the same world. Sitting on this quiet side street a stone's throw from my father's house, LA seemed so far. Adam, further still. So afraid was I of facing him—and in him, myself—that I had actually silenced our thread. Our friendship, our intimacy, was a contract, and I'd broken it.

Leili nudged me, knee to knee.

"Where'd you go?"

"Nowhere. Here, maybe."

"Why are you here? You don't have the look of someone on vacation."

I looked away. The fruit vendor across the street was washing the sidewalk. He paused awhile to water the tree in the median in front of his grate. It grew greener and taller than the trees down the block.

"Is your uncle traveling?" she went on. "He usually waters the plants in the courtyard every night around nine, you can see him from my balcony."

"He's my father. He's in the hospital."

She clucked sympathetically. "What's the issue?"

"He's in a coma."

"Poor thing."

I didn't know whether she meant him or me. I got up to collect our trash. The glass bottles clinked, kind against kind. We started back.

For a block we walked in silence, footsteps out of sync. Then suddenly there was a motorcycle zooming toward us out of nowhere, and Leili grabbed my arm, and we pressed against a double-parked car. After a breath we dusted off our manteaus.

"You okay?"

I laughed. "Maybe I'm not used to things around here after all."

We kept going, the air between us lighter.

"The Indian woman," Leili said a few moments later, when we'd reached the top of our block. "Who is she to you?"

"His wife. My mother."

"It doesn't show."

My body stiffened.

"What I meant is—" she said. "You have a nice complexion."

The acceptable range here went from white to olive. My mother was darker than that, while my father was "a true Caucasian," as he liked to boast. (This suspect "truth" was at any rate lost on America, which doled him his fair share of racism.) As though genetics were as simple as mixing my mother's morning tea, I'd come out right in the middle, milkier than her and browner than him. Passing for olive, for full-bred Iranian, as national myth conceived it.

"Look," I said—but I didn't know what to say. *Don't open your mouth like a fish*, my mother used to say to me as a child. The pond that settled on our lawn after the spring rain seemed wider to me then than the whole world did now. Every east has an east, every south a south. Everyone had someone to fetishize and oppress.

"They were doctoral students," I said. "In America. That's how they met."

I kept my silence and my stride for the rest of the block. At my father's gate, I thanked Leili for dinner.

"The sun's aggressive here in the summer," she said. "You have to water the garden every day."

She followed me in uninvited, and the automatic lights blinked on. Bending to find the head of the hose amidst the leaves and flowers, Leili traced its curved back to the western wall, fingering in the vines for the tap. I said good night and went inside.

A squeak and soon the hush of water—I could still hear the water's whisper as I lay on my mat in the parlor. Squeezing through the closed windows and through the slips between the blinds, the sound found its way in. Water pushing past a thumb pressed against the mouth of a hose; water pushing forward and fanning out, a force redirected but undiminished, spread so thin and fragile that it would, at the edge of its arc, in its final docility, deposit a dew delicate and diamond on the life growing in the garden, so many small moons catching what light they could in the night.

١٠

Friday, August 9

WHEN I WAS A girl of twelve or thirteen, my father came down with the flu. A bad flu that kept him in bed for a week, my mother sleeping on the couch.

In sickness my father was reduced to the neon moods of a petulant child. He woke only to bark demands. They were simple desires. Lime to cool his tongue, a cloth to wipe the sweat. Yet I found myself resenting the wishes of an incapacitated man. I'd always been his emissary to the kitchen, and the old seeds of dissatisfaction soured in my stomach. Fetch the salt, the sugar, a glass of water served iced, on a silver tray— for all her feminism, my mother had taught me that.

I did his bidding, taking my mother's post when I got home from school. I imagined I was righting some wrong that had been done to my mother, addressing some broader injustice. I felt important.

At that age, I schematized our family as a brain. My father, the left brain. My mother, the right. At school they said that the left and right brain complemented each other, which was another way of saying that they were opposed.

NOW I YEARNED FOR those days as the thirsty thirst. I wanted my father to wake and bark for a tall glass of water on a silver tray. I wanted him to swat the feeding tube that sustained his limp body and demand chelo kabob, charred good and black on buttered rice. I wanted my mother to cop his grilled tomato and watch it explode under her fork.

Instead the room stood calm. The sheets clean and white. My mother sat at her post.

The air hung like cut peonies, subject to processes of decay no less chilling for their placidity. Souring by the day, feeding, and yet somehow also, already dead.

۱۱

Saturday, August 10

ON THE SIXTH DAY of our vigil, my mother broached the topic of my actual work.

"You might tinker with that dossier of yours. Some of the fall deadlines hit as early as Labor Day."

She shut her laptop and rose to stretch her legs. I hadn't so much as opened the documents in question since we'd spoken in June.

"Good idea," I said.

My laptop was at the house. Nevertheless succumbing to the notion that I had something to do, I clicked on my silenced thread with Adam. Nothing new, his last message waiting for my reply.

Can we talk?

Three days had gone by. Otherwise, there was a compilation of cat memes from another friend sent expressly to annoy me, which warmed my heart, and an invite from a spreadsheet entry I thought I'd laid to rest, more a sign of his desperation than my success.

A nurse came and went. My father's responsiveness, still zero. I got up to stroll through the corridors.

AN HOUR LATER I texted the friend that I was in Iran because my father was sick. I told the date I had a family emergency. I waited for the friend's thread to go bold with new messages. But it was the middle of the night in Los Angeles.

Left with no choice, I sifted through my email until I recovered a recent version of my job materials. I read and reread the research statement.

" . . . elucidating the precise means by which sexual identity is policed by Western ideas of selfhood in a globalized economy of art and literature . . ."

". . . an urgent critique of how local queerness gets un-queered by Global South participation in the normativizing field of so-called World Cinema, from submitting to the Oscars for best foreign feature, to . . ."

None of it made sense. Or rather, it all made sense in its own obnoxious way, but I couldn't remember why I thought that mattered. Back in undergrad I'd turned to Comparative Literature because studying English in an English-speaking country had struck me as kids' stuff, or just an easy lay. Now, I was sitting in moneyed Tehran trying to talk about books and films made in Tehran—I was contemplating Farsi at the heart of the Persophone empire. My subject held little sparkle.

The screen flashed on my father's phone with a missed call from my aunt. My mother and I hadn't been answering his—admittedly few—incoming calls, and the other day, she'd simply silenced notifications. Only the adhan got through, the great Cairene calling each untimely prayer with the same intonation.

"I guess eventually we'll have to tell them," I said.

"The Iranians?" My mother looked up from her laptop. "Yes, you should."

And thus all diplomacy was left to me.

١٢

A Saturday in 2014

MY PARENTS NEVER WENT to the movies. They considered mainstream media beneath us, whether Hollywood or Bollywood. I received that education via the mosque, at sleepovers with friends from Sunday School, and I didn't dare tell my mother. Movies were for pedants.

But a film screening—that was different.

Once a year the undergraduate film club at my mother's college held an international film festival, licensing both classics and new releases. For a week my family lived in the gum-encrusted chairs of the auditorium, squeezing in homework and lesson planning and a frozen dinner so rare it seemed a delicacy each night in time for the six-thirty screening. On Sunday, for the finale, I even got to skip the mosque.

On occasion we had some felt connection to the national cinema at hand. My father's eyes brimmed with tears at the latest Iranian tragedy to ride the festival circuit—thus is the power of "imagined community"—while an old Satyajit Ray would move my mother to spend hours frying puri that weekend, even though, as far as I knew, her family wasn't from Kolkata and she didn't speak Bengali.

Mostly we lost ourselves in the strangeness. It was a relief not to be the most foreign objects in the room. We watched Wuxia, hearts soaring, and sank into samurai stories. We learned to laugh at French humor. Accosted by sex scenes, we screwed one eye shut and pretended not to know one another.

THE SATURDAY EVENING SLOT was the festival's crown jewel. That year, the year I turned sixteen, featured a family drama. Not from our parts of the world but from somewhere where all-too-familiar ideas lurked nonetheless. The basic plot was this: a girl marries the wrong man, going against the wishes of her family, and she is punished sorely by fate for doing so.

One evening when she is well into her wifely tenure yet childless, her husband stops by the bakery on the way home for her favorite treat, some kind of cookie. After dinner he makes an advance. Gently, brushing a hand across her breast. She demurs. He presses on. She says no. He presses on. Succeeds. She stays quiet. Her in-laws are sleeping in the next room. She hasn't even had time to digest the cookie. It's still inside her, lapped by acid.

Afterward, over ice cream, my mother said she found the whole thing pandering and distasteful. Sucking up to the judges at Cannes, and the dolts who voted on the Oscars (she refused to call them the Academy). My father took issue with the program notes.

"Intramarital rape," he said in English. "What does that even mean?"

He spooned off some Neapolitan. Though by then my parents shared little beyond a bed, when we went out to ice cream, they still shared a sugar cone. Two spoons, and at the end he ate the cone alone.

"Muslims—" my father said, in the pedantic tone he usually reserved for infidels or interfaith events. "Muslims have no such thing."

My mother put her spoon on the picnic table.

"No, not legally," she said. "Not according to the marriage contract."

"And what about kindness?" I said to my father. "Human decency."

My mother answered for him.

"Kindness is not codifiable."

With a professor's forced detachment, she explained the basic terms of an Islamic marriage, classically defined: the woman provided sex and childbirth, the man financial support. A woman didn't even have to raise her own children—she could charge her husband for breast-feeding. But whether for pleasure or procreation, she was to make herself available.

"What if she doesn't feel like it?"

"The point of a contract is to clarify, not confound."

She put her fingers to her temples as if to dissuade a coming headache.

"Its logic is not affective."

"Hocus pocus," my father said.

He hated it when my mother jargonized. I swirled the new word around under my breath: *aa*-ffective, stress on the first syllable.

"Do *you* understand what she's saying?" he asked me in Farsi.

"More or less," I said in English.

"But not all the way. And you were born in America."

My father took a big bite of his sugar cone. The vanilla inside had melted, leaving a viscous pale fluid that dribbled down the bite marks.

"Your mother," he said in English, "is a genius of language."

My mother grabbed the cone. There was such purpose in her eyes I thought she might crush him then and there. I imagined her fist clenching, heard the crack of the shell, saw the cream oozing down the webbing between her knuckles, down over the flat of her wrist.

Instead she took a bite. Modest, controlled.

"You don't mind, no?"

She continued in her manner, small bites and equally small swipes of a napkin. When she finished, her hands were still clean.

۱۳

Sunday, August 11

WATCH THEM BEND HIS KNEES AND ELBOWS.
Watch them pedal the legs to imitate walking.
Watch them coil the fingers to imitate grasping.
Lest "the system" atrophy too much to recover on waking.
(So we were still hoping for that, the waking.)

THE THEORY—AS THE NURSE informed us—was that thus stimu-
lated, muscles engaged of their own accord, and the body was kept
in shape. The exercise was meant to help my father. And yet it was a
terrible sight to see, a gross ventriloquizing. This man-sized rag doll
manipulated by manicured hands. Subjectless movement, an impotent
semblance of the will.

My mother left the room whenever one of the physical therapy
nurses came in. For all her fortitude, that was when she happened to
need the bathroom, or chose to walk the hallway.

I begrudged her this capacity for self-preservation. A martyr, I
stayed put.

Date #92: The Eid of Sacrifice

LEILI FOUND ME AGAIN that coming Monday, August 12, the husk in her voice reaching through the intercom like a diva's through the radio. She waited in the courtyard as I got dressed, watering my father's garden—already we were shaping a routine.

That day at the hospital someone had come round with a box of profiteroles for Eid, the only indication inside that outside, in the realm of the healthful, it was a holiday. Eid al-Adha, the Eid of Sacrifice. Outside, sheep's blood signed the streets in an elegant cursive. Inside stayed sterile and blank.

Now, as I surveyed my lingerie options before redonning my tired manteau, it occurred to me that the only layer on my body I had any real agency over anymore was the underlayer. I listened to the hose hissing in the courtyard and saw, through the blinds, the press of Leili's fair fingers on its mouth.

I went for florals and underwire, high femme. The thinly veiled metal pressed against my chest.

LEILI WAS LEANING AGAINST her car when I came out, my father's gates open. She drove a Daewoo compact in bing-cherry red. Not the fanciest, but given import tariffs and the exchange rate, pricey nonetheless. (Nowadays a Camry sits by her studio, despite grotesque inflation, just as the pomegranate tree flourishes despite the drought.)

She'd left the car idling.

"So I see the gas subsidy's still going?" I said, climbing in.

"What do you know about subsidies, Miss America."

She shifted into first.

"Let's get out of the city. You like kabob?"

DARBAND IN SUMMER. A rainbow of taillights and light-up signs crest the mountainside north of Tehran, each car carting city dwellers into the crisp mountain air. Child eyes stalk street vendors through open car windows. Sour and sweet fruit leather sold by the meter. Fat black mulberries. Fresh walnuts fished from the jar, where they float in brine like brains suspended in the sweat of their own labor. Friends and lovers, entire families, all four generations—they gather on restaurant terraces laid with low plinths and plastic sofas, sitting cross-legged on weathered rugs, backs against cushions dense as stones. Oil-fingered and charcoal-lipped, they suck on soda straws and shisha nibs, flirting through wisps of candy-apple nicotine, trading barbs and poisons. Profiting from the mountain cool, the dark.

That's what you came for. For the night that hung over the tea houses and past the pullover parking. For the night that hid behind the neons, as indifferent to your desires as to your lack.

IT TOOK A SOLID hour to get out of the city, to the foot of the Alborz Mountains. Thirty minutes later, and we were still scaling the main drag through Darband, Leili's hand gripped the gearshift. Up up up, we inched in a coy progression. Passing one after another kabob house—her friends were waiting for us at one of them. My stomach growled.

After the last neon, and after even the afterglow had faded, just when I thought there could be no more mountain for the taking, Leili turned off the paved road. I could hear rocks clamoring under her

Daewoo—we were sure to puncture a tire, at least. She flipped the headlights off. All that guided us now was the weak light of a crescent moon.

Soon it became clear that Leili knew the road, and for about a minute we sailed through the darkness. But we took the next bend to see the towering grille of an SUV, and it flashed across my mind that my father and I might die in the same week.

We jerked to a stop. Calmly, without honking, both cars restarted, backed up, and moved on.

"Where are you taking me?" I asked.

She laughed.

"Two minutes, I promise."

IN FIVE WE SLOWED to a stop.

I expected to see, emerging from the darkness, the outer walls of a private villa, the sort that served as illicit event venues.

According to my uncle, who hosted his daughter's wedding at his personal villa in summer 2015, you had to factor in the police bribes in your budget. A pop-up liquor license, if you will, and the going rate was climbing faster than inflation. My father was scandalized. Not by the sacrilege of drinking, he claimed, but by this open endorsement of corruption. On the wedding day, roped into my father's protest, I'd suffered through the ceremony only to be pulled away from the party.

But now when Leili pulled into the unmarked lot, all I saw was an ordinary open-air restaurant. Far from the glamorous underground I felt I was owed, this was an exact replica of every other place we'd passed on the public road, complete with a blinking pink neon: کباب—KABOB.

The spot lay over several weak mountain streams, with plinths sewn into the stone wherever the land was dry and flat. String lights drooped throughout, stretched between straggly poles. The plinths were spread with rugs and sofras, in the old style. The streams, the plinths, the people upon them, each network floated atop the other like lace.

As we approached, I could hear streams dribbling under the chatter. If my father was any indicator, Iranians were obsessed with the sound of running water. He'd do anything to get himself by a river, or creek, or tacky suburban fountain. He would've liked this place, despite himself.

We ascended the stone stairs, shown to a plinth by a waiter. Leili's friends were already seated. Forty-somethings in bold, oddly tailored fabrics I took to be fashionable, bodies as pert and at ease as the piles of mint and marjoram that sprang from the plates of nūn paneer sabzi on the sofra. The only one wearing anything less pretentious was the trans guy I recognized from the first night, who had on a navy tee.

Seeing us, the group cheered and raised their (completely legal) drinks in salute. The glass bottles of soda and nonalcoholic beer made a satisfying click, but the doogh only came in plastic. My uncles' manufacturing since '91, this continued windfall from fizzy whey had more than paid for my cousin's wedding.

"Salaam, salaam, salaam"—I went around the circle with a loose handshake. Names I was sure to forget tumbled along the sofra.

Leili wedged us into the group. I sat with my feet tucked under me, embarrassed by my expired pedicure—I realized I hadn't done my nails since LA. And I just as soon learned it didn't matter: as the night wore on, Leili's friends hardly looked at me at all.

They talked, I listened. They joked, I laughed.

I watched their movements. The way their fingers curled around the hilt of a fork. The way knees overlapped but feet stayed close. You lived in your body according to the language you were given. They relaxed when I would've tensed, stayed small where I would've let loose. But it was age, too; maybe even history. Leili was of the generation born during the War. These bodies had hid in bomb shelters from time to time as children. I didn't have a body like that.

Or maybe I was just essentializing. "This poor boy didn't get enough milk as a baby," my father had whispered at my cousin's wedding, eyes on the groom. "God damn that bastard Saddam."

The groom happened to be short.

THE REAL FOOD CAME. Kubideh on heaping plates of buttered rice that twinkled under the string lights. Tomatoes fired till their skins peeled and onions served quartered and raw.

Conversation turned to half-Iranians, and I wondered whether Leili had briefed them on me. There was a parliamentary bill due for ratification that would, for the first time, grant citizenship through the maternal line. I didn't want kids, but I'd always known that if I changed my mind, my offspring would have no formal tie to this nation, no legal stake in this land. Citizenship was a privilege reserved for the children of Iranian men.

And yet what was that privilege, anyway? Ten days in and I was beginning to wonder. The right to be a tourist? To see a few pretty mosaics stuck on an old mosque? To see my father sacrificed to a coma because the doctors didn't catch that he was bleeding from the brain. Because he couldn't get a CT scan. Because the US restricted this country's access to hospital equipment.

اصفهان نصف جهان

Isfahan was worth half the world, the saying went. But on the international market, what was the value of an Iranian life?

"What a relief," I said to Leili's friends, the first I'd spoken all night. "Isfahan nisf-e jahān. God forbid I have a child, the kid won't die without seeing Masjid-e Imam."

Leili laughed. But the friend who'd first mentioned the news only looked at me.

"There's a refugee problem here, maybe you're not aware?"

He broke into a patronizing smile. A tea tray had emerged, and he took a glass and two individually wrapped sugar cubes.

"The impact of the legislation is domestic, to protect all the natural-borns who don't have documents because their fathers are Afghans." He popped a sugar cube onto his tongue and took a sip of tea. "If comfortable foreign residents profit, it's only incidental."

I felt heat on my cheeks. Leili leaned into me with a playful nudge to lighten the critique, and instinctually I drew my feet to the other side. The tray was making its way around the circle. I took two teas, serving Leili first, and passed it on behind her back.

IN SEVERAL HOURS, AFTER the evening had taken its course—tea, talk, sex—I'd return to my father's house to lie on my father's mat as my mother lay upstairs, sleeping in my father's bed by my father's windows. Broad locked windows behind which a green garden stood dark, and inside the garden, the pomegranate tree, perhaps a nest, a bird, her unborn tucked into thin eggs.

To all this our eyes stayed closed, mine and my mother's, each in a bed that was chosen for us, even if we had, one day, willingly come.

١٤

Thursday, August 15

PNEUMONIA HAD CAUSED SOME sort of fluid to fill my father's lungs. Yellowish and viscous, thicker than blood, than water—call it black bile; for all its gadgets, modern medicine seemed to me a medieval thing.

The morning prior a true fever had taken hold of my father's body. This time not my mother but the nurse had noticed. They took him for a CT scan. The private hospital had more than enough. My guess was, an X-ray would have done. But now that the patient was paying, the same perverse logic of care that could be taken for granted in the US ruled here: anything to escalate the final bill.

To remove the excess bile, the doctor pierced the thin skin of my father's chest, and through the incision, threaded a garish syringe. The plunger pressed down and fluid flowed out, from high to low pressure, a simple, mechanical matter; basic physics. The doctor disposed of the bile in a receptacle neatly labeled BIOHAZARDOUS WASTE, destined, doubtlessly, for the same landfills as all the other junk in our lives. Or maybe burned so that the toxins could poison whoever was poor enough to live nearby. The process, I was told, was "uncomfortable."

My father's face draped like laundry on a dusty summer day. His tranquility was a lie: comatose, the body could not express its pain.

But the pain had to be accounted for. So I bore witness to this undocumented suffering, forcing myself to watch the workers work on his body.

AT SOME POINT THEY rolled my father to another wing of the ICU, contemplated a second surgery, and rolled him back to his private suite, uncut.

١٥

Friday, August 16

WATCH THEM CART THE BODY TO AND FRO.
Watch the nurses attend to it attentively.
Watch them wipe it with a clean rag.
Watch them snap two fingers to test reaction.
Watch them knock a knee to check for reflex.
Watch them watch the machines to look for signs of life.

۱۶

Saturday, August 17

WITHIN DAYS MY FATHER'S body deteriorated to what was deemed an unredeemable state. Diagnosis: brain bleed, deep coma (stage one), infection, pneumonia, lung fluid, etc, etc. Prognosis, grim.

"Unfortunately in such cases . . ."

The doctor didn't need to finish.

Two weeks into my trip, with my mother's consent, they decided to stop draining his lungs.

THAT DAY WE BROKE routine and my mother and I went back to the house together for lunch. I had the cabbie pull over at an American-style grocery when I recognized that we were nearing the neighborhood, approaching not from Sohrevardi but the other side. Some ten minutes later, supplies for an omelet divvied between us, we started south by foot.

A lanky guy in acid-washed jeans spit by my mother's feet before we'd had a chance to clear the next crosswalk. She was in shalwar kameez again, after a week of jeans and men's button-ups.

"Let's just find another cab," I said.

In fact I'd never hailed a cab off the street. Most weren't official taxis, and I'd always called a trusted car service or taken the metro.

"No," she said. "We could both use the walk."

She had heels on.

For several blocks, we walked the main road in relative silence, cocooned in the usual chorus of horns. At the first residential street, I veered us into the neighborhood.

"That toxic smell," my mother said. "It takes me back to that summer we came to meet your grandmother."

It smelled like gas and exhaust.

"Is that a good thing?"

My mother let out a laugh. We'd never discussed this.

"She wasn't very nice," I ventured. "To you, especially?"

"She was proud."

We reached the gate. Handing me the eggs, my mother jiggered the skeleton key, trying to get it to engage.

"If only she'd known the story behind this place," she said.

The gate gave way and we entered the courtyard. I crossed to the folding table and set the groceries down. She was being unusually coy.

"What do you mean?" I asked.

It took some time before she responded.

"Pretending she still owned," my mother finally went on, "was your grandmother's last shred of dignity. To discover that I was the one behind the purchase—"

"I thought Baba was doing okay back then."

"He wasn't. Certainly we said he was, on the loan application. But he'd been having problems at work for months." She came closer, brows furrowed in pity. "Your father wasn't being cruel. I was still in graduate school. Buying this house didn't make any sense."

Bailing my grandmother out had been my mother's idea. The one woman I thought my father had done right by owed her happiness to another woman. I drew a finger across the eggs, feeling their clean talcy shells—despite the supermarket's pretensions, they'd come in an open carton.

"Then what?" I asked. "Who paid off the loan?"

My mother smiled.

"You can do the math."

"And she treated you that way, you let her—"

Now it was my mother's turn to interrupt.

"Everyone assumed he was the breadwinner," she said sharply. "It would have embarrassed her to know."

Gathering the eggs and other groceries, she ordered me to unlock the front door so we could eat.

THAT NIGHT I LIFTED the lid off the cold pot of ghormeh sabzi to confront white mold eating at the meat. Flesh rotted first.

۱۷

———

Sunday, August 18

MY FATHER SURVIVED THE night, each night now a question. Returning from lunch yesterday, I'd sat vigil with my mother and slept at the hospital. Fitfully, in an armchair, city life clamoring at the window, rude and unrelenting. A mourning dove cooed, and I gave up, rising to meet the day.

LATER I ANSWERED MY father's phone for the first time. It was my uncle's wife.

"Khūbī, khanum doctor?" she asked after I introduced myself.

I smiled at the ribbing. My father must have bragged when I graduated.

"So that's why your baba's been so hard to find," she went on. "When did you arrive?"

"A few weeks ago. With my mother."

I took one deep breath and dove in, summarizing my father's decline.

"Unfortunately in such cases"—I deployed the doctor's phrasing. Citing the hospital and room number, I excused myself, and the line went dead.

18

Monday, August 19–Wednesday, August 21

FREED TO TAKE ITS course, the pneumonia ravaged my father's body. His breath grew labored. His lips became a bruise on his face.

The logic was that my mother and I needed to be there, to sit there, by virtue of our attachments. Attachments that were legally and socially inscribed, beyond our piddling emotions.

So I sat. I sat and watched my father die. At some point I ate lunch.

Evenings the callers called, fulfilling the contract of blood ties.

Night fell, and the callers left.

BUT WHAT WAS LYING beside us was not my father. Whatever sticky grain of sand it was within him that refused to be metabolized or dislodged—his soul, for lack of a better a word—persisted, but his consciousness was not intact.

And still, it went on, the turnings, the doings—alive, I was obliged to take them on.

House, hospital, house, shower, sweat, shower, her bed, my bed: this was the sun's cycle. I bought bread from the bakery and milk from the corner store. I made my mother breakfast. I brewed second and third teas. I wore lipstick. I made phone calls, I received phone calls. When they came to the hospital bearing flowers, I made small talk.

I sat.

I watched, I witnessed.

I listened.

An angel's black cloak brushed against cold tile. Quietly, but heard.

I began to understand: the pain would not stop until there was no subject to seat it.

Date #93 . . . and -4 and -5 and -6: Identical Rhyme

THE SEX WAS NEITHER like fucking nor like making love.

On the cold cement floor of the basement parking with aching breaths. On the pink stone tiles inside the balcony door, curtains open, lights off, shielded by darkness. In the kitchen fluorescence against the German cabinetry whose drawers slowed of their own accord when you slammed them shut.

Leili Leili Leili, sang the spreadsheet. Leili.

I snuck back in slips of darkness, switching off with my mother throughout the night. I showered and changed my underwear. (Black with white contrast stitching, plain navy mesh, Sunday, Monday.) Afterward I showered again. (Black on black embroidered lace, Tuesday. Sheer the color of water, Wednesday.) My body ached to be used. To be admired. Like a morning glory whose one-day bloom—whose death— will go unseen amidst the vine.

١٩

Tuesday or Wednesday, Probably

APRICOTS YOU COULD SMELL at arm's length, cherries so sweet they
were black. Palm-sized cucumbers and Saturn peaches and green
grapes as small as pearls. Nectarines smoother than a fresh wax. Yellow
peaches and sunset cherries for diversity.

I came back from the hospital sometime that week—the days were
blurring—to see that someone had stocked the fridge. Though my
father had the deed to the house, everyone still had a key.

Someone had toted clear plastic bags filled to breaking point across
the hard courtyard tiles and into the kitchen, shoes kicked off at the
front door. Someone had emptied the bags into the sink, and soaked
the fruit in soapy water, and waited for the soap to do its work. Someone
had rinsed and dried each peach, each cherry, each slender cucumber;
loaded the chill bins; and shut the fridge, locking the doors on the
way out.

It was a level of care so habituated as to be automatic, evidence of
a woman's hand. To profit from that care was a bachelor's privilege, or
a guest's.

۲۰

Thursday, August 22

DEATH WAS IN THE room. You could sense the Angel of Death pacing the linoleum floor, wings folded undercloak. You could hear the rustle of His hem, His footstep now unabashed. You could feel His indifference.

They came to greet Him. Not just family now but strangers—to me, at least. His fifth-grade teacher, somehow still kicking. An old friend from high school. His first cousin, twice-removed.

They filed past my father's bedside to hold a limp hand or attempt to talk. Some came with false cheer, and others false solemnity. Life can fill any gap, and to this they'd long assimilated their stride: my father had left them for another world once before. It was Death they owed their homage to.

They tossed me plastic smiles and routine politesse—I was their blood, after all, or next best, a compatriot. They skirted my mother.

Death walked, and waited. Patient. At ease.

Take care not to catch His hem with your toe.

Date #97: Catalexis

THAT NIGHT ON LEILI'S bed—a virginal night, for once; nothing happened—my mascaraed tears slipped to stain the pillowcase. I didn't know where they came from, from what corner of my sadness.

I was losing my father, and with him, I knew, something more would be taken from me. So many pending goodbyes. To others. To selves foreclosed. Though Leili lowered her face to mine, I could not meet her eyes.

I left to pass the night alone.

٢١

Friday, August 23

MY UNCLE FINALLY CAME to pay his respects Friday, first thing. He'd been traveling for work. China or Turkey, somewhere easy to do business. Friday meant the weekend, the first since my father had been reduced to palliative care. Meaning my uncle didn't have to miss work to come.

Striding through the door with his salaams, he kissed me twice on the cheek as customary. My mother shut her Quran and rose to greet him. He declined to meet her handshake, hiding, head bowed, gaze lowered, behind a faith he had no faith in. (If there's a villa, then there's alcohol, and if there's alcohol, then there's mixing.)

"You'll have to excuse me," my mother said.

Accepting his tinny modesty with grace, she mirrored him. Spurred by the same humanity that had moved the man opposite to deem her, in a mistranslation that nevertheless signified, untouchable.

THAT AFTERNOON NOTHING THOUGHTS crowded my mind.

I was sure that as soon as my father died, his house would again meet its fate as a commodity. Sold and the profits split, my mother and I receiving our apportioned shares. Some to his sister, more to his brothers; that was the way of the law. The law was the way of the Book. The Book again lay open on my mother's lap, guarding centuries of reading and misreading. Meanwhile my studio in Los Angeles was sitting there, sealed to sun and air. Paid for, at this point, for only another week.

But Leili, Leili was a daughter with a house of her own.

I considered what it would mean to be with her. To stay. Washed of my current duty, my workday could be refilled. Reading, thinking, learning—I could take on a course or two at the university, my father's alma mater. Even now my mother's laptop sat on the bedside table, at the ready. Surely under all the jadedness and rejection, of my love for my work I could muster something yet.

I imagined a life of two languages. Of kisses by the kiln and streetlamp-lit soujouk. Of watching over my father's pomegranate tree from the neighboring balcony.

Date #98: Watermelon Seeds

SHE COOKED FOR ME. Simple fare; hardly cooking, really. Nūn paneer hindūneh: bread, cheese, and watermelon. A meal so light that only the weight of summer could trick the body into thinking it dinner.

She laid a sofra on her balcony. Set down trays of sangak hot from the toaster oven and watermelon cool from the fridge. Cross-legged on hard stone, we picked pebbles out the flatbread and seeds from the melon's red flesh. We cut from a block of soft cheese still in the carton.

We let the night grow cold.

٢٢

Saturday, August 24

THE MIND MAY SLIP, slit by slit, unnoticed, but the body does the soul's bidding. Tight-gripped and thin-lipped, it clings to this world, clay to clay, kind to kind.

But what will not be given is for Death to take.

Unfurl the hook, pin the joints straight. Let gravity work the skin. Let it sag, both the bag and its load, bones and blood and bile pale and yellow and brown. The silklike milk already rendered impotent by time, the pus in the lungs that suffocates from the inside out, the shit left in the intestines—they drip, they sit.

The Angel's hands stay clean. Nails short and pink, filed. In His grip the soul's soil turns to powder, the body's struggle goes dry.

Dust to dust. Let it sink.

I WAS NOT IN the room when he died. I was not there because I'd left to fetch myself a glass of water. Iced water sourced from the desk nurse in a real glass. There was a tap in my father's en suite bathroom. I didn't want that. I wanted a tall glass of water served on a silver tray. This was the closest I could get.

My father died at maghreb. Not Shia maghreb, not local maghreb, but precisely at sunset, when the caterwaul of a long dead Cairene muezzin sang through my father's phone. All the mosques across town lay silent yet.

He died, my mother later said, because he choked on his own vomit. A clear vomit of feeding tube nutrients, his throat evidently responsive enough for that. It was unusual for a body so far gone to have this reaction, according to the doctor, but at last gasp, nothing was unheard of.

She was there, of course, my mother. In the room, at his side. Opposite her sat my aunt, his blood sister. I'd thanked her earlier for the fruit.

The premature adhan stretched a taught thread and the silver thread of life glistened against the black night and my father's choke broke and my aunt shrieked and my mother said "quiet please" and the bed alarm sounded, though which of them hit it I'd never know—I heard it all from outside the closed door, where I stood, iced water in hand, unwilling to enter. I waited long seconds. I heard the nurse's footsteps nearing from down the hall. I heard the patter of the Angel of Death circling my father's bed. I heard the final line of the adhan attest, There is no God but God. I heard a hush fall. I heard ice knocking against glass inside the cold sweating cup I held in my trembling hand.

I took a long sip of water and walked in.

HE LOOKED THE SAME, my father, and it was this realization that made my throat hurt. His face was lax. He was pale. The feeding tube was still in him. I saw a sick man, a small man, a thing.

There was too much commotion to cry. My entrance had broken my mother's spell of silence, and my aunt was now angling the bed toward the qibla, cutting the room into strange pockets. A nurse had followed me in, and now a doctor followed the nurse. From a few paces away—my body refused to near his—I recited the Fatiha by reflex.

My mother had made it to Tehran in time to see him, speak to him, even if the words between them were, by now in their marriage, few. They'd shared a cab. A phone. The selfie and voice memo he'd sent me had come from her number.

I was too late from the start.

MY NEXT THOUGHT WAS to message Adam. Right there at my father's bedside.

My mother was watching the doctor tend to his business, the business of documenting death. There was nothing to translate. I fished my phone from my bag. My aunt noticed, glared. I tucked myself into the en suite bathroom.

Adam's name had by then fallen further on my list of open threads. I scrolled down. And down. I found it. My thumbs hovered over the keyboard.

My father passed, I found myself typing.

"Passed" was a precious way to put things, and I didn't respect myself for it. I sent the message. *Died* was the word I wanted. *Death*. How often had this word occurred to me this past month, whether in one language or another? How steadily had it walked with me through the corridors of my mind?

In the bright light of the sterile bathroom I set my phone face-up on the counter, willing Adam's name to appear. The bathroom was equipped with only a Western-style toilet, the usual squat toilet forgone for reasons that likely had as much to do with class as disability. I flicked the lid down—there was one, as in a hotel. I sat. I tried putting my head between my hands; that was my image of grief. I didn't feel any better. I checked that the Wi-Fi was connected, that the text had gone through. It had. I put my phone back down.

Saturday, August 24, according to my lock screen. Just after seven. I'd never switched to the Iranian calendar. Twenty minutes had gone by, past local maghreb. I considered finding somewhere to pray. But I'd sat on the toilet fully clothed, and now my manteau was impure. Back in LA it was what—eight, eight-thirty. It took me inordinately long to do the math. Too early, at any rate, for Saturday morning.

The bathroom was gray and white. Clean lines. A mirror the length of the counter. I saw myself, blank and gray, in a room that could just as easily be here, in this private hospital in a so-called developing country, or back in America. I was a cardboard cutout in a box made of modeling paper. Across a paper curtain a man called my father lay small, so small, smaller than a speck of dust in a seamless universe pocked with infinities, and here was I, smaller than even that.

My phone began to vibrate. Adam, a video call.

Morning sun. It washed over my screen and out into the room. Adam was outside, still adjusting the camera. Blue skies, palm tree in the distance—in LA, could be anywhere. I wanted to be there. Finally he came into full view. His cheeks bloomed, blood born of exertion. In the corner of the screen hung my face, sketched by a painter who couldn't be bothered with shading.

For some moments we were quiet together. He was out of breath, and I could hear the birds chirping, cutting through the microphone.

"Talk to me."

I couldn't. I knew my voice would betray me. The camera flipped. Los Angeles revealed herself, downtown rising like a tide about to break.

"I was on a run. I'm at the top of Barnsdall."

The image began to pan. A palette of grays and blues and dusky purples traced the cityscape to the edge I knew to be the ocean. Rendered in the sfumato of smog and haze was the city I'd called home for so long.

Adam flipped the camera back so I could see him.

"I'd ask you how you feel but I know that's not what you're after."

The wan frown on his lips. The wetness brimming in his eyes.

"Okay, facts. Let's start with that. Where are you?"

I breathed, registering only then that I'd been holding my breath.

"At the hospital," I managed.

"Where's the hospital?"

"Tehran."

"Fuck." He took a sharp breath. "When did you leave LA?"

"Three weeks ago. Right after the beach."

"So you're in a hospital in Tehran. In the lobby."

"No," I said.

My background was a blank wall.

"The hallway?"

Adam was right. Here were questions I could answer, answers I could understand.

"I'm in the bathroom."

I angled the camera down and bunched up my manteau so that the toilet lid was visible.

"On the shitter," he said, "to be precise."

I choked out a laugh. After a pause, Adam went on softly.

"He was sick?"

"Heart attack."

"When—when did it happen?"

The pressure behind my eyes began to crest. I swallowed.

"Weeks ago. But the—he's been hanging on. Until now."

Tears sunk down my cheeks. Salt soaked my lips.

"I'm sorry," he said, clear and quiet. "I'm sorry."

He wiped a hand across his cheek. Silence suspended between us as a rope bridge over a stream. The line sputtered but was not cut.

"It wasn't really his heart," I said after some time. "He had a brain bleed. We didn't figure it out till later. A whole day later."

Why hadn't I woken him up? Just to say salaam, I'm here, how are you? I stood and started to pace.

"Since then, it's been all complications. Coma, pneumonia, who the fuck knows. My mother even came out to try to manage things."

I had the clarity that comes with a good cry. Everything before me in high definition. The texture of these white walls, cakey like too many coats of foundation. The memory of the windowless room at the state hospital, sallow as a worn dollar bill. The night-blooms' perfume in my father's courtyard. The charcoal on my teeth in the mountains with Leili. The kiln's cold touch on my skin.

"It was doomed from day one," I said. "The staff was stretched thin. They didn't do a routine CT scan because there aren't enough scanners."

"Jesus."

What bubbled in me was now hot and red. How was it even possible that in this day and age, under the constant vigilance of privatized care, you could die from what was basically a cold? And yet it wasn't my father's people who had invented the term "Third World," and they hadn't defined the terms by which its inhabitants were forced to live.

"So yeah, God bless America." I could taste my bitterness, its futility. "He was pretty much killed by the sanctions."

For a long stretch there was nothing but our breath. Mine, dense yet quivering, a stone on a riverbed about to be dislodged.

There was a knock at the door.

"Hey, I know things got—" Adam stopped. "I was getting worried."

Looking at Adam I had the sensation of looking in a mirror. Of course not on the surface, but somewhere underneath. To see the naked self in someone else: all the poetry of humanity lay along this asymptote. But my throat was again too tight to speak.

A sharper rap. My mother saying my name.

"You should go."

"Right," I whispered.

I cleared my throat, wiped my face.

"I'm sure she already has a checklist for me. One-a, face reality. Three-b, look death in the eyes."

He smiled. "That's the spirit."

I held his gaze for another beat and hung up.

دو

DOU

TWO

١

Sunset to Sunset, August 24–25

ONE, THREE, SEVEN, FORTY: this is how mourning is counted. From maghreb to maghreb we tallied the days.

DAY ONE WE BURIED my father.

In mere hours they'd removed the body from the private hospital and sent it for the usual ablutions. The workers whose work it was to wash dead bodies washed his, my father one among many purified and prepared for the grave that day. His people took care of the details, leaving us foreigners to nurse our sorrows.

And to pick up the bill. Counting from the stacks of toman she'd kept in my father's sock drawer, my mother paid. For the private hospital. For the ablutions. For the shroud. For the coffin that carried the body through the sprawling cemetery south of the city, early Sunday morning. For the white gladiolas I placed on fresh dirt. For the Styrofoam containers of gheimeh polo passed around the parking lot for the mourners, standard funeral fare, little more than lentils on rice. For the single-serving tubs of sweet sholeh zard, the happy scent of saffron thought to spit in the face of heartache. For the gravestone that now lay over my father, level with the ground, meant to be walked on by the living.

But the grave, my mother didn't pay for. My father had bought a plot for himself.

THAT EVENING A SMALL group accompanied my mother and me to the neighborhood mosque, to offer a prayer and read the Quran. In the economy of grace, blessings are fungible: we each read only a chapter or two but asked God to consider the good deed my father's, and in this way, ensured that he'd get credit for finishing the Holy Book cover to cover, at least once. For those who couldn't make it to the mosque, chapters were also assigned via Telegram.

I could not concentrate. Between verses that my father had considered divine poetry, I found myself turning to a couplet Adam had texted, caught on the second hemistich: "Only poetry knows how to pair itself to this space." Adonis, translated by Khaled Mattawa.

The message had reached me mid-morning. Late night, LA-time—I could see Adam in bed, cradling his phone. I was sitting on the garden ledge, back from the burial. Each petal, each leaf was brittle with thirst. I hadn't seen Leili in two days, and no one else had watered the flowers, the tree.

I sat there long enough that at some point I heard the low tones of a fist knocking on metal. I knew it was her. My uncles had hung the typical black banner over the gate to indicate a house in mourning, and it was no secret that my father was dead. I didn't answer.

Leaving for the mosque my mother had opened the gate to find a bunch of cut tuberose without a card, the petals already curling. "Courtesy of your friend"—she'd handed them to me. Wordlessly I took them. Wordlessly I filled a jug with water. We'd never discussed my nights out. Don't ask, don't tell.

Now I sat on the worn carpet in the women's section at the mosque, my mother beside me. Verse by holy verse, I read and reread until I could read each verse once without stopping. Finally taken by the current, I thought of no one, not even myself.

MEANWHILE, IN A GRAVE across town, the Angel of Death tried to pry my father's soul from his body as two lesser angels read my father's scrolls of deeds and misdeeds. All his life they'd hovered on his shoulders, the one on the right recording his kindnesses and devotions; and on the left, his wrongs. Blessings and sins, each person was the sum of these two volumes.

We read, and they read, and finger by finger, tongue and toe, the Angel of Death untacked my father from the world I lived in.

٢

Tuesday, August 27

DAY THREE, MY FATHER'S phone died. I unplugged it myself that
morning. All day it sat on the dining table, a black stone. Maghreb
went unremarked.

Except I could see the last of the sunlight leaning against the windows. I opened them and stepped outside. I took the hose and pressed
my thumb to its lip. I turned the water on full throttle. Felt the force
against my thumb and watched the water fan, heard drops drumming
against the leaves.

My phone buzzed in my pocket. Adam's daily digest—the couplets
had continued. Yesterday, some contemporary poet I hadn't heard of,
lines that nonetheless moved me. Today, Hafez.

The sorrow in my narrow heart stems from this
That I have no friend to speak such sorrows with

It was a joke. I hated Hafez, found his cleverness dull, and now
Adam had sent me the ultimate sad-boy lament, Quatrain 10. He'd
even cobbled an original translation together, working from published
versions.

I reread it. The poem was a perfect circle, and that tautology was
where the humor lay. The speaker's sad he doesn't have any friends to

tell that he's sad—so is he actually sad, or just upset there's no audience for his performance? It was, actually, funny.

Watering my father's garden, nursing my own commonplace sorrows, it struck me that Adam's love for Julia, fucked up as it was, had at least been thick. Mine for my father was a liquid so slithering that I'd run it through the machinery of graduate school to have something to hold on to. What did my father know about me, other than my favorite flavor of juice? He certainly didn't know I didn't like Hafez. He'd never met my friends, he didn't understand my politics, he hadn't read a single word that I wrote. My research on Iran was nothing but the locus of this loss.

I sensed a gaze on my back. I turned. Leili was watching from her balcony, cigarette in hand. I held a hand up in a staid wave, and she did the same. The orange ember of her cigarette flared like a firefly and died.

ג

⸺

Saturday, August 31

DAY SEVEN, MY MOTHER and I went to the cemetery to say goodbye to my father. We had flights booked for later that night, each to our own home. She wrote me a check, down to the cent, for my flight and any change fees as we waited for our ride. I refused to take it.

My uncle had promised his car, and we were outside, on the street. It was still dark out. To beat traffic, we'd arranged to leave at daybreak. You had to traverse the entire city to get to its dead.

At long last, my uncle's late-model Mercedes sailed down the alleyway, whiter than the white thread of dawn. He'd upgraded since 2015. I could hardly imagine at what expense—on luxury brands, he'd once humble-bragged, import duties doubled or tripled the cost of the car. In dollars.

The tinted windows rolled down to unveil my uncle himself. So he'd had the decency not to send the driver. I took the passenger's seat, my mother, the back. Handing me a chocolate milk from those my uncle—or more probably, his wife or secretary—had packed for us, my mother again tried to slip me the check.

Though it hurt my pride, I took it.

AT THE CEMETERY, MY uncle said he had business to discuss with me afterward.

My prayers were brief, pro forma. With my father, I no longer knew where to start, and the same went for God. I said my Fatiha and sat still. We were all three crouched before the grave like frogs, one hand on my father's tombstone. My mother's rising was the signal that I could rise, too.

My uncle started shuffling with his briefcase as soon as we stepped away from the grave.

"Your father," he said to me, using the formal *you*, "made a will four years ago. I'm responsible for carrying it out."

"I'll meet you two at the car," my mother said.

Unlike the doctors, my uncle seemed to understand her English. It was the language of business, after all. He offered her the keys, and she started back the long way, navigating the grid of narrow walkways that partitioned the cemetery.

The American side of my father's worldly possessions had long been sorted. At age nine I was told that my parents had notarized wills. At my college graduation I'd received a photocopy of each. The documents mirrored each other: when one died the house went to the other; when both, to me. Tucked deep in the Midwest, it wasn't worth much anyway. Given inflation, it may have actually depreciated.

Now my uncle consulted a brown leather binder stamped with his company crest. Domestic-make, judging by the mismatched zipper.

"The bottom line is," he said, "the house here is yours. Sole ownership."

I knew few specifics when it came to the local real estate market, but I did know this: Tehran had a housing crisis. After the Revolution, I'd learned in my research, millions had migrated from the provinces to the capital, typical twentieth-century urbanization. Which was to say, the house—a house, not an apartment, and in a central district, no less—was worth something. Even converted from toman to dollars, in the wrong direction of capital flow. This wasn't money that could change my life in LA. But I could pay my rent for some time.

Consulting the binder, my uncle went on to report the balance of my father's local bank account.

We started toward the lot, my uncle carving a straight path across the flat gravestones, and I, hopscotching around them like some child. Death was not to be fetishized; the buried were part of the earth—but I couldn't get myself to step on the stones. My American sensibilities, I supposed. I could still see my mother in the distance, across the vast and shadeless plane. In my father's courtyard, the dew from last night's watering would've dried by now.

"And what about my mother?" I asked.

"As far as I know," my uncle said, "your mother gave up her rights a while ago."

I wondered whether he meant her guaranteed share as a wife, or the rights she'd bought by paying off my father's loan. Maybe rumor had gotten out.

"Your baba, at any rate," my uncle went on, "held the title."

He brandished the binder, and I gathered said title was inside. By then we'd reached the parking lot. The car must have been sweltering despite the early hour, but my mother hadn't even rolled down the windows, much less turned on the AC. She sat erect behind the tinted glass, reduced to a shadow.

Regardless of what she'd once told my father, in my understanding, my mother could now, changing her mind, contest the will and win her due share. Not the whole house but her own little splinter. As could my aunt and other uncle.

"What about everyone else?" I asked. Relying on an idiom that now sounded only too apt, I went on, "Have you all also withdrawn your hand?"

"Leave that to me."

The eldest surviving son acted as representative: his was the collective hand.

"Your father wanted you to have a place here," he said. "In the homeland."

"The fatherland."

"That's the same thing."

An acid anger fizzed inside me. The sun beat down on my head.

My uncle asked what I wanted to do with the cash. Considering the sum was mere "chump change" in dollars, he advised that I keep the account open in my own name for maintenance, gardening, incidentals. Assets had upkeep.

"I doubt I'll keep the house," I said.

He shook his head.

"No, you don't understand. The title comes on condition—it was important to him that you don't sell the house."

I stared at him. By definition a house was not a liquid asset, that was enough trouble. But to have an illiquid asset then frozen into stasis—it was an anchor. What right did my father have to decide where I belonged?

The air between us was still. Unbreathable. This far south of the city, the mountains were mere memory.

"Well?" my uncle asked. "What have you decided about the account?"

"Could I get back to you before I leave?"

I was scheduled to fly to LA at midnight. He zipped up the binder.

"As you wish."

۴

A Couple Hours Later

BACK AT THE HOUSE my hands itched for something to do.

Leaving Tehran wouldn't take much. In retirement my father had lived simply. A razor in the medicine cabinet, a row or two of books on the bookshelf, a single wardrobe's worth of clothes. My mother's and my footprints were even shallower, bound to be the work of an hour. Neither of us had ever fully unpacked, our suitcases splayed like fish we gutted and restuffed throughout the day.

As my mother rested downstairs, I set to work sorting through my father's belongings. Most I tossed, some I let stay. I dumped the contents of the fridge; the French dressing my father kept in the door to spite his cholesterol, the last of my mother's milk. I trashed most everything in the bathroom but saved the fat horsehair brush he himself must've saved for sentimental reasons. (When my father had hair, Reaganomics was still fresh.) I didn't touch the bookshelf. It was work too crass to have contemplated before the seventh day. Now it wasn't yet noon and I was almost done. This house had long been staged for unoccupancy.

I returned to my father's room to find my mother had moved upstairs, abandoning the hard baroque couch in the parlor for his bed. I'd never known her to nap, and I could tell from the tension in her body that she was awake. Curled in on herself, back to me, she looked almost frail. But her shoulders weren't shuddering, and I figured she wasn't crying. It was a relief.

We never touched each other's things, under the pretense of privacy, but I decided to finish packing her bag for her. I gathered the day and night creams she had laid out on the dresser, wiping them down as I had the kitchen counters. They, too, were coated in a film of pollution so thin it looked clear, until you saw the black residue on the washrag. Quietly opening my father's sock drawer, I took out her stacks of toman and the legal pad under them. The cover was inscribed not in English but Farsi. My father's handwriting. I set the money on her suitcase where she'd see it and flipped through the notebook. The pages were clear. On the cover, nothing but the family name—my name—and this address.

All summer I'd been searching for stability and now I had a house. It was that simple.

I stepped outside my father's room and looked around the second-floor foyer. It was sparse and functional, traditionally decorated: no furniture, just a rug underfoot and some pushtis against the wall for your back, like at the kabob house. I sat down by the socket where I'd left my phone charging. I leaned back against the rough wool of the pushti. It occurred to me that in my position—uninsured—my father would've fared even worse in America. What waited for me in LA but bills and the certainty that sooner or later I'd end up brain-dead after some horrible accident because I couldn't afford a CT scan? My mind was my livelihood, my lifeline. Maybe here I stood a chance—the public hospitals might be incompetent but at least they'd try to treat me. And until catastrophe hit, I could read and write and think. Not in Leili's house, but my own.

Adam had left a voice note while I was cleaning. In LA, it was still Friday night.

"Hey there, can't wait to see you tomorrow."

The day's poem followed. He'd held his phone up to a recording of Victor Hugo. "Demain dès l'aube"—Adam was getting lazy.

"A father at his daughter's grave?" I texted. "A little twisted."

I didn't admit how nice it was to hear his voice.

AFTER A SHOWER TO shake the dust, I entered the courtyard. My mother had collected herself. As on my first day, she was sitting on the ledge under the pomegranate tree. But now it was past noon, almost midday—as defined by the Islamic clock, when the sun was at its peak—and the tree cast only a sliver of shadow.

I took a seat next to her in the sun.

"Congratulations," my mother said. I realized she'd known about the conversation with my uncle, knew exactly what his briefcase bore. "You are now a bona fide capitalist."

I laughed. Genuinely laughed—for the first time, it occurred to me, in a week. Her eyes were veiled by big brown sunglasses, but she was smiling. I gathered my hands to my knees. I wanted to ask her advice. But I was shy. She'd done her part. Mothered me. Buried my father. Bought the very house in which we were sitting.

"It gets the best of us, don't look so glum."

She put a finger under my chin. I wiped away a tear.

"This house," I said. "It should be yours."

"Not by the law of this land."

I thought of the Quran she'd read and reread day after day at the hospital.

"There are higher laws," I said.

And yet civil law here claimed that same text. That was the bind, being Muslim in a country like this.

My mother rose and plucked a leaf from the pomegranate tree. Rubbed its dark lips between her fingers, held it to her nose.

"Your grandmother loved this tree more than anything."

"More than us."

"Don't feel sorry for yourself," she said. "Justice is a dangerous thing."

She let the pomegranate leaf drop, and took off her sunglasses to look at me.

"Your father and I talked about this again before you came. I've never laid any claims to this place. Consider it a gift."

Someone in Leili's building had their windows cracked, and the midday prayer tolled on state TV. My mother sat back down, next to me. We listened to the adhan. When the block was quiet again, she spoke.

"Two Muslim cultures. We thought it was enough. But a marriage takes more than two. You're now a woman in your own right, remember that."

I reached up to pluck a leaf from the pomegranate tree. It smelled like nothing. But it was green. Alive. First my grandmother, then my father—someone had cultivated this garden, and I had inherited the charge.

"What if I don't want it?" Even to me, the question sounded childish. "Everything here, it's a whole different life."

She shrugged. Her eyes grew cold.

"Things fall apart," she said. "Just let it rot."

THAT NIGHT I SAW my mother off at the airport. I'd canceled my own flight, and now time folded cleanly on my mother's departure. These were the last hours of August.

As the taxi pulled to the curb, she reached into her bag.

"I have no use for this."

She handed me the toman I'd left out on her suitcase, the various denominations now bound together by a rubber band. There was enough to last weeks, given I wasn't paying rent.

Alone in the dead of night, heading back to an empty house, I checked my phone by reflex only to remember that I still hadn't switched my SIM. All this time I'd been either at the house or the hospital, on Wi-Fi, hardly tethered to the city herself. Tomorrow I'd finally buy one, along with some fresh groceries.

"It won't bother you if I open the window?" I said to the driver.

"Make yourself at home, khanum."

Night poured in, washing over me. I said a prayer. Unthinkingly at first, assigning meaning to the words as I went on. That my mother might arrive safely, that my father might rest in peace. That I might find a little peace myself, here, in this life.

دوباره

DOUBĀREH

TWO, AGAIN

۱

Sunday, September 1

SUDDENLY I LIVED IN the freedom of newfound solitude.

My mother gone, I served the tea to my taste. Strong and black in naked glasses, neither tray nor saucer. Caffeinated, I unpacked. For the first time my clothes hung in the wardrobe, my toiletries stood sentry before the mirror. Reality was made of iterative performance: To see whether I could live this life, I had to play at living this life.

I sat down to study, making a desk of the dining table. I fiddled around on my laptop, clicking on folder after folder, document after document. Book proposal drafts, article stubs, the dissertation itself—I opened each only to close it, shut out by the shadows of my own mind.

The spreadsheet stood stuck on Date #98. By now over a week had passed since I'd eaten at Leili's sofra the night before my father's death. After the seventh day of mourning, there was a lull till the fortieth. I was again free to do as I pleased.

As if summoned, a new message from Adam appeared on screen.

How's the flight?

It was framed by heart emojis—he was trying to make up for the pretension of untranslated French.

I typed something up about moving to Tehran on a lark and deleted it. The idea sounded ridiculous when you put it in words. And yet the

logic was irrefutable. In trying to marry rich, I'd asked for the prover-
bial room of my own, and now I had one. Here.

Delayed my departure, I finally wrote.

Anytime I even applied to a job outside LA, Adam's face fell—and
Bumfuck, Arkansas, was more accessible than Tehran.

My message got a thumbs-down.

Till when?

Long story. More soon.

I powered down my phone and stared at the mess of documents on
my screen. None of this work lived anywhere but there, in my own private ether. I hadn't published a single line since that article my second
year of grad school, apparent to me now as beginner's luck rather than
the promising sign I'd then taken it for. I thought of how hard it must
have been for my mother all those years ago, deciding to abandon an
entire almost-done PhD in the sciences to follow her passion, English.
In her telling, the critic wasn't a leech but a storyteller in her own right.
To critique was to honor the world with some minor truth.

I considered the story I'd been crafting this summer: "a queer
adjunct professor decides to marry rich . . . in order to write a book on
companionate marriage based on her dissertation." It wasn't difficult to
see where the logline lost verve.

A researcher in search of a subject, I returned to my father's shelves.
Maybe I'd missed something last month, looking for hospital reading.

Again, I confronted his old textbooks, lugged here all the way from
America. But now I understood why. They stood spine to spine, spoils
of war. The religious volumes rested on the top shelf. A dua book with
supplications for every occasion, standard issue Shia. A Quran, the
universal Arabic paired with a Farsi translation. A second Quran that
didn't quite fit, wedged in at the end. I took it out. It was the one my
mother had brought with her. She'd left it here. Somewhere that was
now to her nowhere.

I pulled both Qurans and turned to page one, the Fatiha. Page by page, language by language, I read. Arabic, English, Farsi.

Reading the text of my life, I'd see a character who'd not only pursued Farsi to fill a hole left by her father, "the" father, but who'd fallen in love with literature in the first place—fallen in love with English—in pursuit of the absent mother. Obviously, I had abandonment issues, any armchair idiot could diagnose that. But what this month had exposed was the precise nature of my abandonment: my parents had always been there without ever really being there.

At some point I slipped into the Farsi alone as into a cold pool, forcing myself to grow accustomed to it. Despite the subject of my PhD, I was slow at deciphering written Farsi, and the work was plodding. Soon I began to read the Farsi text for not sense but sound, as I did Arabic. It was a kind of nonsense, rendering language into meaningless music. Arabic gutturals softened or were elided when converted to Farsi. I let those rhythms ripple through me and comprehension pass over me. I was but plankton, and the text was an ocean undisturbed by our encounter.

Outside darkness had fallen like an ax, Shia maghreb. I opened the windows and kept reading the Quran on the sofa, night's chill on my cheeks.

Mankind. A creature created in God's image, so the story went. But how sloppy the cast, how fractured the mirroring. My father dead a week, and all I could think of was me.

Selfhood was a trap of small comforts. You had to pry them from the clay of life, knives out.

٢

Monday, September 2–Tuesday, September 3

I ENTERED THE WORLD.

I RESTOCKED THE FRIDGE.

I swept the courtyard.

I tossed the tuberose.

I moved around some furniture.

I took a needle to trigger my SIM tray and switched to a local number. My own, not my father's, not the family's—the number at the house had never changed. I pulled the cord on the landline.

I went on a walk and wandered into a gallery.

I gave Adam my number but not Leili. Not yet. After the bouquet, I knew, it was on me to make the next move. But I couldn't ask myself, much less her, whether what we'd had had been a tryst or the start to something real until I made a commitment. To this place. This version of me.

I faced the fact that fake Jazzercize via YouTube was not the same as long-distance running, and decided to hit the gym.

٣

‌

Wednesday, September 4

MIDWEEK I RETRACED MY steps from summers ago to find the posh gym where I'd spent a not insignificant portion of my research stipend in 2015. Due to gender segregation, the gym was only open to women every other night. This was my lucky night. I pushed my femme face in front of the security camera and got buzzed in.

Forty minutes later, I was finishing up on the treadmill, my time and endurance miserably reduced since my last run in LA. My old trainer passed by, doing a double take when she saw me.

"What're you doing in these parts, khūbī?"

Her pedagogy more a matter of barking at you than demonstrating, she wore full makeup—foundation, blush, the whole nine yards—and I liked her all the more for the absurdity. Now she flashed me a peach smile, cheeks contoured like trompe l'oeil.

"Nothing special," I said. "Family stuff."

I was still catching my breath, but more so, I didn't have the energy to receive condolences. Instead I complained about my training setback. I'd fallen far short of the ten-mile marker I'd reached that day at the beach.

"A month ago I made it to"—I did the conversion—"sixteen kilometers."

"Sixteen! That's almost half a marathon."

She checked the red digits flashing on the treadmill: twelve kilometers. As in, seven and a half miles.

"You're practically there already. The rest is easy." She laughed as she walked away. "You Americans, you run yourselves ragged."

I WOKE UP AT midnight, every muscle in my legs screaming, my abs sore. This was progress.

٤
_____

Thursday, September 5

I IMPORTED MY COFFEE habit, digging at the back of the cupboards until, sure enough, I found a lifetime's supply of dark roast Folgers in a red bucket big enough to caffeinate an army. Leave it to an immigrant to buy in bulk. A white drip coffeemaker stood next to it, yellowed with pollution, adapter attached. That, too, he'd brought from America.

I plugged the coffeemaker in, aware that the last hands to touch it had been my father's. The plastic was warm with summer. I stood there, listening to the coffee tinkle till the machine's last sputter and spit.

◊
—

Saturday, September 7

THOUGH I KNEW ALL too well that the chick flick class was dead, I returned to my syllabus. Those who can't do, teach.

The friends-to-lovers unit was nearly fleshed out. Ditching Hollywood for Bollywood, I decided to rewatch *Kal Ho Naa Ho*. Via VPN, I tracked down a copy.

The plot centered on a love triangle. In this case, two best friends—played by Preity Zinta and the even prettier Saif Ali Khan—who eventually meet their destiny as man and wife. New Yorkers Naina Catherine Kapur (Zinta) and Rohit (Saif Ali Khan) are friends from their evening MBA class. Heartbroken by her father's suicide, Naina finally falls in love for the first time when a new neighbor moves in: the charmingly goofy Aman, fresh from India and staying with his uncle. (Enter Shah Rukh Khan.)

But their love is doomed. Secretly in New York to seek treatment for—what else—a heart problem, Aman arranges for Naina's happiness by playing Cupid. Rohit, conveniently, has recently realized he's in love with her. Aman entrusts his new friend with his beloved, helping him get the girl.

Naturally Naina finds out and gets mad. Then she finds out that Aman is dying and also gets mad about that. After a lot of to-ing and fro-ing, she agrees to marry Rohit under the assumption that she will eventually grow to love him as more than a friend.

One potential husband (S. R. Khan) gets swapped for another (S. A. Khan), and the married couple lives happily ever after in the shadow of their mourning. Essentially love is lent from one couple to the next, a kind of currency.

Mixed into the marriage plot, there's a running joke that the two Khans are consistently mistaken for a gay couple. They first meet on a wild night out with Naina, complete with a Bollywood blowout disco number, which ends with the two men in bed. Aman is "crashing" at Rohit's, and the maid almost faints finding them under the sheets the next morning. Next thing you know, the bros are so close that they're often saying "I love you."

The last time I'd seen this movie I was tucked into a sleeping bag. Now I, myself, was mourning my father, but with little of Naina's sugary idolatry. Sipping the dregs of my second coffee, I had that same sense as the moment before realizing I'd lost a necklace—I knew I was missing something but wasn't sure what. My books were all back in LA. I clicked on the folder from my comprehensive exams in a poor imitation of scanning my shelves. Among the illegal (i.e., free) PDFs, I spotted Eve Sedgwick's *Between Men*.

I reread the intro. This epic book from the eighties, this bit of baby queer theory, argued that relationships between men were typically triangulated by a woman: she acted as both the conduit for homo-erotic desire and as its veil. Or to put it another way, as the guys' beard. So that was it. *Kal Ho Naa Ho* wasn't about the straight couples at all. Zinta is just the cipher for the two Khans to express their gayish desires.

But by the same theory, I'd all these years been madly in love with Julia. I supposed every theory had its limits.

And yet. Adam and I had talked as recently as the other night, chatting about nothing and everything until I fell asleep, phone in hand. By now he knew I was testing this life out. But I still hadn't mentioned Leili.

Need some time offline, I now texted him. *Don't be alarmed.*

I was tired of fucking around. Death had a way of setting a person straight.

۶

Sunday, September 8

MY BODY CRAVED RIGOR.

On days off from running, I patronized an outdoor pool operated by the Sepah, a branch of the military that evidently moonlighted in personal fitness. My father used to come on men's days. (For the sauna, of course, not to work out.)

Set within high walls to guard everyone's modesty, the place was cheap and crowded, with an air of Soviet simplicity. Flabby mamanbozorgs paddled in the shallow end, while at the deep end, their twiggy granddaughters learned to swim under the harsh direction of a drill whistle.

Between them, I swam laps, pushing memories through chlorine like air bubbles.

V

NIGHTS, I FELL LIMP. Where the threat of my father's death had driven me into my body and my desires, mourning left me dry. I did not knock on Leili's door.

My father's was the only bed in the house, and I still slept on my mat. My second night alone, I'd moved it to the upstairs foyer, where the old-fashioned dushak made sense among the rug and pushtis: everything cut close to the floor.

Some nights I tried to wake my body up, fantasizing about exiting these gates and turning sharply to the neighbor's. Tonight Leili answered on the first buzz. Explanations, apologies, all that was due was given. And something more. Kisses, yes, but also an offering. Say, a ripe fruit from the pomegranate tree in my father's garden. Come fall, the hard green seed-sacks that now hung from its branches in the dark night outside the window by my father's bed would redden and enlarge, liquifying on the insides into a wetness that made you pucker.

But this was where the fantasy glitched. In reality, I'd never been here in the fall, and I didn't know whether the tree outside bore fruit worth eating. It was the LA tree I was imagining, outside my apartment, where I'd staged my dating app selfie at the start of summer.

Each LA autumn I picked the best two pomegranates and left the rest for my fellow renters. One, I gave to Adam; the other, I kept for myself.

It might sit in my fridge for months before the right moment arrived. Only then would I cut into it. Trying hard not to pierce its insides with five or six shallow, vertical cuts, like my father had taught me, to keep the knife hovering skin deep so that when you chopped off the head and bottom, you could pry the fruit open, and each section would come out, seeds intact. Failing, inevitably, so that the juice spurted under my knife, thick and dark and wet and red. A liquid thread unraveling, unending.

ᚠ

Tuesday, September 10

ON A LISTLESS AFTERNOON I opened my laptop like usual to discover that my VPN wasn't working anymore. The university had kicked me off its rolls.

I set out for the nearest metro stop in search of bootleg DVDs, descending with the waves of commuters into the sweat. Underground peddlers lined the passageway neatly as kiosks at the mall. Volcanic foot pumices that were probably a million years old and palm-sized fans bound to break in a day. Bright swirly straws. Candylike hair barrettes. And my personal favorite: broad sheets of homemade fruit leather that were folded and rolled like architectural plans, the vendor half-blind, which was supposed to make you trust that the food wasn't poisoned. I bought two, barberry and cornelian cherry. I could smell the sour through the plastic.

Finally I found the DVDs. Bootlegs of all the recent legal—a.k.a. censored—titles were spread out on the vendor's sofra. I lingered. I loosened my shawl. I played with the front of my hair, though the pixie didn't leave much to work with. Eventually he got the message, and from some unknown pocket or shadow, a slim case of contraband was procured.

"Khanum, be quick."

I grabbed the first movie I saw and left without waiting for my change.

WHAT TRANSPIRED ON MY father's TV fifteen minutes later was *Four Weddings and a Funeral* dubbed in Farsi, Hugh Grant's voice dropped an octave, and Andie MacDowell's, raised. Despite this squeaky gender norming, MacDowell remained a Lothario of a woman. One whose infidelity led not to her demise, but to true love. And here was Farsi-speaking Hugh, a heartsick dweeb pining after his love, like Majnun for Leyli. Richard Curtis scripts read through medieval romance—a whole unit of my syllabus was taking shape.

> Week One: Female Fuckboys and Fey Straight Dudes
> Week Two: Copulating and Kicking It

That was, after all, the strangest thing about this movie. It married the genre of the rom-com to death. Not only that but the friend who dies is gay. A gay guy dying suddenly and unexpectedly in the early nineties—that couldn't help but summon the specter of AIDS. So *Four Weddings and a Funeral* was about femme bodily rights and the AIDS crisis?

And about how love can't be divorced from death.

9

Wednesday, September 11

THE FIRST COOL EVENING amidst my new routine, I treated myself to
a soujouk sandwich at the Armenian spot, paid for this time with my
mother's dwindling wad of bills. I was nervous I'd run into Leili. But
eight p.m. was too early for dinner on a summer day, and I was the only
one at the shop.

Ass against the low, hard stool, I wondered when I'd become such
a coward. Of course it wasn't that I meant to ghost Leili. I was simply
waiting for—what exactly, I wasn't sure.

I wasn't sure about anything anymore. Whether I lived here, for
one.

AND WHETHER I WAS Iranian, I thought a half-hour later, back at
the house gate and trying to get the skeleton key to fall into place.
Belonging was as much about who claimed you as what you claimed
to be.

I got in. The doors clicked shut behind me.

١٠
‗‗‗

Thursday, September 12

READING THE QURAN, I skipped to the end. Juz 30, the final section, with only the Farsi translation open on the dining table, next to a glass of tea.

At sura seventy-eight I stumbled.

"And We created you in pairs . . ." That old cliché printed on every Muslim wedding invite since before the Mayflower, or would've been, if the first Muslims in America hadn't been enslaved.

According to the Platonic idea of soulmates, all humans were once two-faced monstrosities with four legs and four arms before the gods cleaved them apart. The Islamic view was more or less the same, minus the horror show. But I'd never believed in soulmates. I still didn't. Reason wouldn't let me.

I also knew in the marrow of my bones that my parents' collective tragedy was that they'd each married the wrong person. That didn't mean there wasn't a right one. Or two, maybe—you had to choose who to love.

I started over, reading aloud.

> *And We created you in pairs*
> *And made your sleep rest*
> *And made the night a cloak*

And made the day for work
And built over you seven strong skies
And there made a burning lamp
And sent down from rainclouds rushing water.

As though to spite my cynicism, this time my breath caught. It was in the Word, but also in the Farsi.

Flipping to the front matter, much to my surprise, I saw a woman's name. Translating God's word was typically a man's job.

I took out my laptop and began to translate, working from this translation of a translation of God's truth. He had manifested Himself in language, and that divine language, Arabic, had been put into Farsi—now I formed the latest link on this eternal chain.

Though I'd quoted from Farsi texts for years in my academic work, roughly rendering a few lines from a novel or movie into English to serve my argument, I'd never tried translating for its own sake. Yet I was strangely at ease. Line by line, I tweaked, I tuned. Draft after draft, I blew it all up and put it back together again, anew.

I started a fresh spreadsheet, minimizing my list of dates. I entered every variation of every verse into the clean cells, the sura rendered as an infinite grid of possibilities. Rather than pale in comparison, the record of my summer struck me as its own kind of poetry.

I worked late, too consumed to remember hunger, thirst. By midnight I had a text I could stand by.

Putting myself to bed, the experience seemed uncanny, in the Freudian sense. Translation was a homecoming. Existing in both worlds at once. Not having to choose.

۱۱

Friday, September 13

IN THE BLOOM OF night, I revisited the scene with Leili and the pomegranate.

The scenes unfolded like a series of miniatures in a museum, torn from the manuscripts that made sense of them; jarring and displaced.

In the first folio I saw Leili perched on the balcony, watching me over the yellow brick wall of my father's courtyard. In the next I stood at her door, pomegranate in hand. In the third, at the top of the slope to her underground parking, waiting for her to come down.

Courtyard to courtyard, I exited one frame to enter another. The pomegranate, the critic in me noted, was an Orientalized symbol, with its feminized wetness and jewellike seeds. Except my Oriental fantasy hinged on an American pomegranate, and thus the copy exceeded the original—Benjamin, flipped. (All my capital-T Theory was coming back to me.)

But any which way, these images weren't my own. I knew almost nothing about Leili beyond the niceties. We hadn't even gotten to the point of having a fight.

When I flipped to the next page, instead of Leili and a pomegranate, I saw Adam.

Adam in the passenger's seat with that goddamn donut, Styrofoam-white cream on his lips.

۱۲

Saturday, September 14

SATURDAY WAS MONDAY, SO I got to work. I took the metro down to Enghelab. To the University of Tehran.

The clean white folds of the modernist concrete gates looked like origami, this effect dulled, albeit, by the black iron bars that stretched along the bottom. Rather than try to get past the guard, I contented myself with the bookstores that crowded the nearby streets. For some reason I hadn't ventured this far—and it wasn't really that far—in 2015, when I was ostensibly in Tehran for research. Then, I'd limited myself to the bookstores closer to the house, with cutesy knickknacks and curated tables fit for any mall in America. Now I knew that whatever I was looking for, it lay beyond my father's bookcase.

I went from shop to shop, at first without buying anything, luxuriating in the spartan shelving, the dust. Ugly volumes printed on cheap paper and sold just as cheaply—I picked through fiction and poetry, I fingered the paper. This was how a bookstore should be. Available, affordable. A few authors were familiar. Most were not.

I paused in the smallest shop I came across, jammed floor to ceiling with books. There were several versions of Hedayat's *Blind Owl*. I skipped to a page and read the phrases my eyes snagged on. It was as though I were encountering the book for the first time. Suspicion settled on my skin. My degree was a bad joke. Any lay reader of Farsi had read more than I'd read. Any fan had seen more films.

Of course, I had a few tricks in my pocket. So many flimsy, fancy theories I knew how to spin. I could cloud an argument behind layers of jargon, shuffling them like a stack of cards. Just as I'd thought I could reason myself out of my emotions.

I reshelved the Hedayat and walked over to poetry.

Unlike the other bookstores on the block, this one had a woman behind the desk. She was dressed plainly, in a khaki manteau and the same black maghnaeh worn by many of the students I'd seen passing in and out the university gates outside. Crooked over the closest display table, I now realized that most of the featured poetry was by women.

But of the names I recognized, there was one conspicuous absence: nothing by the midcentury writer Forugh Farrokhzad. Poet, feminist, filmmaker—she was such an icon, her face could be on T-shirts, Ché-style, in fierce silhouette. She'd put the body on the page in Farsi. She'd changed the course of culture. Since Forugh, free verse in Farsi was never the same. But she was nowhere here.

Like a pang of hunger, I decided I wanted the definitive volume of Farrokhzad, a solid complete works spanning the fifties and sixties. I turned to the shelves. There, too, I came up short. The only Forugh—quietly folded into a busy row of books—was a collection of her unsexiest poems. Given the oeuvre, it was slim.

I approached the register. I made my inquiry with the shopkeeper, literally translating the phrase "complete works."

For a moment she studied me. Lips pursed, hands still. Then she turned, wordlessly, and, brandishing a key from her manteau pocket, disappeared behind a locked door.

Long minutes passed. I wondered how many books I needed for my research that would have to be obtained this way, should I stay.

The shopkeeper had paused to vet me, I now understood, to make sure I wasn't a narc. I knew Forugh wasn't exactly a revolutionary favorite, but this, I had not expected. She was contraband, like some cheap Hollywood romance.

I imagined my local analog, my doppelganger. My—her—research was on gender and sexuality in Iran; was, indeed, a critique of normative binary gender and heterosexuality. How would that be received beyond the university's black bars, behind those folds of white concrete? What conversations would be curtailed? What could I teach, what could I publish? Was my other self damned to the realm of the "independent scholar," that euphemism for the independently wealthy, the dilettante?

The shop grew hot. I flapped my shawl against my chest, trying to create a breeze around my neck.

I thought about my failure to land any fall teaching, and about my mother's critique of my personal statement. In the US, one was also forced to self-censor—if not in the name of the state, then the market: the publishing market, the job market; in America there was never any shortage of markets. Academic presses feigned freedom from such concerns, but what else did it mean to ask whether a book "had an audience?" You were asking whether it would sell. Hiring was no different. If you made it through the hoops—floated to the top of the pile for a first-round interview, clawed your way to a campus visit, got the job—you wrote and taught what they wanted you to write and teach to keep it. Here, there, there were forms of power so insidious that the policed did the policing: that was the sign of their success.

"Voila, *The Collected Works of Forugh*," the shopkeeper said as she set the thick book on the counter, my amateur Farsi corrected with the more elegant turn of phrase.

I paid for the Forugh, plus everything I'd picked up at random and the best bilingual dictionary she could recommend.

WEIGHTED WITH BOOKS, I stepped out onto the busy avenue. I'd ventured out in the middle of the day, a rookie mistake, and my nervous sweat from inside the bookstore yielded to the simpler fact of sweating under the sun. There was no way I could manage the metro.

But a cab wasn't any easier. In busy areas like this—I was, in my own reckoning, properly downtown at this point, though I wondered whether that was actually true, or just another distortion from my father's map of Tehran—most people used line taxis that went up and down the boulevards like buses, with folks hopping in or out along the way. I didn't know the routes, what avenues intersected with what to get me back to the house.

"Khanum?"

I turned to see the shopkeeper, poking a head out to ask if I wouldn't prefer to have the books sent by courier. She held a notepad out for me to write my address.

"Thank you," I said. "But that won't be necessary."

I was too embarrassed to expose my childlike handwriting. With a pondering step I headed toward the metro.

Here, there, nowhere to go. But maybe there was something to be said for choosing the hell you know.

١٣

Sunday, September 15

WAKING TO THE SOUND of horns the next morning, suspended still in the bubble of half-sleep, I checked my phone for my daily dose of poetry only to remember that I'd told Adam not to text me.

Why? Because it was an axiom of adulthood that you needed to be alone to figure out what you wanted. But in a romantic comedy you could run from one lover to another without censure. No one cares how many other folks Harry and Sally see before getting together. That's part of the joy: desire proliferates.

I turned to my other side, to the light struggling through the blinds. I was still sleeping on my mat in the foyer, and the stone floor under the carpet cut into my hip. I punched my pillow to fluff it. Real life was no fun.

۱۴

Monday, September 16

MONDAY AT THE GYM on what was actually Monday, I again ran into the trainer. She came to me in the locker room, all play, bumping into me bicep to bicep.

"You were really working out there, I like it."

A stripe of my sweat now glistened on her skin. I smiled and ran the faucet. I still hadn't made it to thirteen miles. No matter how hard I worked, my legs gave out at ten.

"When do you leave?"

"I'm not really sure."

"You'll be missed."

Water dripped from my chin where a moment ago there'd been salt.

"I might be back soon."

"Here? Either you're crazy or in love."

Face buried in a clean towel. I heard her rummaging in a locker behind me.

"Love is a terrible thing," someone else said.

I looked up to see a middle-aged lady buttoning her manteau. The trainer laughed.

"See what I'm saying?" she said. "Mehri khanum knows." She shook her head mournfully. "No wonder you look so depressed."

"Dastitūn dard nakoneh," I said, rolling my eyes, smiling. *You're too kind.*

I grabbed my things and finished dressing. Everyone around here was a font of wisdom.

۱۵

Tuesday, September 17

TUESDAY I STOPPED BY the vegetable seller for herbs on the way home from the pool. I meant to set a pot of ghormeh sabzi on the stove, foregoing my father's dry mix for fresh greens. Coriander and fenugreek, cilantro and parsley.

The vendor's grate was already lowered partway. Tonight he seemed to be closing early, or rather, less late than usual.

"Excuse me," I called through the grating. "If I could just grab some sabzi?"

The same old man I'd seen watering the tree on my first real date with Leili walked over and lifted the gate, his movements confident, a body preserved by exertion.

"Khasteh nabāshīd, thank you," I said.

But he didn't return the courtesy, and we finished our transaction with few words.

IN THE KITCHEN FIFTEEN minutes later, herbs washed and chopped, I found myself making pesto. Or rather, an approximation of pesto, rigged with what I had at hand in my father's kitchen. Walnuts for pine nuts, grapeseed oil instead of olive. In search of pasta, I boiled egg noodles intended for āsh. Over the days I'd discovered corners of cabinets

I hadn't thought to check when first clearing my father's things. My father's pantry was fully stocked. He even had golpar.

But if he was going to start playing chef before he died, why not a couple decades prior? The hours my mother must have spent learning to cook his cuisine. Immigration, emigration, exile—whatever you wanted to call it, his life was rife with such illogic: sticking to strict gender norms abroad only to abandon them back home.

I counted three weeks and change since my father's funeral. *It felt like yesterday*, people liked to say of time. But for me it felt like tomorrow. I was still in his house waiting for something to change.

The failure of my parents' marriage had become my fear. If I wove my fingers through a friend's like I already had my daily life—then what? It was to risk everything. You couldn't game the game. I stabbed the last of my fusion pesto-pasta and cleaned up.

۱۶

Thursday, September 19

MY LANDLORD SENT ANOTHER email, this time with a more menacing subject. It was September 19. Rent was long overdue.

The balance of my savings account was maybe just enough, but I couldn't check at any rate; without VPN, I had no way to log into the bank app. Which also meant I had no way to pay. I wondered how many months you could miss before getting evicted—one, likely.

I took a walk to Haft-e Tir, leaving the apartment-lined blocks of the neighborhood to go south and west along busy arteries of the city. As a child I'd gone shopping there with my parents, marveling at the gleaming vitrines and white marble floors. Returning in 2015 to buy the shawl I now wore, the crowded area sparkled with mystery. Like a tourist or settler, I thought that here, life was alive.

Now I noticed fingerprints on the glass and dust graying their doorways. Shiny wrappers littered the streetside gutters—thanks in no small part to my uncles—with these same products reproduced on the billboards overhead in ghastly proportions.

The manteau-rusari chain I'd last shopped at was still there, and I stepped in for a new square scarf to replace my worn shawl. Technically I wouldn't come out of mourning until October, but even black and white would be an improvement.

Most of the wares were folded in a glass case. Ninety centimeters, one hundred, one twenty: the square scarves were organized by size, measured along the diagonal. I asked the salesman to see a few in full, acutely aware that each scarf I had him unfold built the expectation of a purchase. But I had no sense of how small or large the measurements were.

In the fitting room—evidently ninety centimeters rendered a triangle so tiny it exposed my neck—I overhead two women about my age enter the store. They knew precisely the size and print they wanted. But when the attendant tried to ring them up, they balked.

"I bought this same scarf last month for twelve toman," one said, where twelve meant twelve thousand. "Now you're trying to charge fifteen?"

"Inflation," the salesman said, "it's really not in our hands."

Back outside, my new 120-cm hibiscus-print scarf on my head, I wondered what my father had found here. Everywhere I turned was tinged with Third World patina, the patina of not an heirloom but a penny.

What I found charming in LA repulsed me here. The dirt and grime and poisonous air—this wasn't the veneer of casual neglect and corruption but rather shabbiness through and through. The advertising was dated, the cars looked like toys. Anywhere cool in LA, you had to hide your happiness behind a mask of indifference, but these people looked like they were ready to stab you. New Yorkers were the same, I told myself. It was a sign of urbanity. And yet the exchange from the shop echoed. Soon I'd exhaust my mother's money, and my father's account wouldn't last all that much longer as a sole source of income.

"Careful, khanum!"

I stopped in my tracks—I'd almost knocked over a senior with a cane making his way over the gutter grille and onto the sidewalk.

"I'm so sorry."

I stood by as he leaned on his cane for a few breaths. It occurred to me that here in Tehran, the most minor hiccups paralyzed me. Why hadn't I tried, for example, to simply download a new VPN?

"Please," I said. "After you."

"Allahu akbar." The old man sighed, and in that chiding prayer, I heard my father.

We parted ways.

Looking, from behind the veil of my sunglasses, into the faces of the men I now passed—gray eyebrows bushy as runway models', cheeks sunken like bags of sand—I realized my father had been after that. Sameness. In the US he would always be a foreigner. Here, "back home," he'd become one. But my difference was inescapable.

This house was a letter in a language I didn't want to understand. The small dreams he'd wanted for me in America: a marriage two kids a mortgage, those were legible. But this?

"Comfortable foreign resident"—I thought of the rancor with which Leili's friend had spoken to me, of me, at the kabob house. Justifiably, perhaps, now that I was a freshly minted property owner in a city with a housing crisis where I hardly belonged.

It was one hell of a climate for a summer home.

WHEN I GOT BACK, I emailed my mother. I'd never before asked her for a loan. I explained my situation. Plainly and brutally, putting aside my pride. I'd been laid off from teaching, I had no immediate prospects, and I wanted to go home to LA.

How many hours we'd passed together and how little had been said.

17

Saturday, September 21

MY MOTHER EMAILED A few days later to assure me that she'd paid the rent.

This missive took the form of a forwarded PayPal receipt with the subject line: "Failing a job, find a husband."

۱۸

Later That Day

THAT AFTERNOON I FINALLY got it up to apologize. I poured a pot of fresh coffee into an old jar, grabbed two tea glasses, and buzzed Leili's. No response. Maybe she was in the studio, at the kiln. I stood there for long minutes in the street. No one came in or out. Afraid that if I left her gate, I wouldn't come back, I buzzed the other units, her tenants. On the ground floor I got someone.

"Excuse me, I'm looking for khanum—" I realized I didn't know Leili's last name. "Leili khanum."

I explained that I was their neighbor, and wanted to drop something off, but the woman remained suspicious.

"Why don't you try her cell?"

When I admitted I didn't have Leili's number, she grew curt.

"I'm sorry, I really can't do anything for you."

I turned back. Hosing down the folding chair and card table, wiping them dry, I set up under what shade I could muster from the pomegranate tree. I composed a letter in English—I was sorry for ignoring her, for not being in touch earlier, and I was leaving. Using my new dictionary, I then translated my letter into Farsi, on a fresh leaf from my father's legal pad.

The English to Farsi translation came out poorly. Bilingualism was a river; it only flowed one way.

I left the letter squeezed into the door sill at Leili's, between gaudy flyers for pizza and fried chicken.

THAT NIGHT, BACK FROM the gym, now stuck at twelve miles, I got my reply. A pretty piece of heart-shaped stationary was posted to the gate with a slip of tape, the message made out to a pet name Leili had never called me: جیگر—jīgar. All around Tehran, the word "liver" rolled off the tongue like "babe" in LA: here it was the liver that was the seat of emotion, rather than the heart.

Between this dedication and her signature, both in Farsi, the note was brief. Two words in the flowery cursive of ESL English:

"Fuck you."

I laughed. Fair enough.

۱۹

Sunday, September 22

MY UNCLE CAME BY unannounced the night of my flight. For two days I'd been trying him at the number listed on my father's speed dial, reconnecting the landline only to get the same nonplussed secretary. I'd all but given up on sorting my father's affairs—now, admittedly, my affairs—when he turned up.

"We have our own oil here," he said, grabbing the remote to the AC. "You don't need to conserve."

I brewed tea and served him. The silver tray had gathered dust since my mother left. Now it sat, rinsed and dried, on the coffee table by the branded leather binder my uncle had brought to the cemetery.

We sipped our tea in silence. Emptied, two waisted glasses clicked against their saucers.

"At this point, it's practically your father's fortieth. You've stayed this long, what's another week?"

There were twelve whole days left until my father's fortieth day of mourning.

"Unfortunately I have a lot of work to do," I said.

"As you see fit."

I'd booked the cheapest flights possible. But there was also this, that I wanted to keep one ritual for myself. One, three, seven, forty—only the last remained.

"The title's in here, under the other paperwork. Don't lose it."

My uncle unzipped the binder. A short stack of papers was on either side pinned by an elastic band. Originals on the right, copies on the left. Under the gale force of the AC, they gasped like butterfly wings at the hands of a lepidopterist.

"About the account, then, have you made a decision? As I said"—he went on before I could respond—"I really do recommend leaving it open to cover costs here."

"Sure, let's do that."

Making a point of circling the balance—lest, I gathered, I later accuse him of skimming—he suggested I set a new PIN.

"Here's the old one."

Holding down the top page, he jotted the numbers ۱_۳_۶_۷ in a corner.

Thirteen-sixty-seven—1-3-6-7, my birthyear according to the local calendar. A twinge of melancholia tugged at my side.

"To be honest," I said. "I'm not sure when I'll be back. Maybe you could handle things, taxes, whatever, and just withdraw directly from the account?"

"So don't change the PIN?" He raised his eyebrows. "I think the bank might require it. For security purposes."

I rose to grab the legal pad from the dining table, where it lay next to Forugh and the open dictionary. I'd been translating when he got there, as I had been almost nonstop for two days, working late into the night and pausing only to eat and drink and exercise and shower and shit and sleep. Now, laboring on the Farsi numerals, I wrote ۲۰۰۶ on a fresh sheet and, in an English that was just as belabored and unnaturally neat, my email. It seemed a fresh indignity that I had no work email to offer in trade for his business card, but then again, you didn't need a dot-edu to send a translation to a slush pile and hope.

"Okay," he said, this one word in English. "Ask my secretary whenever you want to check the books."

I thanked him. "Just have her email me if the balance ever falls short."

"Don't be disrespectful."

Though he laughed, he folded my email into his breast pocket. I put a hand on the left side of the binder, on the copies.

"Could I take these for my records?"

"But of course."

Pulling the copies, he zipped up the originals and gave me the binder. The documents and their skin, an inheritance as unearned as any.

I saw him out. In my work haze I'd again forgotten to water the garden, and the soil at the foot of the pomegranate tree was dry. I turned on the hose. The water that came out for the first few seconds was warm—what was stuck in the hose had been sunning all day. I watered the garden until every leaf was wet and every root had had its fill, water pooling on the soil.

Finished, I sank onto the cool stone ledge and stretched my legs. They were sore. I folded over them.

Today I'd come close, my closest, to hitting the 13.1 miles of a half-marathon: 12.4. For days I'd been stuck on twelve flat, and now I'd broken the wall. I grabbed my bare feet by the soles. Pulling my torso forward and my hamstrings back, my calves back, all the minor essential muscles I couldn't name, back, everything shifting in mechanical order, I pushed past pain into release.

An alarm dinged on my phone, warning me that my flight was leaving in just a few hours. By the time I arrived in LA, yet another long flight later, it would be Monday. On Thursday the university quarter would start, and I wasn't teaching. I also wasn't engaged, still stuck on #98.

On the surface everything was the same. Except nothing was the same.

Nearly a hundred dates across two continents, and after all that, my final prospect—my eternal hope, now wandering weak as a fruit fly in a hurricane of my own making—was to fly back and get my man. A white man. This white man, yes, but in the eyes of the world, a white man like any other, just as privileged and, in the queer way of power, just as pained.

I thought about what brought me here, to this moment. In the late aughts at the Ivies, white guys were in abundance. Maybe the odds were always stacked against me. I showed up one night in my navy blazer to thank some dying old men for their money and walked out having given a Jewish boy from LA my—liver, I supposed. Now I wanted nothing more but for him to take it.

I looked up at Leili's balcony. There was no one there, and the lace curtains were drawn. Light seeped out like liquid.

I kept looking.

And then there, slipping outside through the lace, moonfaced and curly-maned, was Leili.

MAYBE IF I LEFT a key with the neighbor, she might water the garden. I wondered if her generosity went that far.

Date #99: Unspoken

I WAITED UNTIL I'D called the cab to the airport to try her one last time.

The night was uncharacteristically cool, almost cold. Summer was past its prime, overripened and ready to fall. I'd locked up the house, and now I stood outside the open gate with my backpack on. My carry-on was in the courtyard, full of books. I had donated all the clothes I'd packed for the sake of my father, taking nothing with me but what I had on my back and the new floral scarf on my head.

As I waited, I screenshotted my itinerary and sent it to Adam with the caption *coming home.*

Leili answered on the third buzz.

"Sorry to bother you, but—" I hesitated. "I was just leaving and—"

"I'll come down."

Her voice was businesslike, the way you'd talk to a delivery boy. I waited on the street, my American phone number scrawled on a tear of paper and a copy of the gate key—my mother's, unpaired from the set she'd left on the bedside—pressed hard into my left palm. My own keys were in my backpack, zipped into an embossed leather binder with a title that claimed that the house, the courtyard, were mine.

Leili's gate sighed open. Confronted with the question of how to greet each other, our bodies stiffened. I held out a hand. She met my shake with a loose grip, stepping onto the street dressed like some Euro club kid, soft midriff on full display, thighs lost in nylon cargos.

"My condolences," she said formally.

"I meant to thank you for the flowers."

For a moment I held her gaze. I was sure she could see the traces of the past weeks written lightly and definitively on the thin skin under my eyes, as I had in the mirror. Lines like those that had wrinkled the tuberose petals she gave me before their time was due.

Leili broke away. Her fingers fidgeted with a pack of cigarettes, extracting one, only to slip it back, unlit. My backpack weighed on my shoulders.

"It's only natural that you should go. Anyone who can, does."

"Except for you."

She let out a laugh like a hiccup. A car turned into the alleyway. The brush of its wheels, the whine of an old engine.

"Your work is excellent," I said. "Maybe I never said that."

"I know."

"Maybe someday you can give me a friends-and-family discount. I'll put the plate right in the middle of my twelve-person table in Beverly Hills."

"My prices will have climbed so high you won't be able to afford it. Even on the dollar."

A smile broke through her placidity, the sun through a marine layer. I basked in the warmth. A second stretched into a lifetime.

The faded Peugeot I took to be my ride beeped from down the block.

"So why don't you pull up?" Leili yelled, flicking her hand at the driver.

I stepped into the courtyard for my things. The driver loaded them into the trunk, still arguing with Leili about who was at fault. The key was slick with sweat, and time was fleeing, and still, I was ashamed to ask something of her.

I took a last look at the pomegranate tree. At the unripe fruit that now ornamented its spindly branches, green skin streaked with red, each seed inside still hard and illiquid and, nonetheless, a promise.

Summer was stone fruit season, hard with pits. Summer was dry season. Hot season. When pleasure was ripe for the picking. When laughter fell to the ground. Summer was night season, when darkness hung from the boughs of life, low and wet and sweet.

Pomegranate was winter fruit. Giving you succor when you least expected.

"Leili jan," I said, "would you do something for me?"

I opened my hand. The key glinted, catching the ambient city light. The crushed paper breathed.

I asked whether she might water my father's garden. The flowers, the vines, the tree. Asked without asking whether she'd steward these lives—these bodies—full of charm and beauty for which my life had no place.

"But of course," she said. "We're neighbors, after all."

LATER, ON MY FATHER's fortieth day of mourning, a snapshot from Leili would brighten my phone at home in LA. Pomegranates in full blush, the last of their greenness gone forever.

Back from my run—13.1 miles finally complete—I'd pause in front of my building to hear the hush of seagulls taking flight all at once from the power lines, thinking that they must've lost their way to have strayed so far east. On the pomegranate tree in the courtyard of the house I owned, I'd see, by way of a photo, the first ripe fruit of the season, skin red and deep and leathery, with liquid inside that, though unseen, was at least thick enough to make the gray branch bow.

POSTSCRIPT

Monday, September 23, 2019

ADAM WAS WAITING FOR me on the other side.

When it comes to LAX, even a promise isn't a promise, and his only response had been to heart my text. But there he was, standing in a sun-streamed Terminal B, holding a brown paper bag with a grease stain for a beauty mark. The sight of him sent a charge through me, from the heart to the liver. Blue button-up like a cloudless sky. Black curls like ink. A man my father had never met. Would never meet.

Seeing me, Adam broke into a smile, then frowned, as if remembering the occasion. I leaned in for the usual absurd bise. Instead he pulled me into a hug. My body sank into his. Into the smell of sweat and aftershave, the laboratory definition of *man* failing, wonderfully, to veil his own individual musk. Into the trust rippling from his body to mine and back. I sank into the care that beat through the veins on his transparent arms.

A KNOT OF GRAY under a blue sky, the tangle of highway interchanges lay on the landscape like an overturned oyster shell on ice, matte and rough-muscled, majesty overlooked. Barreling along the foot of the smog-smeared mountains on whose lesser slopes rich-people house lights twinkled by night like the fireflies of my childhood I'd been taught not to catch; driving into the climate-change heat of a California September gearing up to another fire season that rekindled old fears of divine justice—from the 105 to the 110 to the 101, from east to north to west, side by side in Adam's Insight, we sped home.

There was a spot on my block right in front of my building, condolences from the parking gods. (Tomorrow when I'd check for my car, I'd realize the spot had been mine, my Focus just recently towed.) Adam switched the engine off and turned to face me, his hand on the leather console between our seats. Friendship had taught us this boundary. Strong and dense as fishline, but taut now. Taut to the point of breaking the riddle that lay between his tented fingers and my clothed thigh, between my gaze and his lips.

Adam took a breath.

"Will you come to City Hall with me?"

"What?"

We hadn't talked the whole way home, hiding behind the music purring through the radio.

"That's not what I meant. Like, not *not* that—" Another ripple fell down my spine. He was blushing. "It's my mom. She's getting married."

I felt my lungs deflate.

"Today?"

"At five. In Beverly Hills."

My connection had landed after one, and it was already well past three.

"Seriously?" I gestured to my jeans. "It takes hours just to wax my legs."

I opened the car door and got out. Adam popped the trunk. I reached for my carry-on but he stopped me, setting the book-stuffed bag gently on the sidewalk. He toyed with his turquoise cooler, then changed his mind and slammed the trunk shut.

"What's that," I said, "my new heart?"

We stood on the street in the frank afternoon sun, my arms bared to the warmth. I'd taken my manteau off during my first layover and dumped it in the airport trash. My new scarf I'd tied around my neck like an oversized kerchief.

"Please," Adam said. "I can't do this without you."

Nervousness flickered in his eyes, or maybe, fear. I broke away and led us through the gate.

"If that's what you want."

Fear was good. Fear pointed to desire.

I DIDN'T BOTHER TO ask after the groom until we were tucked into the Insight, zooming down Vermont for a pit stop at Adam's so that the son of the bride might appear in something more respectable than faded jeans and canvas footwear. I was in go-go boots and a shift dress, hairy thighs be damned. (And any semblance of propriety.)

Sharon had a roster of eligible exes. The suit who fancied her his manic pixie dream girl, postmenopausal edition. The leather bomber who drove a Mustang and cooked quinoa for breakfast, obviously manopausal, given the Mustang. The shy physics teacher, who never really stood a chance. All in all, they weren't a bad lot; solvent, and nice enough. Maybe one of them had finally come around after a second divorce.

"So who's the lucky guy?" I asked.

"Who knows. She met him yesterday."

A matte gray McLaren honked as Adam cut it off to run a red. I'd never seen him drive this way.

"Yesterday," I said. "Meaning when exactly?"

"She tried to introduce him to us. That night we went to Venice for dinner, right before you left?"

As in, the night Sharon downed an unbecoming portion of piquette—evidently in nervous expectation of her son meeting her new beau—while Adam tried to alchemize his mournful mix of manly pride and separation anxiety from the placenta-pink floral sofa of his boyhood into char and smoke. The night I recognized the guy walking through Sharon's gate as the same guy I'd picked up after my hooding

ceremony two years ago. The night I almost lost my best friend by con-
fessing that I'd kissed his maybe-ex. The night that ended one of the
longest days of my life, the last I'd lived without knowing my father
was dying.

At this point we were pushing sixty coming on the next traffic light,
also yellow. I weighed my confidence in the quality of the Insight's
brake pads against the likelihood that the LAPD would pull over a
white guy.

"Just go," I said, and Adam went, zooming through the red and into
the intersection, cars on either side slowing and swerving so as not to
smack straight into us.

"He's an infant," Adam said, as we rejoined the flow of traffic on
Wilshire. "Like actually Gen Z."

Adam screeched to a stop in front of the Gaylord, parking by a
hydrant. I'd been wrong to underestimate the Insight.

"So what's this guy's deal?" I asked.

The flashers clicked desperately. Adam stared straight ahead, gaze
aimed at the windshield.

"He'll outlive me. Her himbo is going to be chilling on the moon
when we're all dead from some curable cancer our healthcare was too
shit to get treated."

"Male model?" I said, feigning innocence. "Silicon beach bum?"

There were some things you never needed to learn. That I'd slept
with his step-dad was likely one of them.

"Well, he calls himself a poet." He shook his head. "Her son's a
poet, and she's marrying a poet who's younger than her son. Textbook
midlife crisis. It's too boring to psychoanalyze."

Swinging the car door open, he threw his phone on my lap, screen open
to a grid of beach and biker shots alternating with sentimental haikus.

"What kind of a poet has two thousand followers?" he said.

I took one look and clicked the screen black.

"I'll watch the car."

Adam went up to change.

Stretching my legs on the sidewalk, I pulled up my summer spreadsheet on my phone. "9/26" cast an angry glare, now but a few days away: this very Thursday. Leili's name lay on line ninety-nine. Line one hundred begged to be filled.

So we'd been playing the same game, the stranger and I. He'd struck out with me, but Sharon was no small catch. A beachside bungalow in the Gold Rush State's best city as the world rushed toward destruction: it was a room of one's own in the golden hour of humanity, and it was now more or less his. In this country, the surviving spouse reigned supreme, and what was once Adam's inheritance would soon enough belong to this specimen.

Which, naturally, also meant that Adam had little to share. Nothing but himself.

ON OUR WAY OUT from my place, I'd checked my overstuffed mailbox. As Adam did whatever was taking him so long, I reached into the dash to sort through the stack. The Insight's long nose served as my desk, overdue bills on one side, recycling on the other—until I found, nested in the lures of various credit card offers, a crumpled manila envelope. I smoothed it out to read my mother's office number in the return address. I ripped it open. Folded into a blank sheet of Xerox paper was a check for $8262.50, the precise amount I would've earned teaching one class that fall. The UC salary scale was public.

Fishing for my uncle's business card in my wallet, I toggled my keyboard back to Farsi and jotted a brief, surely error-ridden email asking his secretary to ask him if he knew of any local refugee nonprofits that could suggest tenants for the house in Tehran at low to no rent. Then I set a calendar alert to look it up myself Wednesday morning. Tomorrow I planned to spend the day translating and running errands. I needed groceries and a new plant. The aloe was predictably dead.

I felt a hand on my arm and looked up to see Adam behind me, standing on the asphalt in his best suit. He looked sharp as a pencil on the first day of school, shoulders square in powder blue linen, waist cinched by a belt. His mother had instructed him to be her something blue—but casual; the groom was wearing shorts. The suit was Adam's rebellion.

"You look nice," I said.

Ignoring the compliment, he walked past me to the trunk, and returned with the turquoise cooler. He lifted the lid to expose a bouquet of fiery dahlias on a bed of ice, stalks curved from sleep.

"I didn't want them to wilt," he said, "waiting for the right moment."

I eased the bouquet out of the cooler, the skin of my fingers wakened by the cold. Adam held my gaze, eyes soft as the sighing side of life.

"I never wanted to be friends. Back in college, I mean. But like, life happened. You couldn't date, I met Julia—." He shut the cooler and set it down, standing before me, hands open at his sides. "What I'm saying is, you're not the one who was the substitute. You're the why I write for."

The Y poems. It was so simple and cheesy, Adam falling back on cliché.

I felt the warmth of a tear on my cheek. He wiped it with the pad of his thumb.

"Can we start over?" It was almost a whisper. "Or just—again?"

Finally I found something to say, laughing through my tears.

"How's Thursday?"

Adam held the door for me, and I climbed in. I leaned back, taking comfort in the worn skin of the seat, in the air crossing through our two open doors as Adam climbed in next to me. Above us a blue sky shone, obscured by the peeling roof, unseen, unspoken, and yet known.

We started the engine. The doors kissed shut.

ACKNOWLEDGMENTS

Many thanks to the folks who helped make this book happen, whether for work or love. Listed from A to Z, people like Danielle Bukowski, Evan Hansen-Bundy, Lena Little, Bobby Mostyn-Owen, Nadxieli Nieto and Kathy Pories, plus my teachers this past decade: Hilton Als, Paul Beatty, Ali Behdad, Richard Ford, Heidi Julavits, Binnie Kirshenbaum, Nasrin Rahimieh, and Sherene Razack. From Z to A, friends like Jenny Xie, Justin Torres, Shivani Radhakrishnan, Tara Menon, Angela Flournoy, plus too many more to list. I'd be remiss not to cite Megana Rao and Casey Modderno as early readers and Bryan Washington for bringing me to Danielle, to say nothing of Ari Bolotin, Darice Murphy, and Heather Peterson's gracious hosting and Sharanya Durvasula's keen-edged design instinct. Mona and Jacob, for standing by me always.

Sam, for everything.